OFF TRACK

NEIL BULLOCK

Endless undulating sky,
Shapes gray and white and black.
They sing to me, these things outside,
And dance for my regard.

—Unattributed.

PART ONE

ONE

NOW

April 30th

IT'S NEARLY FULL dark.

The only illumination comes from the sleek black train quietly hovering three feet from the ground out in the street. There is a glowing white light running down the side, just under the rows of windows that line each carriage.

The supermarket behind me is a dead place, empty and silent, its parking lot filled with cars that will remain exactly where they are, forever. The streetlights offer no respite from the darkness; the power went out a few days ago. I forget when exactly.

Somewhere nearby, a soda can rolls around in the gentle breeze. I glance from side to side nervously, almost wishing

there were someone else here to verify what I think I'm seeing. Impossible, of course. There is nobody else.

I know this train. I dreamed of this train five nights ago. It was just a dream, though. How could it have been anything else? How could it be real? How could it have found me here, at the end of everything? I run my thumb over the glossy label on the bottle of Oxycodone I took from the supermarket pharmacy, then pocket it and begin making my way slowly toward the locomotive.

FOOD COURT APOCALYPSE

April 25th

I arrive at the food court at eleven-thirty, exhausted and hungry, but excited. My best friend Alice and I grew up together, but we're both so busy that we almost never manage to get together anymore. This is the first time in months that our meticulous planning hasn't fallen apart at the last minute. I scan the food counters, then go to the one I've been craving for weeks. There, I obtain an oozing, glistening monster of a cheeseburger, fries coated in powdered awesome, and a strawberry milkshake in a shiny metal cup. That's three of the four basic food groups right there: fat, salt, and sugar. If only they served alcohol here. I carry my heart attack on a red plastic tray to the most remote table I can find and plop myself down facing the door, then pull out my phone to check that Alice hasn't canceled on me.

There are no messages from her. Thank God.

I start on the fries, dipping them in the inadequate puddle of ketchup I was provided, then munching on them while I struggle to remember the last time Alice and I got together.

It was a couple of weeks before Thanksgiving, I think. I remember inviting her to my mom's place for dinner. Mom and Nana consider her a surrogate daughter, but they see her even less than I do. I spot her then, across the food court, hurrying through the door in the process of extricating herself from the tangle of her coat and the messenger bag slung over one shoulder. She scans the food counters in much the same way I did, notices me, then throws her coat over her arm and makes a beeline through the crowd, much to the chagrin of everyone around her.

I stand, and we crash into each other, grabbing hold and hugging tightly, then releasing. "Sorry I'm late," she says. "You know how it is."

I nod. "The life of a hot-shot doctor."

"Something like that. Guard my stuff? I'm starving."

"Sure."

I watch her thread her way through the crowd and approach a noodle vendor. She has the busiest life of anyone I've ever known. She never seems to be at rest, working every hour available to her. When she's not working, she's planning her wedding. I wonder what her next project would be, though I suspect I know.

"So, how's it going?" she asks in an expectant singsong. I hadn't even noticed her return to the table, her own red plastic tray piled high with food. She sits.

"Exhausted, actually," I say. "I had bad dreams all night. Well, not bad. Just weird."

"About me not turning up?" She grins, but I see an uncertainty behind it.

I smile reassuringly. "Nothing like that. Something about a train." I shake my head to remove the stark monochrome images that still linger from the dream even now, hours later.

"Weird. You were going somewhere?"

"Nope. I wasn't on the train. Just following it, I guess. Like a movie."

"How'd it end?" She slurps a mouthful of noodles.

"It hit me, and I woke up."

"Huh. I guess that thing about dying in your dreams isn't true then."

"Well, give it time," I say, then start on my burger. It is, as I'd hoped, wonderful. Salty and greasy and savory and the perfect thing for my tired brain. When I'm done chewing, I look up to find Alice looking at me with an amused expression.

"You eating that or fucking it?" she asks.

I'm surprised into a laugh. "What?"

"You moaned."

"I did not!"

"Did too. Don't worry, I won't tell anyone." She grabs more noodles with her chopsticks and slurps them suggestively, closing her eyes, tipping her head back and performing her own exaggerated moan of pleasure.

The mom and dad of a trio of young children three tables away fixes Alice with a glare and I burst out laughing, quickly covering my mouth with one hand. They look away, annoyed.

"You're going to get us kicked out," I say, grinning. Then, noticing something is different, I grab Alice's left hand and pull it towards me. "You finally decided on a ring!" I inspect it in all its gleaming splendor, then allow her to retract her hand.

"No, no, the official story is that he finally got around to buying me one," she says. "Nothing to do with me."

"Ah, that version." Making a decision has never been a strength of hers.

"It's pretty spiffy, right?" she says, smiling a little tentatively and examining it herself. I remember this uncertain, almost shy girl from childhood.

"It's beautiful."

Her smile gains more warmth and she nods, apparently satisfied. "Thank you. I have something for you." She rummages around in her bag and produces a small plain white envelope with the word *Eden* written on it in swirling script. She hands it over.

"You set a date?" I can barely contain my excitement and struggle not to rip the envelope from her hand and tear it open with my teeth. Instead, I delicately wipe the grease from my hands on a napkin and pick up the envelope, open it as slowly as I can manage and pluck out the tiny piece of pink card within. It's not an invitation, just a save-the-date, but setting a date is a big step for Alice.

"I'll have to check my calendar," I say, joking, but I guess there are some things you just shouldn't joke about. She covers the crestfallen look quickly, but I still catch it. "Of course I'll come, you idiot! You couldn't keep me away."

"Good," she says, then looks down at her food. "Because it wouldn't be much of a wedding without the maid of honor."

My heart skips a beat. I would be lying if I said I hadn't spent some time imagining this conversation. I'd convinced myself that she would pick someone she sees more often, maybe one of her friends from the hospital, and I'd convinced myself I'd be fine with that. But of course, I wouldn't have been. I can't wipe the stupid grin off my face. "Me? You mean it?"

"Who the hell else would I pick?"

We lean awkwardly across the table and embrace. When we part, she reaches back into her bag and pulls out more envelopes. One for my Mom, another for Nana. "You'll pass these along?" she asks, the tentative note returning to her voice.

"Sure, of course. They'll be thrilled," I say, and they will. They won't understand why she never comes to see them, or why she didn't come to invite them personally, but I've come to realize that Alice suffers from a constant pressure to *achieve*. Her parents were never particularly encouraging about anything, let alone pressuring, but I've come to understand that was part of the problem. Alice's parents aren't even alive anymore, and conditioning her to always be searching for approval where none is forthcoming is one of the shittier things they saddled her with. I started to suspect that she's simply acting out a desire to make the people around her proud of her

when her visits to see my family started to dwindle. Now she only sees them at significant life events, ones where she can show she's reached a milestone of some kind. Her graduation, her wedding. Will the next one be her baby shower? What's after that? Since I realized this, I try to avoid saying things that will make her feel bad. Rather than suggesting she should come see my family and invite them to her wedding in person, I simply agree to deliver the save-the-dates.

"Thanks, Eden," she says, and slurps more noodles.

We both eat for a little while. I finish off my fries and munch my way around the outside of the burger – the middle is the best bit – then we move onto more mundane matters.

"So, any tours planned?"

"Probably something in summer. We're about to start rehearsing a couple of piano concertos, I think they're booked for next month sometime, but they're local."

"I should really try to make it to one," she says, and I don't agree or disagree. "I used to love listening to you play."

"Not when we were kids you didn't."

"Well, no. But when you got good." She looks wistful.

I am a violinist in the Oregon Symphony, something I've been training for since I was five. By Alice's reckoning, I got good around age thirteen. "I'll email you the dates."

She nods and sips her Coke. "Cool. It'd be nice to do something cultural for a change."

"What, you're bored of saving lives?"

We're both suddenly startled by the sound of a stack of the red plastic trays clattering to the floor. Someone apparently

stumbled and knocked them over. People around the scene of the accident clap and cheer sarcastically and I roll my eyes. People are so good at being assholes to one another.

We turn back to our food and I'm about to pop the center of the burger into my mouth when another noise causes us to turn again. This time it's a stack of plates, and this is much louder and far messier. It's quickly followed by a scream. I imagine someone cutting themselves on the shards.

"What the...?" Alice stands and looks around, meerkat style. "Oh, shit," she says, almost absently, and moves around her chair and in the direction of the scream. I stand too, putting my burger-middle back down uneaten, and watch Alice moving across the room. She's hurrying, but she is blocking whatever she's heading toward. As I'm adjusting my position to get a better view, another scream pierces the air.

I glance in that direction, but I can't see anything there either. "What's going on?" I shout after Alice, but she doesn't turn. People are getting agitated now. More people are standing. The family three tables away look confused, but also quite annoyed. Maybe because Alice said a bad word.

I stand immobile for a second, then sit. There's still some agitation, mostly over by Alice, who is now obscured by a low dividing wall intended to separate the dining area from the area where you line up for food. I pick up the middle of my burger, consider it, but put it down again before standing. I walk over to see what Alice is doing and freeze as I reach the wall. She's leaning over a woman's body that is bleeding heavily from the eyes, nose, mouth, ears, basically anywhere blood can escape.

Alice is trying frantically to find some cause for the hemorrhage and apparently having no luck.

Someone from the rapidly forming crowd asks, "What's wrong with her?"

Alice turns, her face flushed but fierce. "She's bleeding to death. Somebody call 911, for fucks sake!"

I pull out my phone, unlock the screen and dial the numbers, put the phone to my ear as I stare, horrified, at the dying woman on the ground. I hear a busy tone in my ear.

"It's busy," I say as I glance around the room, watching more people getting up from their tables and coming over. A few gasp, but most are content to be silent, horrified onlookers.

"What?" Alice turns to me. "What do you mean? How can it be busy?"

It didn't occur to me until she asked that there was anything odd about that. I feel a little dazed. I shake my head. "I'll try again," and I do, with the same result. I notice one or two other people around me get their own phones out and try, removing them from their ears moments later. We share a worried glance, then turn back to watch my best friend tell a dying human being that everything will be okay seconds before she takes her final breath.

When Alice stands and turns toward the gathered crowd, she looks defeated. Blood is smeared all over her hands.

"What do we do now?" someone in the audience asks.

Alice blinks. "Is there anything we can cover her with? We still need to get an ambulance here. I need everyone to step back, too. There are some hemorrhagic fevers that might do

something like this, and they're not something any of you wants to catch."

"What about you?" I ask.

She shakes her head and shrugs; a shrug that says *this is what I signed up for.*

A bald man with red cheeks and dressed in an apron stands at the edge of the gradually retreating crowd and tosses a blanket Alice's way. "Thank you," she calls back, then turns to cover the woman with it. Then she stands, wipes her bloody hands on her pants and pulls out her own phone. I wait. Moments later, Alice pulls the phone from her ear and glances at her watch. "The hospital isn't answering."

"Oh. What does that mean?"

"I don't know..."

We stand there, not really knowing what to do when Alice's pager starts to beep loudly. She pulls it off her belt and consults the screen, then dials another number on her phone. When nobody answers, she shoves the phone in her pocket, which is when somebody else cries out, way back against the food counters where the crowd has migrated. I see a large man fall to the ground, clutching himself and hyperventilating. He emits several awful, pained shrieks as the crowd around him scatters, faces pale and frightened. I hear some muttered swearing and heavy panting. As people move faster, they start to panic more, and the noise level increases.

"Is this the same thing?" I ask, dodging fleeing people, but Alice is already running for the man. I hear a cry of agony from somewhere else, followed by another scream. I turn. There are

now several people on the floor, and probably a hundred others running for the exits as fast as they can. I see one older lady fall, making eye contact with me as she gets trampled to death. I can feel every blow she suffers in my chest. I find it hard to catch my breath, to move, even harder to know what to do now. Alice has moved on from the man who fell near the food counters to another woman lying near the table where the best part of my burger sits uneaten. She looks up at me and her face is a mask of pure anguish.

I cross the room to her. "We need to get out of here," I say.

"I... I should try to help."

The arms of running people jostle me as I stand there. "You can't. Is she the same as the first one?"

Alice nods and looks around at the sheer number of people now lying on the floor. The noise is deafening and horrible.

"You can't help them, then. We need to get out of here. What if it's a chemical weapon or something?" Her eyes bulge, and she nods again. I take her bloody hand. "Come on."

I take us to the double doors that lead back out to the concourse, then freeze when I pull them open. Beyond is a scene from a horror movie. No, worse. Beyond is like witnessing a genocide. There are hundreds of people, most lying on the ground gasping, groaning, crying, crawling, or simply dead. The ones not already dead are dying, that much is obvious.

"Oh, God," Alice gasps behind me.

My heart races. My legs propel themselves without my brain's involvement. "This doesn't change the plan. We need to get out. We just need to find a different way." There's no clear path

out of here and as much as I feel for these people, I know there's nothing we can do. The last thing I want is for one of them to grab at our legs as we pass, maybe pulling us over.

NOW

When I reach the train I can no longer deny that it's real, because I'm close enough to touch it. I can feel its presence, too. It may seem completely motionless, but there's something keeping it suspended in mid-air like it is. It's not exactly perceptible, but there's something tangible about it all the same. A slight fluctuation in the air pressure, perhaps.

"What *are* you?" I ask the train.

It doesn't respond.

I reach out and place one finger tentatively against it and find that it's cool to the touch. It feels like metal, but it's impossible to tell what kind. The entire train is painted a shiny black, like an expensive piano. The only deviation from this color scheme is the bright white line that runs along the side of each carriage.

I'm standing at the very front of the locomotive, which slopes almost to a point, like a bullet train. I walk along its length and find there is no door, no windows. Then I walk back the way I came, around the front to the other side. There's nowhere for a driver to go. I crouch and look under the train. No wheels. Nothing to keep the train suspended like it is.

Walking down to the place where the first carriage begins, I note the presence of a door. Finally, something explicable.

It would be easy to jump to conclusions. Here before me is a train that should not be possible. A train floating three feet from the ground with no obvious place for a driver to go. A train that I dreamed about the night before everybody died. In my dream, I only remember seeing the train rushing along on its way to wherever a train like this one goes. I woke when it became apparent that I was not on board, but instead standing in front of it as it hurtled toward me. My eyes flew open when it plowed into me.

Should I not climb aboard? Is it dangerous in some way? Was the dream a warning?

How much of what has happened is related to this train? The fact that I dreamed about it the night before Alice's death, and the fact that it is here now seems to suggest that everything that's happened in the past few days is linked. How can that be? This isn't the way the world is supposed to work. Things like this aren't supposed to happen. This is nonsense. Perhaps the last week has finally taken its toll on me and I'm hallucinating. Perhaps I'm somewhere else, on the edge of death myself, and this is what my brain's final horrible misfires look like.

I close my eyes and relish the darkness.

I open them.

The train is still there.

survivors

April 25th

We manage to get out using a fire exit, run across the roof, then descend to the ground by ladder around the back of the building where it looks like deliveries are made. We walk slowly around to the front of the mall, not speaking. We're both still reeling from whatever we just witnessed, but I'm clinging to the idea that 911 was busy because whatever happened was being reported by lots of people and when we get to the front of the mall, we'll see a long line of ambulances and people in hazmat suits. We'll be taken to hospital and everything will be fine.

Except when we reach the front of the mall, what we see is not that. What we see is a parking lot much the same as it was when I arrived, except it is now the scene of a number of low-speed crashes. The area in front of the mall where there's a playground for children, a small picnic area and a large, paved area with benches is dotted with mounds of blackened sludgy flesh. I can still make out the people some of them used to be, folded or contorted into hideous poses as they succumbed to their fate.

We stop and stare.

"They're... are they melting?" Alice asks.

I watch closely and see that, yes, some of the piles of black horror seem to be flattening out. Spreading. I see one working its way slowly down an incline, leaving a glistening trail behind it like a hellish slug.

"Do you know of anything that could do this?"

Alice shakes her head. "Not like this. Not so quickly."

"Could it be some kind of attack?"

She doesn't respond. She's staring at the remains.

"Alice!" I shout.

Her head snaps to me. "Sorry. Yes, yes. Maybe something like that."

"All right. So why are we seemingly the only ones unaffected?"

She frowns at that, looks around. "Are we?"

"I think so." I scan the area again, but there's no movement that draws my attention. I realize I can hear the sound of cars idling, one of them only a few paces away. I walk in that direction and peer in through the passenger side window. On the driver's seat is a puddle of black goo which has leaked into the footwell. Alice comes over. "It must not have been limited to inside. I wonder how far it goes?"

"This doesn't make sense," Alice says.

"How we're not affected?"

Alice once commented on my ability to be calm in a crisis, complaining that she'd had to endure endless terrifying situations as part of her medical training to learn that skill, and I seemed to possess it naturally. It's not innate, though. I did learn it, but much earlier than Alice, and much more privately.

"Exactly."

I ponder this. "Do you think there are any survivors left inside?"

"I think there have to be. I don't know of anything that would work this way, to kill a mall full of people, plus everyone out in the parking lot, but leave two people alive."

I pull out of my phone. "All right, let's see if we can attract someone's attention."

"Wait, though," Alice says, holding up a hand. "If this was an attack, like you said, we seem to be immune. Or maybe there's a delayed onset. But bringing more people into the situation might not be the best idea..."

I nod, then then look around again. This place should be alive with movement, with noise. The fact that it's mostly silent and completely still is starting to make me feel uncomfortable, like just the sheer absence of life is sufficient to rob me of my own. I pull up various apps on my phone and scroll through some pages of information. "Nothing in the news about this."

Alice nods as if she expected as much. "Not much of a surprise. Do you see any reporters?"

I continue to tap at my phone's screen. "Nothing on social media."

"Maybe try posting something?"

I nod, then click on the Messenger icon and consult the list of friends who are online right now. There are several, and I select Martie, a cellist in my orchestra, at the top of the list. I tap out a message asking if anything weird is happening where she is and wait.

Meanwhile, Alice starts pacing, checking cars, getting much closer to the rivers of ick than I'm comfortable with. I watch her while I wait for a response to my message, but the longer I wait, the more concerned I become that Martie hasn't even seen the message. "What are you looking for?" I call to Alice.

"Just looking. Trying to understand what happened."

"Just... try not to get too close, okay?"

She mumbles something, then continues to watch the closest pile of sludge to her.

I shuffle over to a raised flower bed and perch myself on the brick wall that surrounds it, then write the following message on Facebook.

My name is Eden Lucas. I'm in Portland, OR with my friend Alice. Everyone here is dead, possibly the victims of some kind of attack. Does anyone know anything? Can anyone help?

I read it back a few times, add some hashtags, then post it. When I look up, Alice is walking back toward me. "This is so fucked up," she says.

"What is?"

"Nothing I've ever seen could do this. Melt flesh, turn it to that stuff," she points at one of the gently flowing puddles. "Not this quickly. It's like they're rotting, but sped up many hundreds of times."

"No acids or anything?"

"Not like this, no. This is organic matter decaying, not being burned."

I stand, then consult my phone. Martie hasn't seen my message. Nobody has responded to my post. "What do we do now?"

"I think we need to look for survivors."

I shake my head before she finishes speaking. "I don't want to go back in there."

"You don't have to. I will."

"Alice, no! Think about it. If these bodies are rotting, won't they become a disease risk all on their own?"

"That's a myth. Dead bodies pose less risk than the living when it comes to transmission of disease. If we're not already dead from the same thing that killed them, I think we're reasonably safe."

I frown, frustrated. I want to get out of here, find someone in charge of something useful, like a hospital, and hand this mess over to them. I want to know what happened here, and I never want to come back again. "All right, but what if it's an attack? What if there are people on their way here right now to make sure that it had its intended effect, that everyone's dead?"

That makes Alice hesitate, but I can see she's not convinced, and honestly, neither am I. I think that kind of clean-up crew is good for the movies, but no purpose would be served by eliminating any witnesses to what happened here. Indeed, if it's a terrorist attack, our retelling of what happened will form part of the purpose of the attack: scaring people. I add, "And where is everyone? If there are people alive inside, why haven't they come out?"

She blinks. "I don't know."

I check my phone. Still nothing. "This is worrying me, though. Why has nobody replied to my post? I have a lot of friends who are apparently online right now."

That seems to set Alice's mind on a different track. She frowns deeply, then her eyes bulge. She pulls out her own phone and taps the screen a few times. She puts the device to

her ear, listens, waits, then repeats the same process three more times. "Mark isn't answering."

Mark is her fiancé, and my worry kicks into a higher gear. I already wondered how far this extends, but I hadn't stopped and really thought about it until now. "Shit," I say, then call my mom with the same result. No answer. I try to tell myself that my mom doesn't keep her phone on her. She could be out in the garden, she could be taking a nap or watching television. Not answering isn't a sure sign of anything.

"Come on," Alice says.

"Where are we going?"

"My place."

I trail behind Alice for the first part of the journey. I'm struggling to get my head around what's happened. Whenever I let my mind wander, it's not the people who turned to black sludge that I think about, it's the woman trampled underfoot as everyone tried to get out of the food court. She looked at me. I wished so badly that I could help her, but now it seems like she actually got the better deal. Not the *best* deal, though. That seems to have been reserved for me and Alice. Why do none of the news outlets have anything about this? Why has Martie not seen my message? Her icon shows she's offline now. Why has nobody responded to my post on Facebook?

I occasionally stop my obsessive thoughts and look around. The further we get from the mall, the more obvious it is that this wasn't as localized as I want it to have been. Every street we turn down has more of those awful puddles of gloop. In every window I peer through and every car on the road. It's as if the population of Portland was judged and found wanting, so this is their punishment. But what about me and Alice? Did we pass the test?

Alice occasionally tries to call Mark, but her calls don't go through. I decide against trying to contact mom again because I don't want the feeling that is obviously building in Alice with every frustrated step, with every failed connection attempt. She's going to explode if we don't get to her place soon.

We quickly determined that driving to Alice's place was not feasible. We'd never have got either of our cars out of the parking lot, not with all the stalls and crashes blocking the way. The public roads are much the same story, so we're walking. We both want to run, but there are too many slippery puddles of people.

"Alice," I call, stopping, squinting at something in the distance.

She turns, still heading homewards, then stops, but says nothing.

"I think something moved."

She turns to face the same way as me, then turns back. "A person?"

"I don't know. Maybe."

She starts walking again and I follow after staring into the distance long enough that my eyes begin to water.

When we reach Alice's house, we stop on the sidewalk, staring up the path that leads across the front yard. The place is immaculate as always, but there's an almost palpable feeling of dread that surrounds the property. After a minute of this, I start to imagine my own version of this ritual. When you've walked God knows how many blocks and every person you've seen has melted into oblivion, it's hard to remain optimistic about what you'll find behind your own front door. Alice has to be steeling herself to walk up the path and inside. The only thing keeping me from breaking down right here is that Mom and Nana live sixty miles away, and that maybe this was just local to Portland. The longer nobody responds to my Facebook post, the less I believe that, though. I have friends all over the country.

Alice finally starts to move forward. She's apprehensive, but she fumbles her keys from her pocket as she walks. When she reaches the door, she slides the key into the lock and pushes the door open, then collapses to her knees.

I can see it, even from the end of the path. The puddle is just on the other side of the door, like Mark was on his way outside when he was taken. Maybe he was trying to escape this, like everyone in the food court. Like the woman who was trampled.

I run and crouch next to Alice, wrapping both of my arms around her. She remains stiff and immobile for a second, then shifts and grips me tightly as the tears start to flow.

It's dark when we finish cleaning up the remains. I'm glad Alice has hardwood floors and not carpet, but it's still a wretched, horrible job. I manage not to throw up, but it's a close call. I try to do most of it myself, because Alice can't stop crying, and it seems like this isn't something she should have to do. She insists, though.

When we're done, Alice sits at the breakfast bar in the kitchen while I turn on the television in the living room.

"Shit," I say without meaning to.

"What is it?" Alice calls weakly from the kitchen.

"News channels are all off the air."

There's no response, but I imagine she's probably inferring the same thing from this information that I am. I don't know where these things are broadcast from, but I'm fairly sure they're not all in Portland. That means this extends beyond the city. When I can't get anything out of CSPAN on the television, I allow myself to think for the first time that maybe the worst has happened, and this is at least country wide. I try the CSPAN website on my phone and discover the radio section, but it's just broadcasting silence.

When I turn around, I find Alice standing behind me. "Do you want me to come with you to your mom's place?" she asks, and I almost have to laugh. It took the end of the world for her to be the one to make the offer.

Immediately, I feel horrible that I even thought that. I nod. "If you wouldn't mind."

"Of course not. We can leave at first light. I'm going to bed. You can sort yourself out?" Every few words she says have a minute pause before them, like she's on the verge of losing herself completely, and who could blame her?

"Sure. Good night."

She looks at me for a beat too long, then turns away. She hurries out of the room and up the stairs when her eyes begin to tear up and her face begins to crumple into devastated, helpless anguish once more.

Alice seems better in the morning, but I can only imagine it's a veneer. She smiles weakly at me as she enters the living room, then proceeds to the kitchen and clatters around. I didn't sleep. I lay awake thinking about the woman trampled underfoot, replaying the moment I lost sight of her over and over again. Wondering if she's the only intact body left in the food court, a fleshy island in the middle of an ocean of decay. The more I focused on that image, the less real everything else seemed. Everyone dead? Not possible. I witnessed a disaster, sure. Something I may never understand, but it was only the mall. The memories I have of walking to Alice's house are hazy and insubstantial, like we floated the whole way here in a dream. If I go outside now, I wouldn't be surprised to find the world continuing as normal. Children playing, parents mowing lawns, dogs barking. Alice makes coffee and sets a mug in front of me. "Is this it, then? The end of the world?"

And just like that, my fragile fantasy world is shattered. One thought I did have before my brain compartmentalized the events of yesterday is that perhaps there's a genetic component to what happened. Alice's parents died years ago and she's an only child, but maybe if I'm alive, other parts of my bloodline are too. "I hope not."

Alice watches me, expecting more, then sighs. "Jeez, I'm sorry." She's apologizing for suggesting my family might be dead.

I wave her apology away and take a sip of coffee. It's bitter and strong. "When do we leave?"

"Whenever you want."

"You still want to come? I'd understand if you want to be... here."

In response, she stands and walks over to the front door, the spot where her fiancé died. She pulls the engagement ring from her finger and sets it down in the center of the stain that still adorns the wood. To me, the act feels like she's breaking off the engagement, giving the ring back, but I don't question it. If it feels like the right thing for her to do, then it is.

"All right," I say. "Thank you."

We check Google Maps before we head out and I make sure I have an app that doesn't require an internet connection, plus downloaded maps. The roads are gridlocked which initially gets Alice's hopes up, but I tell her that Google figures out the traffic by how many phones are on a particular piece of road and how quickly they're moving, and it probably just means people died on the road with their phones. When we leave, Alice doesn't look back.

Alice doesn't live in Portland itself, but in an area called Bull Mountain, which is southwest of the city. It's an offensively bright and sunny morning when we leave her house and start walking straight west. As the name of the place suggests, it's hilly out here, which slows our pace. We walk mostly in silence, occasionally stopping to catch our breath after walking up a steep incline. We brought no supplies and we're hoping we'll find places to sleep on the way. It's going to take two or three days, at least. A few hours in, I realize I'm walking alone. I turn and find Alice sat on the ground behind me.

"Alice?"

She looks up, waves me over, and I go.

"You okay?"

She smiles a sardonic smile. "Ish. Just needed a rest. I just realized that I'm never going back to that house. It hit me kinda hard."

I sit down beside her, smile sympathetically, then cock my head. "Do you hear something?"

She listens, shakes her head. "What's our plan, Eden? What happens when we get to your mom's place?"

"I don't know."

"I can't stop thinking about what comes next," she says. "Can this really be the end?"

I shrug rather than repeat myself. "Maybe not. Maybe it's just the US. Or maybe just this continent."

"Even if that's true, nobody's going to let us into their country if they think we might be carrying something with the capacity to wipe out humanity."

That silences me. I watch Alice plucking blades of grass from the soil, rolling them between her fingers, then discarding them. "Then we survive here, on our own. Maybe we look for others. If we're alive, there must be other survivors, right?"

"I guess."

I listen again to the wind, but whatever I thought I heard is gone.

We stop a couple of hours later and this time we both hear the noise. It sounds like someone shouting. We both turn back and spot movement in the trees we just passed through. "What do we do?" Alice asks.

"Wait, I guess."

"What if he's coming to kill us?"

"Then he won't be the first thing that's tried to kill us in the last couple of days."

It starts to seem cruel, both of us standing there, watching him run up a hill to reach us, listening to him panting and gasping and wheezing, yet still trying to shout, "Wait! Please, wait for me!"

When he does finally catch up to us, he bends over double, hands on knees, and breathes heavily for several minutes.

"Hi?" I say when he's calmed down a little.

He looks at me incredulously. "Why... Why didn't you wait? It looked like you heard me the last time you stopped. I thought you'd seen me. I thought you stopped to wait for me. Then you just got up and started walking again."

I glance at Alice, who shrugs. "Sorry. We didn't see you. Who are you?"

"My name is Greg. I followed you from Portland." He pulls out a compact pair of binoculars to demonstrate how he kept track of us from afar.

He's dressed in jeans and a plain white t-shirt with pit stains, presumably from all the running. He carries a light jacket. He has short sandy colored hair and kind hazel eyes. He doesn't seem to be a threat, and he's clearly a survivor. "Eden. Alice," I say, introducing us.

"So, you survived," Alice says.

"You, too," he says.

"Did you see anyone else?" I ask him.

He moves his head around and I'm not sure if it's a nod or a shake or something else. "I think so, but I couldn't find them. Then I see you two walking off into the distance. Where are you headed, anyway? Do you know something? A safe place to go?"

Alice says, "No. We don't know anything, just that the world seems to have ended."

He winces.

"We're headed to my mom's," I say. I can't decide if Greg's appearance gives me more or less hope that Mom and Nana might still be alive, so I don't elaborate on the plan.

"Where's that?"

"About as far west as you can go. Oceanside. Come with us if you want. If you have nowhere else to be."

He appears surprised at the offer, maybe even more than I am at having made it. I hadn't intended to, it just kind of came out. I guess we survivors should stick together until we know what's going on.

"You're okay with that?" he asks.

I nod, then look to Alice for her thoughts. "Whatever. Just try not to turn into a psycho killer. There's been enough death." She turns and starts walking again. Greg and I share a glance, then we start after her, giving her some space.

I try for a minute to come up with a way to explain Alice's abruptness, but I figure it doesn't really need explaining. "Where are you from?" I ask, opting for mundanity instead.

"New York. Syracuse. You?"

"Here. Well, I was born in California. Fresno. I don't remember it though. We moved when I was young. Why so far from home?"

He doesn't respond for several seconds. "Visiting friends. They're... well, you know."

I nod. They're dead now, like everyone else. "Any theories on what caused this?"

He shakes his head and raises his eyebrows. "It doesn't feel real. It's like a nightmare. I keep thinking I'll wake up any minute and everything will be back to normal."

Up ahead, Alice stops, turns and shouts, "It's not though! Nothing will be fine! Everyone's dead. Better get used to it!" Then her legs buckle and she falls to the ground, sobbing. I run for her and bend down, wrapping my arms around her as she bats ineffectually at me. "Get off me! Leave me alone!"

"Not going to happen," I whisper as she cries disconsolately on my shoulder.

She spends the next hour studying the horizon to the east, back the way we came. I let her go when she stopped crying and retreated to give her some time. Greg and I are standing by, not talking, eager to get moving. We're going to lose the light soon, and I'd rather not spend the night outdoors without camping gear.

"Have you guys heard any birds?" Alice asks without turning to face us. Her voice is flat.

I cast my gaze to the sky briefly. I'd noticed the lack of birdsong, but I didn't want to worry anyone unduly. "That's pretty high on the list of things I'm trying not to think about."

"Shit. You think it got the birds too?" Greg asks. At this, Alice does turn with an expression that suggests she forgot he was even here.

"Maybe it got all the animals," she says.

"Dogs? Cats?" Greg looks upset at this.

"Pets?" I ask.

He nods. "One of each. I hope they didn't suffer."

"Oh, they did," Alice says. "Everyone did."

"Alice," I say, because it's not in her nature to say callous things like that. I get that she's upset, but cruelty is uncalled for. She glares at me.

Greg bends down and looks at the ground. "What about insects?"

A bead of dread rolls down my spine and I crouch and begin parting the grass with my hands, looking for signs of insect life.

"So what if it got the insects?" Alice asks, and I look up at her.

"No pollinators, nothing to condition the soil."

She looks at me serenely as if I haven't even spoken. The corners of her mouth twitch, then she gets up. "Come on, we should keep moving."

RESPICE

April 26th

Just as dusk threatens to swallow us, we encounter a huge house surrounded on two sides by enormous swaying trees, on the other two by a tall fence. Through the fence I see a regrettably empty swimming pool and beyond that, tennis courts.

"Up for some breaking and entering?" I ask with mock cheer.

"Always," Greg replies. Alice remains silent, standing dejectedly off to one side, shuffling her feet and staring at the ground. Greg searches for a while and comes back with a hefty rock which he throws through the window of the front door, then clears out the remaining glass with a thick tree branch. He unlocks the door, then when the alarm begins to blare, takes his tree branch and bludgeons the source of the high-pitched siren to death. There are no cars in the long driveway and no evidence of habitation. Hopefully this was a summer home and there was nobody here when the world ended. I can't deal with more of that black slime right now.

Greg goes off to explore while Alice and I make ourselves comfortable in the large living room. "I know it's a stupid question, but how're you doing?"

She shakes her head. "It keeps hitting me. Over and over. Bang! I'm never going to see Mark again. Bang! We're not going to get married. Bang! I'll never have children. Bang! I'll never be an attending physician. I can't stop it, Eden. How do I stop it?"

She looks hollowed out. I know I should feel the same way, but I'm still clinging to the infinitesimal possibility that there's a genetic component to whatever immunity I have, and that Mom and Nana have survived. It's all I have, and it's the only way I can keep it together. If I thought about it too hard, I might just lie down and never get back up. "I don't know, Alice, I'm sorry. I'm so fucking sorry."

She smiles sadly. "There's got to be some booze here. That'll help."

Alice is the happiest drunk I know, and on the spur of the moment, alcohol seems like a wonderful idea. We start the hunt, and by the time Greg returns, we've uncovered a large bottle of gin. I hold it up as he appears in the doorway. "Shot of gin? Ease your pain?"

He laughs, shakes his head, then finally nods.

We slip into something like normal conversation, like we're just three friends drinking and passing the time of day. Greg disappears briefly and returns with three piping hot bowls of canned soup on a tray. It doesn't go with the gin at all, but since I started to feel tipsy, I've stopped drinking it. The last thing I want is a hangover in the morning.

"When do you think we'll leave tomorrow?" Greg asks.

I shrug. "I don't know. Early. It's another fifty miles or so. We did ten miles today, but we only started at lunch time."

"And my feet are killing me," Greg says.

I am forced to admit that mine are too. "All right. So maybe we aim for fifteen miles a day? We can be there on the morning of the twenty-ninth."

I hate that it's taking so long, but I also don't. The longer it takes to get there, the longer I can stay in my fantasy where everything is fine. It's the same reason I haven't tried calling Mom or Nana since Alice and I were outside the mall. Not knowing is easier.

"That sounds doable," Alice says. "Does it flatten out any?"

"Eventually, yeah. Once we reach the woods."

She nods. Greg cuts in, "Are there bears in those woods we need to be concerned—oh."

We're silent as we consider this faux pas. No, of course we don't need to be concerned. All the bears are probably dead. "I guess not," I say eventually.

Alice stands and paces the room. "I don't understand any of this. How can everything be dead? How can I have everything one minute and nothing the next?"

"I don't know," I say.

"It's just... it's so unfair! I was nearly finished. I did what my dad wanted. I became a doctor. I found Mark. We were getting married. We were going to have kids. Now none of that means a damn thing."

There's nothing to say, because she's right. I glance at Greg while Alice's back is to us. We share a pained expression.

"What the hell are we going to do? What the hell is the point anymore?"

I take a deep breath. "We do the only thing we can do. We live. We redefine what that means. We find out how far this extends, and we deal with whatever that entails."

"That's not the only thing we can do, Eden."

I stare at her, shocked. "You're talking about suicide?"

"Sure. Why not?"

"*Why not?* How about because I'd be devastated? You're basically my sister, I love you! You're not leaving me to deal with this without you!"

She looks ashamed as I'm yelling at her. "But... what's the point, Eden? Why go on if—"

"If what?"

Her expression is one of confusion as she shakes her head. "I don't know."

"I think you do," I say, standing up.

She stares. "What—"

"You want to know what the point is if there's nobody around to see, right? To see you hit life's big milestones?"

Alice screws her eyes shut as if I've slapped her, then dips her head. She breathes heavily and a small whimper escapes her.

I sigh. I didn't want to do this, but I might as well see it through now. "Alice, the only person that's ever mattered to is you. I love you and I've always been proud of you. Mom and Nana loved and were proud of—" I exhale sharply and tears sting my eyes as I realize what I've said. *Mom and Nana* were *proud of you*. Past tense. Alice turns abruptly, reacting to the same thing. Her face collapses and she rushes to me. We cling to each other fiercely, sobbing.

A minute later, when we're mostly done, Greg says, "Well, don't I feel like the third wheel?" and our pain is replaced by fits of manic giggles for which we're both extremely grateful.

We eat more soup that Greg prepares, and I apologize to Alice. She waves it away, and everything is okay. I manage to mostly crawl back into my bubble of denial about Mom and Nana by telling myself it's pointless to assume anything until we get there, and I can see what happened with my own eyes. We decide to channel our dwindling energy reserves into coming up with a decent plan before bed.

"Okay, no birds and maybe no other land animals," I say. "We didn't really check for insects."

"What about bacteria?" Greg asks.

I blink. "Shit. If the bacteria are gone, our lives become a lot harder."

Alice looks confused. "Why?"

"No pollinators is bad enough, but no bacteria means no crops at all."

"Oh."

Greg says, "One thing it might mean, though, is that the food we do have won't spoil. Maybe canned food lasts forever now."

I smile. "Ah, silver linings. A lifetime of canned food to look forward to."

Alice says, "All right. So, what about the oceans? Could there still be fish and the like?" She shudders. "I hate fish."

Greg says, "It's good for you."

Alice rolls her eyes. I say, "Maybe. That's something to check, and we're going to the right place to do that. So that's two things to figure out."

Alice nods decisively. "If there's no bacteria, do things that are already growing die? Trees and stuff?"

I shrug. "I'm not sure. Maybe not, which might mean we can find an orchard or something and have fresh fruit. That's a third thing, then. Figure out if existing plants will die now."

Alice seems to be getting into the swing of things now, while Greg appears to be ruminating on something. Alice says, "What about survivors? We should look for other people."

I nod. "Agreed. I should be writing this down."

Greg clears his throat. "What about repopulation?"

I raise an eyebrow. "What about it?"

He looks uncomfortable. "Well, you two are... ladies. You can... you know."

Alice laughs bitterly. "Good luck with that. Eden's gay."

He glances at her, blinks, then back at me. "Really?"

I nod. "Gayer than bubble baths."

He smiles uncertainly. "But still, you can— like, make a kid, right?"

"Oh, boy! I've never heard anything so romantic! I think you've turned me straight! Take off your pants." I start to remove my belt to make a point.

Alice snorts. Greg frowns. "I'm not talking about romance, Eden. I'm talking about the survival of humanity."

"All right. Let's talk. How's that going to work?"

He glares at me while he turns red. "Well, I could—you know, into a cup or something."

"Okay, then what? Because a cup of your baby batter isn't going anywhere near me."

"Or me," Alice announces.

He makes a sound like all the words have got tangled together coming out of his mouth, stops, then takes a breath. "You don't think repopulation is important?" He looks genuinely confused and more than a little flustered.

"I don't think you get to use us as incubators for the rest of our lives."

Exasperated, he turns to Alice. "What if, a few years down the line, we met another survivor and you fell in love?"

She's shaking her head before he's even finished talking. "Nuh-uh. No children for me. Not without Mark, and certainly not in this new world."

"So that's it? You two just get to decide that's the end of humanity?"

I shake my head sadly. "We all have choices to make. Yours is going to be how far you're willing to take this. You seem like a good guy, Greg. Or am I mistaken about that?"

He glares some more and eventually sighs. "No, I guess not. I can't make you do anything. Well, I guess maybe I could, but I don't want to."

"Good to know."

Alice says, "It probably wouldn't work anyway. We don't have the genetic diversity between the three of us. We'd need a couple of hundred other survivors."

Greg asks, "Would you consider it then?"

Alice shakes her head. I say, "No, but hopefully in that case, we wouldn't have to. Maybe there'd be willing participants."

He seems to be coming to terms with the idea that our species is most likely dead. He sighs again and turns back to me. "You never wanted kids?"

"Me? No."

"Why not?"

"I'd just rather not risk that I picked up any parenting tips from my dad."

"Oh. Was he—"

"He was a manipulative con man. Let's just leave it at that."

Greg nods. "Fair enough. Look, I'm sorry I brought up the repopulation thing. It's hard to get your head around the fact we might be the final generation."

I nod and smile, and I'm surprised at how genuine it feels. "Yeah, it is. Don't worry about it."

He returns my smile.

We talk about our plans for tomorrow a little more, then we make our way upstairs. The house has eight bedrooms and Greg picks the one that overlooks the swimming pool and tennis courts around back. Alice and I pick rooms next to each other.

I stop at my bedroom door, turn, and call, "Good night."

Greg pauses down the hall, turns and gives a cheery wave. Alice emerges from her room and offers a tight-lipped smile. "Night, Eden."

I gaze at her for a second, then we all disappear wordlessly into our rooms. When I've fallen into bed fully clothed and am looking around at the unfamiliar space with all its unfamiliar dark nooks, I wish I'd asked Alice if I could share her bed, but I start to drift off to sleep even as I'm having the thought. Before I have time to think about much of anything else, I'm gone.

NOW

I observe the gap between the locomotive and the first carriage. Aside from the coupler, there's nothing there. It seems there really is no way into the locomotive. I turn my attention to the door that leads into the first carriage. While I'm staring up, it splits in two, each half sliding silently open.

A feeling of dread begins at my shoulders and radiates down my spine, but I don't move. I half expect someone to step out and invite me aboard, but nobody does. I can see inside though. There's a vestibule of some kind, presumably with a door that leads deeper into the train. All I have to do is climb the four rung ladder and I'll be inside.

Is that what I want?

I take a step back and look at the silhouettes of trees in the distance.

I only have the two options here. I already know, or at least strongly suspect, there's no future for me on this planet. All forms of life may be at an end. My options, then, are to get on the train, or to unscrew the cap of the Oxycodone and down the contents. The decision isn't an easy one. The only thing I know for sure about this train is that it killed me in my dream. Realistically, that's no different to my other option, the Oxy.

All things being equal, I'd rather a quick death than a drawn out one.

Which is it? Is Oxy a quick death? What about the train?

I don't know what to do.

NEW DAY

April 26th

Like yesterday, it's almost aggressively sunny when I wake, like the sunlight is physically beating itself against the curtains and will break through if I don't open them. I stare at them for a second as the last two days come flooding back. It's tempting to give up, to stay in this magnificently comfortable bed forever, but I have places to be. We have a plan to enact.

I climb out of bed and note that both Alice and Greg's bedroom doors are still closed. I figure I'll allow them some extra time to sleep while I make breakfast. Soup isn't going to cut it if we have fifty miles of walking to do over the coming days.

I walk downstairs, taking in how different the house looks in the daytime. It's bright and inviting, filled with pale shades offset by rich, dark timber here and there. I make my way to the kitchen and hunt through the enormous pantry for calories. Finding nothing, I walk through into another room containing an enormous freezer, which is when I notice the power finally gave out. There's a lot of stuff in the freezer, and most is still cold and fresh enough, so I figure I might as well use it. Rather than play with the gas stove, I take a camping stove outside, hook it up to one of several gas bottles I find out there and stand in the warm April sun cooking bacon by dropping the entire frozen block in the pan and awkwardly peeling off slices with tongs when they warm up enough. I eat some slices as I go, but soon I have a large pile of crispy bacon – a perfectly balanced breakfast. I head back inside with the plate and place it in the center of the kitchen table, then call upstairs. "Breakfast!"

When I hear nothing, I climb the stairs and knock on Greg's door – the closest one. When he doesn't answer, I open the door a crack and say, "Greg? You awake?"

When I push the door all the way open, I see a black puddle close to the edge of the bed. Some of it has oozed onto the floor. "Oh, no..." I repeat this as I start to hyperventilate, each repetition becoming breathier and more panicked. "Oh, no. Oh, no, no, no." I run from the room and throw the door of Alice's room open.

The pile of blackened sludge is almost dead center on top of the bedspread. My lungs force all their air out and I struggle against tears to take more in. I walk across the room, crouching by the bed. The sludge glistens in the sun. Did she suffer? I didn't hear anything. If she'd suffered, I would have expected to hear her scream like the people in the food court.

I remember my last thought as I drifted off to sleep, wishing that I'd asked to share the bed with Alice. I now wish more than almost anything that I'd got out of bed, marched into her room and demanded to spend the night. Maybe I couldn't have stopped this, but I could have done for her what she did for the first victim. I could have told her everything was going to be fine. I could have told her she was on her way to see Mark. I could have held her while she—

When I'm out of tears and my stomach hurts from gasping and sobbing, I sit alone in the silence. The house has turned from somewhere I wanted to be to somewhere I must escape. Every second I sit there listening to absolutely nothing, my fear grows that whatever is happening will come for me. I start to move without being completely aware of it. I run down the stairs, throw open the front door and by the time I think to look back, the house is out of sight.

If this is coming for me, I have one thing left that I need to do.

Later

April 29th, 2019

The last few days have passed in a blur.

Normally, I'm pretty good at hiding from my feelings, but Greg and Alice's demise has screwed me up. I can't stop thinking about it. Why did I survive when they didn't? What's so special about me? Alice was a doctor. Surely, she deserved to live more than I did. Maybe the same thing will still happen to me. It'll take me just like it took everyone else around me. Why would it not? Still, I keep moving forward because I have to know for sure what waits for me at the end of this journey.

I don't know where I am, but I can't be far from my mom's house. I've been slowing down since realizing that. It seems obvious what I'm going to find there, and I don't want to confront it. I've been heading downhill for some time, and I hope that means I'm about to reach Tillamook. I picked up a river yesterday afternoon, which I think will take me into town. From there, it's a comparatively short walk to the coast. You can't see the ocean from my mom's place, but you can smell it. I'm looking forward to that in a weird, guilty sort of way.

I haven't seen a single living organism since Alice. At first, I was a little anxious walking through Tillamook State Forest. It felt like the trees were closing in around me, but I don't even know if the trees are still alive. I slept where I fell from sheer exhaustion. I fear I am alone, at least on this continent, and I don't fancy my chances trying to get to a different one. The only way I can see it happening is if I head north to Alaska, wait for winter, hope the ocean freezes enough that I can walk into Russia. And maybe get eaten by a polar bear.

I stop walking and start giggling.

The idea is ridiculous. I picture myself running cartoon -style across the sea ice, legs spinning and going nowhere, while a confused polar bear watches.

Abruptly, I stop laughing. The silence is all-encompassing.

I start moving again.

My mom's house comes into view, and I find I am wrong – you can see the ocean from here. A tiny portion of it, but it's there. Why didn't I know that? I feel like I should have known that. I approach the front door, palms sweating, heart racing, and knock. Normally, I wouldn't knock. I have keys, but I didn't bring them.

"Mom? Nana?"

On either side of me are beautiful flowers in reds, purples, oranges, and yellows. There is not a single bee in sight. I wish Alice were here. She'd be almost as devastated as I expect to be in a matter of minutes, but she would be here for me, and I for her. I wish Greg were here. I wish someone were with me, for fuck's sake. Is that too much to ask?

I knock again.

There's no answer.

The door is unlocked, so I open it.

The hallway beyond is devoid of life, but also lacks any puddles of that terrible tar-like substance. That's good. I step inside and close the door behind me. I think about Mrs. Castillero next door, how she's usually the first to spot me arriving for a visit. She sits out in her porch swing, sipping coffee for what seems like most of the day. Her absence was almost more jarring than my mom and Nana not answering the door.

"Mom? Nana?"

Cautiously, I move into the living room. It is exactly as I'd expect, though the television would normally be on at this time of day. Nana would be watching some atrocious daytime soap opera or other. The television is off, but I assume that's due to a lack of power.

The dining room is similarly empty.

I find my mother in the kitchen. I know it's her because Nana was getting too old to be able to use the kitchen effectively. There is a jar of spaghetti sauce open on the counter and a pot of water on the unlit burner.

I stifle a sob because my stomach muscles still hurt, then I just stand there for what seems like days. Time ceases to mean anything. I imagine what my mother might have been doing. Clearly, she was preparing food. I try to conjure her up in my mind's eye, but I struggle, and that brings me closer to tears, but mostly I just feel defeated. I stare at the sticky black mess on the floor in front of the stove. I wonder what her last thought was. I wonder if she was in pain. I wonder if Nana tried to help. Maybe she survived and was taken later, like Greg and Alice. Maybe they went together.

I don't want to think it, but I think it anyway: *what if Nana is still alive?*

It can't be true, can it? I venture outside and my stomach sinks as I find Nana's remains on the ground, just in front of her favorite garden chair. She's nestled in among a normally spectacular array of flowers in just about every shape and color you could imagine. It's not quite there yet — it's only April — but I can see the beginnings of how it will look.

Nana would have liked this to be the last place she ever got to be. In her garden among her flowers.

And that is the thought that tips me over the edge.

It was late afternoon when I arrived. I'm vaguely aware of being hungry, having had only the bare minimum of food since

I left Greg and Alice behind. I've tried to stay hydrated, but the near constant headache probably means I've not done a very good job. There's a supermarket a twenty-minute walk from here. I consider going, but I can't face it. I've walked enough. I've been through enough.

Despite everything, despite what's downstairs, I feel safe here. I became an adult in this house. I figured out my place in the world. I basically grew up here, in all the ways that matter. Fresno, where I lived with my mom and dad, means nothing to me. I barely even remember it.

I roam the house aimlessly, finding myself in my old bedroom. Not much has changed since I left for college. Then I'm on the bed, face up, staring at the ceiling.

In seconds, I'm asleep.

I couldn't do it.

I stared at them for such a long time, but I can't bring myself to... to clean up mom and Nana. I did it for Mark because I couldn't bear to see Alice staring at his remains. But... I just can't do it. It feels wrong, like this is where they're supposed to be, and I don't want to take them away. I know that's stupid. I know they won't know one way or the other, but I still can't do it. Part of it is the ick-factor I recall from cleaning up Mark. But most of it is that I just don't want to deprive them of being where they belong.

That means I can't stay here. I don't want to see them like that every time I want to use the kitchen or go into the garden.

I don't know what to do now, though.

I want to stay nearby. I love this place. This is where I belong just as much as Mom and Nana, I just can't stay in this particular house. There are plenty of vacation homes for the rich and annoying in the area, so I guess I'll find one and move in there. I spend much of the day hobbling around the town looking for places where I could be happy. I don't find anywhere, probably because *happy* is now an alien concept.

And besides, even if I found somewhere to live, what then? What is there for me? We had a plan when it was me and Alice and Greg, but if I'm the only person left, survival no longer seems all that important. If all the animals are gone, I can't surround myself with dogs and live as a crazy dog lady. There are no people, so even if I thought I could restart humanity — which I can't — there's one part of the equation missing. Can I really live out the forty or fifty years I might have left completely alone? Humans are social creatures. Why would I do that to myself?

Part of me understands the purpose of the trip before I set out on it; part of me thinks I'm just going out for groceries to begin my new life. I walk slowly, doggedly in the direction of the supermarket. The sun is going down, which makes people's remains less conspicuous. There are cars crashed into other cars, and into walls. I haven't heard an engine since I left the mall back in Portland.

The supermarket parking lot is filled with cars, most in parking spaces. There are some remains close to the entrance doors, but mostly the people seem to have been inside when the end of the world came for them. There's plenty of space to pick my way between them. I grab a hand basket and make my way to the drinks fridge, now silent and room temperature, and procure a bottle of water.

Then I head to the in-store pharmacy.

It's difficult to ignore what I'm doing as I'm doing it, but there's still a large part of my brain that refuses to accept that I'm preparing to die. Maybe not today, or tomorrow, or maybe even this year. But at some point, I'm leaving this life behind, and if the end of the world forgets about me then I want the means to do it on my own terms. I find what I'm looking for quickly – a large bottle of Oxycodone – then I head for the exit.

Outside the store, I freeze.

Out on the road beyond the parking lot, floating three feet from the ground, is a sleek black train that I now remember dreaming about the night before the apocalypse.

"Huh."

NOW

The second to last thing I do in this, my old life, is think about the people I loved. My Mom and Nana. Alice. I didn't love Greg, but he was certainly a major part of my life despite knowing him for only a couple of days. It seems only right that someone think about him under the circumstances, and given that I'm probably the only person left, I guess it falls to me.

That done, I sigh and climb aboard.

PART TWO

TWO

ALL ABOard

ONCE ABOARD, I turn around and watch the doors slide silently closed. Two illuminated buttons are set into a silver panel to the right of the opening. The top button depicts a vertical line with two arrows pointing outward on either side — the button to open the doors. The other button has the arrows pointing at the line — close.

There's a smell in here, like something once pungent has faded into the background over time. I have a momentary panic. This train is nonsensical, so why did I climb aboard? The second I ask myself this question, the buttons dim, and I'm trapped.

I chew my lip while I take in the space. It's a small vestibule, painted mostly black like the outside of the train. The carpet is red and gold and might once have been nice, but seems to have suffered due to wear. Maybe that's a good sign. Maybe there are actual living people on this train. There are three exits from here. The door I entered through, the one directly opposite on the other side of the carriage, and the one to my left, which must lead to the rest of the train. Opposite that door is a noticeboard, though it's not like any noticeboard I've ever seen. It's a matte black panel over which the word "Notices," rendered in bright white letters, hovers about a half inch above the surface. There are no notices posted.

I press my face to the front wall of the carriage and peer sidelong at the noticeboard trying to figure out how it works, but I can't. I lose sight of the word once I'm looking at it from ninety degrees. As soon as I return to looking at it head-on, the word becomes visible again.

I rotate to face the door that leads into the train. What the hell, right? I have nothing to lose that I hadn't already given up on some level.

I slap the top button, and the door glides open.

On the other side is a deserted passenger carriage that's more luxurious than my apartment in Portland. It's more luxurious than anywhere I've ever been, and I'd thought the house where I stayed with Greg had been pretty spiffy. The carpet here is that same red and gold, but it's thick and springy underfoot. Ornate light fixtures jut out from the walls on either side. There are sixteen armchairs in four groups, two on one side of a polished wooden table, two on the other. Experimentally, I sit in one and sink down into it. I feel like it's giving me the best hug I've ever had, which, under the circumstances, is very welcome.

There's a faint smell of something that reminds me of a spring day in a forest, and a pleasant warmth that I can't identify the source of. The carriage is absolutely silent, even when we begin to move. I snap my head to the side in shock, though I don't really know what I expected to happen. Trains go places. It's the whole point. I move to the window seat and watch dumbfounded as we start to rise into the sky, the supermarket outside growing smaller and smaller beneath us until I lose it in the darkness. I don't know how high we are when we stop ascending, but I feel the point where we start moving forward, slowly at first, then gaining speed.

My stomach lurches as we suddenly pass out of what I would recognize as the world and into something altogether more upsetting. Outside the windows are amorphous gray shapes stretching as far as I can see. At first, it's difficult to differentiate one from another, but the more I stare, the clearer the boundary between each one seems. They twist and swirl and seem to advance on the train, then pull back. They undulate and form spirals, then straighten out again. They pulsate. Some flash white. Some dim to near-black. Some resemble horrible tentacles. I touch my fingers to the glass, mesmerized, until I realize the shapes further away are much more languid than the ones close to me. They're dancing for me, vying for my attention. They want me to see them. The feeling comes unbidden: I want them to know I've seen them. I want to open the window and go to them, to float among them. I tap on the window and almost at once, hundreds of them dart over to that exact spot on the far side of the glass, flitting back and forth like ghostly fish in an aquarium. I exhale shakily, then stand. There are thick cloth curtains on each of the windows in here, and I waste no time in closing all of them.

I frown, and gaze around the carriage, hoping to spot the next inexplicable thing that will happen. When nothing does, I figure I'm done in here. I grab my water and my bottle of Oxy, then head for the door through to what I assume must be the next carriage. I'm almost right: it's another vestibule, more or less identical to the first, but the carpet is less tatty, and this one has four doors. One behind me, one on either side, leading to that swirling gray hell, now plainly visible again with no way to block it out, and one directly ahead. To the left of this one is another noticeboard.

I hit the open button and step through into a narrow corridor. The carpet is the same as the last carriage, but the light fixtures are slightly less ornate. Sturdy looking wooden doors line the walls, five to a side. A sleeping car, I guess. Good to know.

I'm about to move on when I notice that each door has a gold colored plaque at eye level, and the one first on my right has three words etched into it.

Eden Isabel Lucas.

I blink. That's me.

"Uhh," I say, mostly out of surprise. What does it mean that I have a room on an impossible train? A room with my name on the door, etched into what I assume is probably brass. Who did that? And when? Did someone know I was coming? They must have. That's worrying. It occurs to me for the first time that just because this train might have living humans aboard, that doesn't automatically mean I want to meet them.

After staring at the door like an idiot for several minutes, I reach out and touch the handle. Nothing untoward happens, so I depress it and push the door inward. My mouth drops open as I step inside, and I close the door behind me.

"What the..." This is my room. Not exactly, of course, but if I had a space this shape and size, this is how I would organize it. There's a bed in the corner because I never quite got over the idea that monsters might live underneath, and putting my bed in the corner means they could only get to me from two directions. Next to the bed is a desk, and this isn't a desk on par with the luxury items I've seen so far. This is a desk that looks like it came from Ikea. My kind of desk. Simple, functional, and affordable. I put the bottles of water and Oxy on it.

In the corner diagonally opposite the bed is a round table and four chairs, behind which is a mini fridge and a couple of cupboards and drawer units. There are no real kitchen facilities, but there is a microwave on top of the fridge.

Next, I cross to the window and pull the blind to block the ghost world outside, because looking at it feels like there's something tugging on my brain. That done, I head to the fridge, pull the door open hard, like I'm accusing it of something, and find it's stocked with all the things I like to eat. Cold cuts, half a watermelon, milk, yogurt, various types of cheese, and a variety of fruit juices. There's even a full bottle of vodka in the freezer compartment, for Christ's sake. This is basically my apartment, and someone has some serious explaining to do.

I turn around and find a violin case in the other corner. I shake my head in dismay, but I must be getting into the swing of things because I'm not in the least bit surprised to find *my* violin in the case. Maybe it isn't mine exactly, but it feels like it. It looks like it. The tiny scuff marks that are on my instrument are also on this one. Everything I need to play is here. Bow, rosin, even a small stack of sheet music. I examine the bow, apply rosin, pick up the violin and play a few experimental notes, then tune it. There's even a familiarity to the timbre that makes it *sound* like my violin. How is that possible?

I move to the bed and sit on the edge — it's exceedingly comfortable, far better than anything I could afford, but exactly what I'd buy if money were no object. I pull all the stuff out of my pockets. My phone – long dead, not even having enough juice to tell me the battery is flat — a few loose coins, and my keys. I put them next to the water and Oxycodone, then flop back onto the mattress.

Even if this train has a driver, I don't know how to access them. There was no door into the locomotive in the first carriage's vestibule. There were no doors or windows visible from outside, either. I'm going to have to hope that another passenger — if there are any — knows something.

I still haven't ruled out the idea that this whole situation is my brain misfiring as it slowly dies, but as everything feels so real, I decide I'm going to treat it that way. I need to figure out what the hell is going on, because none of this makes any sense. Call me crazy, but I like things to make sense.

There are still two carriages that remain unexplored. I debate taking my stuff with me. There has to be someone else on board, or the sign on my door is literally impossible. I don't want to lose the Oxy, I may still need it later. I open one of the desk drawers, looking for somewhere to hide the bottle and instead find a key that fits my room door, and that appears to solve that problem. If I think about it, it seems like that whoever operates this train might also have a key, but I figure I'm not going to be long. I abandon my stuff, leave the room and lock the door behind me.

In the corridor, I examine each of the other nine doors. The first eight all have plaques like mine, but none of them bear words. The final one is a bathroom, identifiable by the little pictographs of a man and a woman on its plaque. Good to know, I guess.

I turn and look back the way I've come. It's a little frightening. The corridor really is very narrow, with barely enough room for two adults to pass without touching. If someone were to enter from the far side, and that someone was hostile, I would have nowhere to go but behind me, into the next carriage, and then where? To the end of the train? Not for the first time, I feel trapped. I shiver and, with an effort, turn my back to the corridor.

I hit the open button on the door to the next carriage and freeze. It's a dining car. There are four polished wooden tables, each surrounded by four matching chairs rendered in dark wood and deep red velvet. There's a bar in one corner and what I assume is a small kitchen or storeroom walled off in the opposite corner, accessible by a plain white door.

At the table in the center of the room sits the room's only occupant: a grinning bald man.

"I was wondering when you'd get here."

THREE

MITCH

"WHO THE HELL are you?" I ask, far more abruptly than I mean to.

The man tips his head back and roars with seemingly genuine laughter, his cheeks gradually turning a slightly redder shade of pink. He laughs for so long that I start to fidget, feeling uncomfortable just standing in the doorway, apparently the subject of some hilarious joke I don't understand. I frown and take a step forward.

When he finally finishes, he looks at me and says, "My name is Mitch. Come in, won't you? Have some... dinner, I guess. The steak is wonderful."

I take a few apprehensive steps into the dining car and peer over the back of the chair closest to me. Mitch does indeed have a plate with a large slab of steak, mashed potatoes and baby carrots, the pretentious kind that still have part of the stem attached. "Where did it come from?"

"I have no idea!" Mitch says with a chuckle and a flamboyant shrug of the shoulders. "I just think about steak and a few minutes later, it appears in front of me."

"Well, that's impossible."

Mitch gestures to his food with a wry smile. "And yet."

I move a little closer. "It's dinner time?"

He eyes me a bit more seriously now. "It's whatever time you want it to be. There is no time on board."

I glare. "Am I supposed to know what that means?" I haven't seen any clocks on board. My phone should have told me the time, but it was dead when I pulled it out of my pocket. It shouldn't have been – I'd been keeping it switched off since the power went out – but I didn't think much about its deadness earlier.

Mitch says, "All right, so... wait, don't freak out, okay? It's a little weird when you first experience it."

I brace myself and wonder what's about to happen to me. "Experience what?"

A grin and a knowing look. "Can you tell me what year it was when you boarded the train?"

"I... of course I can. It was... uh..." I can't tell him. I haven't got a clue. I bring my fingertips to my temples as if I can channel my thoughts like a hokey sideshow mind reader, but it doesn't help. It's not only the answer to his question that's missing from my brain, it's everything that fixes me in time. I can't even remember the year I was born. "What the hell?"

"I know. It's strange, but you get used to it. It turns out time isn't really that important if you allow it not to be."

I'm still reeling from the idea that something has removed information from my head, or rendered it inaccessible, but a question occurs. "You've been here a while, then?"

He grins at me again. "I don't know. I can count the number of sleeps I have, or the number of dinners, that kind of thing. I etched it on the wall of my compartment for a while. I remember that number was close to a hundred, but then one day I woke up and it was gone. I've tried writing it on paper, but the paper eventually disappears. I stopped trying."

I'm not sure how I feel about this. Time is something humans use for so much. I feel untethered knowing that it's suddenly beyond my reach. I resolve to try to remember rather than write down the number of sleeps I have. If I don't write it down, it can't be removed, right? Then again, if my date of birth is missing from my head, maybe nothing is safe.

"Why don't you sit down?" Mitch asks. "You look a little pale."

I surprise myself by joking, "This is my natural shade." It's not a funny joke, but Mitch roars with laughter a second time. I'm getting the impression that he's one of those people it's impossible not to get along with. He shoves out the chair opposite him with one foot and I park myself in it.

"Good. That's better. Now, might I ask your name?"

"Oh, God, I'm sorry," I shake my head slightly. My mom instilled a rigid sense of politeness into me. I think it's understandable that other things have taken priority lately, but I still feel the tiniest bit mortified. "I'm Eden. Eden Lucas." I hold out my hand across the table and Mitch takes it, gives it a gentle shake, then releases it. His hand is ice cold.

"Oh, that's *perfect*. I'm Mitch," he tells me again. He's clearly quite a lot older than I am, but I find it difficult to put a number on that. Maybe that's a result of the inability to use time, or maybe it's just that Mitch doesn't have a very guessable age. He's bald except for the sides of his head, which are covered in thinning gray hair, and he has a scraggly gray beard with flecks of blond. All of that suggests he's maybe late fifties, early sixties, but his eyes are a striking dark brown and his skin taut and radiant.

"Nice to meet you," I say, the familiar rhythms of social interaction making me feel a bit more like myself. "And I mean that. It's been a really stressful few days."

His face assumes a somber expression. "Ah. The stories you hear on this train are some of the most interesting, though often horrible, stories you will ever hear in your life. When you're ready to tell me yours, I will be all ears."

"What makes you think I'm not ready now?" I'm not, but he doesn't know that. Right now, I'd be surprised if I ever want to talk about anything that happened to me again.

"I didn't want to presume. Would you like to hear how I ended up on board? I've told this story so many times it's lost its power over me."

A steak suddenly appears on a plate in front of me. It's accompanied with mashed potatoes and carrots. I flinch and Mitch grins. "Did you do that?" I ask.

He nods, clearly very pleased with himself.

My stomach makes a low rumbling sound, and I realize how hungry I am. I have barely eaten since I left Portland. "I'd love to hear how you ended up here," I say, then start eating. The steak is divine, pink and juicy in the middle and perfectly seared on the outside, with seasoning aplenty.

He speaks carefully, slowly, as if he's afraid he might miss some detail or other. "It was late winter, February or early March, I think, and my wife, Melissa, and I were on our way to visit our son, Thomas. We lived in Chicago, him in Idaho. I never understood why he moved to Idaho to tell you the truth, but there you go. It had been snowing in the days preceding our little trip, and though all the snow had been pushed to the side of the road, there was still a lot of it around. We set off late into the day, which was a mistake as it turns out. The sun was low in the sky already at the time of year, but it was dipping toward the horizon."

I put down my knife and fork and hold Mitch's gaze, not liking where this is going.

"I guess it was the glare from the piled-up snow and the low sun that did it, but suddenly I find myself staring at the back of a semi-trailer and still doing fifty-five miles per hour. I hadn't seen it. We hit it, and Melissa, who was never very good at remembering to wear her seatbelt, was thrown through the windshield."

My eyes widen. I don't know what I was expecting, but it wasn't this.

Mitch drops his gaze to the table. "I wore my seatbelt but it was still a pretty old car. Not very safe. My legs were crushed. I was trapped. I tried calling to Melissa, but she was face down on the road, not moving. I screamed for help, and of course, help came. People crowded around Mel, and around me. I started drifting in and out of consciousness, but I swear the last thing I remember is pulling myself from the wreck of my car. There was nobody around, Melissa was gone, as were the paramedics, but none of that seemed very important. I remember seeing a train, just beyond the tree line at the side of the road. This train. All black, except for a bright red line down the side. Then, despite my legs being crushed, and despite the fact I was trapped, I found myself walking to the train and climbing aboard, and here we are."

I'm staring at him, mouth agape. When he finishes speaking, I say, "My God, I'm so sorry."

"Thank you, Eden. Eat your steak, it's getting cold."

I take a reluctant bite, chew, swallow, then try to figure out how to respond to his story. He said it had lost its power over him, but I don't think that's true. It seems clear to me that he doesn't want to discuss it further, and I can't blame him. I think for a moment. "You said the train had a red line down the side?"

He nods.

"It had a white line when it came for me. Do you know that that means?"

He shakes his head. "No. I know it changes, though. There's a carriage further down the train that has a bunch of displays the same color. I don't know what the point of it is. I can show you later if you like."

I nod eagerly and take a bite of mashed potatoes. They are salty and buttery and wonderful. When I've swallowed, I ask, "So, do you know what this train is? Where it's going?"

His eyes get a faraway look in them, "Isn't it obvious?" My blank gaze must make it plain that it is not, so he continues. "It's not like this in scripture, but I think this train must be our ticket to the afterlife. To eternal paradise. To Heaven. That's why your name is so perfect. Congratulations, Eden. You're one of the lucky ones."

I concentrate on eating my food for some time, trying to make Mitch's assertion fit with my reality. I didn't die. I was the *only one* who didn't. Why would I need a ride to Heaven? If what Mitch said is true, this train should be jam packed with millions, maybe billions of people, but I shouldn't be among them. Given what I know about God, I'm far from convinced a heathen such as myself would be afforded a position in whatever passes for eternal paradise anyway. God never showed much regard for the people who did believe in him. Why would he show me any?

I watch Mitch eating his own plate of food, his motions slow and deliberate. He chews delicately but rhythmically, like a machine. Does this seemingly sweet old man honestly believe that this train is taking him to Heaven?

"It's just what I believe," he says when the silence stretches on long enough that I don't know how to restart the conversation.

I offer a half smile. "It's an interesting theory."

"But you don't believe it."

"I... don't really know what I believe. I mean, everything about this is impossible. I guess I haven't settled on a theory yet."

"That's fair. Well, let me know when you do. I'll be all ears."

I nod and the smile I present this time is more genuine. "Deal. So, is it just you and me, or are there other people on board?"

"Only one at the moment."

"Oh," I say. Three people. Only three people left in the entire world. Mitch seems nice, but I am conscious that I have only just met him. What if the other person is someone I end up not liking? What if he or she hates me? I push those thoughts aside. There aren't many people I can't find some common ground with, and I'll cross that bridge when I come to it.

"People come and go all the time. Some people linger, some people are only here for one stop. Don't worry, there will be others."

I don't have the heart to tell him that, no, there won't be. We three people now on board are all that's left of our species. Unless there are other planets with sentient life, and unless this train visits them — an idea that seems ludicrous — this is all there will ever be. And Mitch probably isn't a young man. Statistically, most people alive are likely to be older than I am, so there's a high probability that I will be left alone again at some point. I wonder how long the shelf life of Oxycodone is.

I return to Mitch's theory and turn it over in my mind. Nothing about it works for me. If the train is going to paradise, why would people get off along the way? I can understand more people getting on, but not off. Rather than question his beliefs, I make it the next item on my rapidly growing list of things to try to puzzle out for myself. "Do you know where people go when they get off?"

"Not specifically. The last guy to get off stepped out into a desert. There was a small town in the distance, maybe a half hour's walk away, but apart from that it was featureless."

"You've never been tempted to get off when the train stops?"

He looks momentarily surprised. "Me? No. I'm here all the way to the end of the line."

I smile and nod, then pop the last bite of steak in my mouth. When I've swallowed, Mitch moves to stand and says, "Come on, let me give you the tour."

FOUR

THE TOUR

MITCH TAKES ME through the fourth carriage, which is an identical copy of the first, and into the fifth, another sleeper car.

"This is my room," he says, pointing at the first door on the right. On it is a brass plaque engraved with three words.

Mitchell Joseph Powell

He doesn't offer to show me inside.

"Who does the signs?" I ask abruptly as Mitch is turning to lead me farther along the train.

He stops in his tracks. "What do you mean?"

"You say you have passengers come and go. Do they get signs on their doors?"

He nods decisively. "They do."

"Okay, so where do they come from? Who makes them? Who attaches them? Who removes them when the passenger leaves?"

Mitch grins, catching on. "I guess the same people who make the food." There's not a lot I can say in response to that. "Come on."

He leads me down the corridor and I note that, like my sleeping car, none of the other doors here have names on their plaques. Whoever the third passenger is must live in another car all their own. We enter the next car which is rendered in bare metal with a smell that reminds me of the times I took my car in for repairs. There are a few metal and wooden crates dotted around, secured to the walls with thick strapping.

"What's in these?"

"No idea," Mitch says without stopping.

I want to ask more questions, like where did they come from? Does the other passenger know what's in them? If not, why are they here? Is there a cargo service to Heaven, too? Does God have to order in from Earth to keep everyone in luxuries? I nearly ask these latter two questions as jokes, but I don't know Mitch well enough to know how he'll take them. I stay quiet instead and follow him into carriage seven.

"This is the one I was telling you about," he says. This car's floor, walls and ceiling are covered in a thick metal grille, behind which is a bright white line running around the perimeter roughly halfway up the wall. In the center of the floor is a black circle inside which is a cross, also glowing bright white.

"This all changes color to match the line on the outside?" I ask.

"I haven't actually left since I boarded, but other passengers have told me enough that I believe so."

"Weird."

Mitch doesn't agree or disagree, he just turns and marches off to the next carriage. Another sleeper car.

"Here we are," he concludes, stopping in front of the first door on the right. I wonder why we all have our own carriage, and why we've all been allocated the same room in our respective cars. On the door is a plaque which reads:

Rona Hamutana

"You'll like her, I think," Mitch says as he knocks. Seconds later an older woman with beautiful bronze skin, dark hair and eyes and a faintly amused expression that reveals an expectation of mischief opens the door.

"Mitchell!" she says, in a deep, sing-song voice. It sounds like she's greeting a long lost relative, not someone she presumably sees all the time. "And you found the new passenger!"

"Hi. I'm Eden." I hold out my hand and Rona shakes it twice, firmly.

"Rona. I saw you get on. I was the one who told Mitch we had a newcomer. It's been a while since we had any new blood on board. It's nice to meet you, Eden."

"Likewise." I turn to him. "This is why you were expecting me when we met? Rona told you about me?"

"Exactly," Mitch says, then to Rona, "We're doing the tour."

Rona fixes me with her gaze, something I find a little unsettling. "There's not a lot more to see, I'm afraid. There's another couple of cars after this, but that's all."

"Oh. Well, it has more than I expected," I say before I can catch the words. I don't want to talk about anything from the time before.

"How do you mean?" Rona asks.

But I also don't want to lie to the only people left alive. "I... I dreamed of this train. A few days before it came for me," I say, hoping that's sufficient.

"You did?" Mitch asks, his voice suddenly harsh, his expression stern. As I watch, surprised, he rearranges his facial features into something more neutral. "That's... certainly strange."

I hesitate. "Yeah. I didn't think anything of it at the time. But then it came to pick me up."

"Remarkable!" Rona exclaims, clapping her hands together.

I smile tentatively. "I guess neither of you did, then? I was kind of hoping I might not be the only one."

"No... no, you seem to be unique in that regard," Rona says thoughtfully. "Listen, I'd love to stay and chat, but I'm right in the middle of something. Perhaps we can all meet for breakfast in the morning and talk some more?"

I can't escape the idea that Rona is trying to get rid of us, but I acquiesce, "I'd like that."

"Wonderful! I'll look forward to it. It was lovely to meet you, Eden."

"You too," I say, and watch slightly bewildered as Rona closes the door.

"That's Rona," Mitch says unnecessarily. "She's often busy with one thing and another."

I think of the violin in my room and wonder if everyone on board gets to keep something of their former lives. I wonder what Rona's thing is. Maybe I'll ask at breakfast tomorrow. It feels wrong to gossip about her with Mitch, though I'm sure he'd tell me. "She seems nice."

"Mostly," Mitch admits, then changes the subject. "You want to see the last two cars? They're not very interesting."

"With a sales pitch like that? Sure."

He grins, then turns and leads me into the next car, which is another replica of the first, then a final sleeper car. Everything is the same as all the other sleeper cars except this one has nothing but blank plaques, plus the bathroom. I gesture at the door at the far end of the carriage. "That doesn't go anywhere?"

"It's locked. I guess if we pick up more carriages, it might be unlocked."

"By the same people who make the food, right?"

He laughs. "You're catching on."

FIVE

THE CLEANSING

"WELL, I USUALLY turn in early and get some reading done," Mitch says.

I wonder what exactly he's going to read. Our tour didn't include a library, and the rooms aren't exactly large. I guess if I have a violin in my room, it's feasible that his room is full of books. Perhaps he was an avid reader in his previous life. It doesn't matter. I'm glad of the opportunity to be alone to try to figure this place out properly. I nod. "All right. Well, thanks for the tour. I'll see you tomorrow for breakfast."

He looks at me for a beat, appearing to consider whether to say more, then nods, turns and waves as he walks away.

I watch the doors slide closed behind him.

First things first: I press the buttons for the allegedly locked door at the rear of the train. They don't do anything. I pull at the door's manual handle, but it doesn't budge. That's probably for the best. I don't really want to fall out into that vortex of swirling horror if I can help it, but I wanted to verify the facts as they're presented to me. Mitch told me the door is locked. The door is indeed locked. That checks out.

I wonder about the rooms. I'm surrounded by vacant rooms. Someone or something prepares them for the passengers. Someone or something puts plaques on the doors. Someone or something prepares the food. What else does this mysterious force do? It's surprisingly easy to think of this as a normal train when I can't see outside, but I need to remember that it isn't. I don't know its purpose, its route or its ultimate destination. I don't know what the rules are.

So, what *do* I know?

I start with the absolute basics. I'm on a train. The train gets around by flying. That, to me, seems futuristic. Could the cooking and room prep be done by some sort of advanced artificial intelligence? It doesn't explain how food can just appear in front of me like it does, and it raises some uncomfortable questions about the ordering process, like can this hypothetical AI read my mind? Who or what has access to the information it finds there?

I decide to head back to my room, figuring I can at least try to find out what else on board works the same way. I pause in the dining room where I met Mitch and pick up a napkin, then I shred it and deposit it on the carpet outside my room, treading it into the plush fabric for good measure. I glance around guiltily before deciding I don't care if anyone saw me. Fuck it. Nobody can expect me to behave rationally given the circumstances, and treading a little paper into the carpet isn't exactly a capital offense.

I unlock and open my door and I'm home, at least insofar as that word still has any meaning. When I close and lock the door behind me, I feel an immediate sense of relief.

"What the hell did I do to end up here?" I ask the silent room. When it doesn't answer, I sigh. I'm exhausted. I've done nothing but walk for days on barely any food. I'm still mostly holding the floodgates of my emotions closed, something that's going to drain me of my remaining energy. I look over at the bed. While I could probably sleep for a week, I feel gross. I quickly go through the drawers and cupboards that line the back of the room and find towels and shampoo, plus an array of lotions.

The bathroom at the end of my carriage is all marble and granite. There's a clawfoot tub in the center of the space, and if I thought I could stay awake long enough to use it, that's exactly what I'd do. I know I'd be asleep in seconds though, so a shower it is. I turn the water on, as hot as I can stand, then double check the door is locked before undressing. I have bruises on my arms and legs that I don't have any recollection of getting. I stand there for several seconds as the room fills with steam, watching the water pour down the drain, then I close my eyes and step forward into the stream of water. I suck air in through my mouth as the sudden change in temperature hits me. I struggle for a moment to maintain my composure, but then I exhale the breath in a loud sob. The floodgates open and I am helpless against the torrent that comes gushing out.

It's a very childlike thought that pounds its fist at the back of my mind.

It's not fair.

I cry for Greg, who I never really knew, but he, along with everyone else, didn't deserve what happened to them.

It's not fair.

I cry for Mom and Nana as I picture their faces at the end. I imagine fear and confusion. I imagine unrelenting pain. They never hurt anybody, and they raised me to be the person I am. Why couldn't there have been a genetic component to whatever it was that happened?

I smash the side of my fist against the wall as the weeping becomes more intense and the muscles in my stomach start to hurt again. Good! Let them. I put my index finger into my mouth and bite down as hard as I can bring myself to. It just brings more mewling.

It's not fair, dammit!

Mostly, though, I cry for Alice. She was a fiercely intelligent, talented woman hindered by the simple fact that her upbringing didn't allow her to believe anyone who told her she'd done well. She kept searching for someone she could believe, but I know she never felt worthy. I hope to any Gods that might exist that she died in her sleep, and not spending her last seconds regretting wasting so much time and effort on those completely unjustified feelings of inadequacy. I cry because, as much as she may have believed herself unworthy in one breath, in the next she would be fighting for everything she deserved. The job, the husband, the inevitable clutch of pale smiling children.

And I cry because I'm here, on this train, with people that I don't want to be with, because they're not the people I lost.

It's not fair.

When I get back to my room, my eyes sting and my finger hurts where I bit down on it. I'm dripping water from my hair all over the carpet because I didn't bother drying it, just pulled my clothes on over my wet skin. Now, as I confront my bed, a new wave of sadness washes over me for the things I myself have lost, mixed with a healthy dose of guilt that I'm even thinking such a thing when I'm still alive.

Still, I can't help it.

I strip off my wet clothes which have now wicked the moisture away from my skin and left me mostly dry. I towel my hair briefly, then I climb into bed, pulling the covers up over my head so everything is dark, and I can pretend I'm absolutely anywhere else.

I try not to drift off to sleep thinking about how I'd have loved to be the cool aunt to Alice's children, despite never wanting any kids of my own. I try not to think about how I'll never make concertmaster. I try not to think about how I'll never experience the heart-stopping wonder of a majestic orchestral piece ever again.

Eventually, I sleep.

The disorientation when I wake is immediate. There is no indication of what time it is. There's no sunlight through the window. I have no clock. The train's lights are apparently turned on permanently with no obvious way to turn them off. Recalling my idea about the AI, I groan, "Lights off."

Nothing happens.

If this were a spaceship, its schedule would at least fake a circadian rhythm. The train doesn't appear to do that. Maybe it's a consequence of time not working. I don't know what time I went to sleep, and I don't know what time it is now. It could be midnight. It could be noon.

It's an effort not to be annoyed by this. I have to tell myself that knowing the exact time isn't a skill that humans have always had. Sure, they had the sunrise and sunset to go by, but there's only one question I need answered right now: do I feel rested?

The answer is, surprisingly, yes.

That makes it morning. If it is actually four in the morning and it's just that I've woken up at a particularly favorable point in my sleep cycle, I can always take a nap later. I need to get used to the idea that it doesn't matter. I don't have a job anymore. I don't have anything. There is no reason to get out of bed, and so if I don't want to, I don't have to.

It hits me then that the disorientation I felt wasn't entirely due to the lack of time. It feels like we're slowing down. Are we about to make a stop? Or maybe this section of swirling gray hell has a speed limit for some reason. I already know we can't be about to pick up another passenger because there are no people to pick up, but I'm still curious.

I climb out of bed and pull on my clothes, squirming in discomfort at the dampness against my skin, and walk haltingly over to the blinds covering the window.

Just a peek, I tell myself.

I lift a corner of one blind slowly and am shocked by the intensity of the sun outside, bathing the world in its brilliance. I pull up the blind completely. Below me, I see an expanse of pristine water that mirrors the clouds. Trees cluster along the edge of the lake in groups, as if daring each other to take a dip. Scattered among the trees are red brick buildings with corrugated aluminum roofs. They look mostly dilapidated, but as we rush past, I try to focus on each one long enough to notice the movement I desperately hope to see inside. Some evidence of humanity, of anything. Some reason to go on.

I don't see anything.

I look hopelessly from side to side, taking in as much of the outside world as I can, wanting to see something that will prove to me that everything is not lost. It's strange, watching the train traverse its surroundings like this. There are no tracks, no obvious navigation of any kind, we're just plowing through the air about sixty feet up, gradually drifting toward the ground. I notice that the train is rounding a corner. From my position near the front, I can see the rear carriages.

How many cars did we visit on Mitch's tour?

The first passenger car, this car, the dining car, another passenger car, Mitch's car, the room with the crates, the room with the white light, then Rona's car, another passenger car, and then a final sleeping car. That was ten carriages. I can see... it must be double that number at least. I don't have time to count all the way to the end because we straighten out and I lose sight of the back.

I wonder if Mitch knows. Or Rona, for that matter. I'm not a naturally suspicious person, preferring to listen to the words people say and take them at face value rather than trying to infer hidden meanings; but how can you be on board for as long as Mitch and not notice how many cars the train has? All our rooms are in the same position in their respective cars. Maybe Rona wouldn't be able to see the back — she's closer to what I now believe to be the middle of the train — but I'm fairly sure Mitch would. How can they not be interested in exploring the train fully? Maybe they know how long it is and just can't get through the locked door. It's not like Mitch specifically told me how many carriages there are, just that we'd reached the end of the accessible ones.

Maybe it boils down to the fact that Mitch isn't looking for answers because he thinks he already has them. I, on the other hand, find my to-do list increasing with every new thing I notice. My immediate question, though, given that the train appears to be making a stop, is: should I get off? So far, I've seen nothing to suggest that I should.

I open my compartment door and find the carpet is spotless again, all traces of the shredded napkin gone. The train AI is responsible for cleaning, too, then. I'd thought it might be. Maybe there are little cleaning robots that run around after everyone's gone to bed. I wonder if there's a way of monitoring how it happens, but there's every chance it'll happen the same way food is served in the dining car; something so close to magic that I can't think of a better word.

I arrive in the vestibule at the front of the first carriage and watch more of the world pass by. Where are we? It's much the same as the landscape I've already seen, I'm just closer to it now. Large bodies of water with tracts of land snaking their way through it, adorned with trees and ruined buildings.

Then I see it.

There's an animal down there! Something thrashing in the water. A crocodile, I think. Or an alligator? I don't know how to tell the difference. I didn't think there was anything left. What if I was wrong? What if this is somewhere far away from Oregon and there are still people here? What if life is going on as normal out there?

The rate of our descent increases, and I feel the train's forward motion slow to a crawl. I need to think quickly. Are we stopping for supplies? Maybe the train's artificial intelligence needs an upgrade. Who knows? Perhaps we are going to pick up another human person after all. If there are alligators out there, maybe there are people. Maybe I was wrong about the end of the world.

Is it possible that the train has brought me here specifically because there are other people? Maybe it's coming to a halt because somehow the AI that runs the place knows what I'm looking for and has delivered me here because it knows I can find it. If that's the case, as soon as I step off, the train might depart. Is that what I want? I would be lying if I said I didn't want to puzzle the train out.

I don't know what to do.

I scan the vista for more signs of life and see none. If I saw an actual human, I think I'd get off in a heartbeat, but so far the alligator is the only living thing I've seen, and those things outlived the dinosaurs. The fact they also outlived humans doesn't tell me enough. The train finally comes to a halt. There's a soft chime from behind me, and I turn and find the noticeboard's display has changed.

Passengers may not exit here.

The doors remain closed. The buttons for opening and closing them do not light up. I couldn't get off if I wanted to. Still, I grab the handle and give it a shove. It doesn't move, not even a little bit.

Sometimes it's nice to have a decision taken out of your hands.

SIX

Breakfast

I MAKE MY way from the vestibule to the end of my sleeper carriage and stand facing the door leading into the dining room. I take a deep breath, hold it, let it out. This, apparently, is how I prepare to speak with the only other members of my species.

I press the open button.

Mitch and Rona are already sitting at a table. They look up as the door slides open and smile at me, Rona rather more warmly than Mitch. The smell of fresh roasted coffee hits me immediately.

"Eden! How did you sleep?" Rona asks.

"Pretty well, actually." I step into the room and make my way to the table, pull out a chair and park myself. Rona has a half-finished plate of scrambled eggs while Mitch has a clean plate in front of him. They both have mugs of coffee and I conjure up an image of one for myself, not believing for a second that such a thing will work.

"Good! That's good. The first night can be... trying," Rona says.

"Not being able to turn the lights off probably doesn't help," I say.

"No, that is something of an oversight," Mitch agrees.

"I'm glad you're here," Rona says. "Perhaps you can settle our little argument."

I raise one eyebrow. "I can try."

"Eden doesn't need to hear about our squabbles," Mitch says, and Rona casts her eyes to the table for a moment.

I glance from Mitch to Rona and back, wondering what I'm walking into the middle of. "You were squabbling?"

"No, not really," Mitch says.

"We were trying to guess where you were from based on your accent," Rona admits, and this time both of my eyebrows reach for my hairline.

"So, you were squabbling about me."

Rona fixes me with a stare for a second and I think I see something pass over her face. An expression I can't read. It's gone almost as soon as it appears, and she breaks into a wide smile. "I suppose we were!"

I frown. "So, what'd you guess?"

"Florida," Rona guesses immediately.

I chew my lip. "Not exactly."

Mitch suggests, "California, right?" He says it as if he knows, not as if he's guessing, and I frown again. I wouldn't introduce myself as being from California. Oregon has been home for two thirds of my life.

"Yes, actually. Originally, I mean. I haven't lived there for a long time. I live in Oregon now." I pause, then add. "Lived."

"That's a very good guess, then, Mitchell," Rona says.

"I'll second that." I don't think I sound like I'm from anywhere in particular. Mitch shifts uncomfortably in his seat, and I'm not sure where to look.

Rona's gaze lands on me again. I lock eyes with her, and she stares at me almost vacantly for several seconds before she seems to come back to life. "Why don't you tell us about yourself, dear?"

I blink. "There's not much to tell."

"Oh, come now. Everyone has a story."

This is starting to feel like an interrogation, but I decide to go with it. "Born in California. Moved to Oregon when I was young because my mom wanted to be close to her mom."

"Family is important," Rona supplies.

I nod. "I studied music. I played violin in an orchestra in Oregon. That's pretty much me." Sure, I've glossed over pretty much everything, but talking about anything from my life in any great detail is going to make me sad. Any people I could talk about are dead now, any places are long gone.

"Oh, how wonderful," Rona says, clapping her hands together. "I haven't heard a violin for, well, a very long time! They're such moving instruments, don't you think?"

I nod. "I guess they are." Then, despite knowing she can't answer, I find myself asking, "How long is a very long time?"

Mitch jumps in. "What were your favorite things to play?"

I blink at the unexpected derailment but turn my attention to Mitch. "Can't beat the classics. But I played some show tunes and movie scores in college. That was fun."

My coffee pops into being on the table in front of me and I pick it up and inhale the aroma deeply. It relaxes me a little. "Not sure I'll ever get used to that."

"Things appearing from nowhere?" Rona asks. "It startles me every time. I remember a time when—"

"Rona," Mitch says, and my spine tingles at the calm tone of authority he uses. "Eden doesn't need to hear about our nostalgia."

I want to tell him that actually, I'd love to hear more about them. I don't want to talk about me. It's too painful right now. I need more time to come to terms with everything that's happened, but I don't want to go against Mitch's surprisingly firm assertion. I glance at Rona who is scowling at the table, but then she notices me looking.

"Forgive me. So, would you care to tell us how you came to be here? It's different for everyone, but I like to keep track."

Like you keep track of who boards and leaves? I almost say, but manage to stop myself. I don't want to talk about this, but as she's asking directly, I don't feel like I have any other choice. "Well, everyone I knew and loved died when the world ended, then I saw the train. Figured what the hell, you know?"

I catch Mitch's wince out of the corner of my eye and find myself smiling inwardly. I blow across the top of my coffee and take a tentative sip. It tastes wonderful, just the way I like it.

"My goodness," Rona says when she sees that I don't plan to say anything else. "You poor thing, that sounds terrible. I can't even imagine."

"Yeah, it sucked pretty hard."

Mitch asks, "What happened, exactly?"

"I don't know. People started screaming, then bleeding from their eyes and noses and fingernails. Then they kind of melted into puddles of black stuff. Me and a couple of others survived, and we traveled together for a little while, but then they died too. I think everyone is dead. The animals, too."

"Wow. That's..." Mitch begins. "Do you... I'm sorry, this is probably very insensitive, but do you have any idea why you survived?"

I shake my head, then wait for the threat of tears to pass. "No," I say eventually, and take another sip of my coffee. I want to end this conversation as soon as humanly possible, so I figure monosyllabic responses are the way to go.

As if Mitch has sensed my thoughts, he says, "Well, I'm terribly sorry for your loss."

Rona adds, "You seem like you're doing okay, though?"

I stare at her. Talk about tone-deaf. I'm not okay. I'm far from okay. If it looks like I'm doing okay, that just means I'm better at pretending than I thought I was. "Have you ever lost your entire species?"

"I... no, I haven't. But neither have you. You have me and Mitch!" She sounds altogether too pleased with herself about this revelation. I stare some more while Mitch shifts in his seat again.

"No offense, Rona, but I don't know either of you. And, again, no offense, but you're not my mom, you're not my Nana, you're not Alice. You're not anybody to me. You are just two people I stumbled on in this fucked up end of world nightmare." Half a sob escapes me before I can stop it, and I slam my palm down on the table, causing the coffee cups to shake and Rona to jump. I stare into the middle distance, trying to dry my eyes.

When Rona puts her hand on mine, I fight the urge to snatch it away and shout *don't touch me!* I don't want to be here. On this train, at this table, with these people. They're both just a reminder that everyone I had in my life is gone. Rona whispers, "Just remember, you have options," then removes her hand from mine and glances at Mitch. I see something I don't like in that look, but it's gone before I can figure out what it means.

I remain silent for some time, calming myself down, waiting for it to feel like I won't start crying as soon as I open my mouth, then I change the subject. "Do you know why the train stopped just now?"

Mitch answers, "The train stops from time to time. Sometimes it picks up passengers, as I said yesterday. Sometimes it drops them off. Sometimes it doesn't seem to do anything, just sits there for a little while, then starts moving again. I think it's maybe refueling, or something like that. Occasionally, people will load or unload some of the crates you saw in carriage six." It sounds like a canned response he's used on every passenger he's ever met.

"What's in the crates?" I ask, not for the first time.

Mitch shrugs. "I don't know for sure. I assume supplies for the meals."

"The train runs its own inventory? Orders its own stock, then makes stops to pick it up?"

He smiles. "I guess so."

I really wish I knew how long they've both been on board. I want to know how much effort they've put into finding out the answers to some of the questions that burn in my mind. I want to *know* why the train stops. I have no use for their idle speculation about it. The more time I spend on board, the more I need answers. I think the general impossibility of the train itself has made me wonder what else might be possible. If a flying autonomous train can exist, and I can be on board, what's to stop even more fantastic things from being possible? I've been reluctant until now to even acknowledge this thought because I don't want to get my hopes up... but what if there's some way the train can reunite me with my family? Who knows what the rules are? Mitch and Rona clearly don't, but I need to.

"What about carriage seven?" I ask. "Anything ever happen in there when the train stops?"

Mitch's eyes narrow for a second, then he shakes his head. "Not that I've seen, no. Why?"

"Just feels like the odd car out. Everything else seems to have a purpose."

They both smile at me, and both smiles feel forced. Mitch says, "I guess you're right. But no, I've never seen anything happen in there. Rona?"

Thoughtfully, Rona drawls, "No... No, I think it's just one of those inexplicable things we're not supposed to understand."

I nod, and decide that based on their answers, I need to check out that carriage further. I change the subject again, because I'm getting a little weirded out by the vibe in the room. I'm not sure what I'm picking up on, but there's more to these people than meets the eye. "Do you think it'd be possible to get off the train the next time it stops, but get back on again before it leaves?" I ask, thinking specifically of the number of carriages I saw out of my window versus the number of carriages Mitch took me to. Maybe I can get off the train the next time — that is, if the doors actually open — then run along to carriage eleven and get back on.

Mitch makes some considering sounds and rubs at his face. "I think it's probably risky. What if the train leaves without you? I doubt it'd find you again."

I ignore the implication that I'm an idiot who wouldn't have considered that and change the subject again. "So, Rona," I say, and she looks surprised. "I've heard Mitch's story. How about you? How did you come to be aboard? Everyone has a story, right?"

It feels petty to repurpose her words, but I would be lying if I said I didn't get some measure of satisfaction from it. Rona glances at Mitch, then throws another of her unsettling gazes at me. She inhales deeply.

"I lived as part of an island community. It was thousands of miles to the nearest landmass. My people were starving, and disease was ravaging the island. The seas were often too stormy to catch fish, and we didn't have enough wood to repair our boats."

I can feel the isolation in her words as she speaks them. Once again, this story feels completely alien. I would never have guessed at it, much like I would never have guessed at Mitch's.

Rona continues, "I discovered a book in our town hall. I couldn't read it, but I could feel a sort of power coursing through me as I held it. I took it, and I learned to read it over the following months or years. Some of the letters were like ones I was used to, and some were pictographs which I eventually puzzled out. By the time I was done, the population of the island was less than a third of its peak. But I learned something from that book. I learned of a... a ritual, I suppose. It seemed like it might help."

I frown. It's starting to feel like a work of fiction, but I suddenly realize I have no idea what time period we're talking about. If time doesn't mean anything, maybe Rona has been here fifty, sixty years. She looks like she could be old enough.

She goes on. "It took a long time. We had to dig down into the earth and erect big stone tributes, I guess you'd call them. They were really focusers of energy, I think. Anyway, one day when I was at the bottom of the hole we were digging, a man I had never met descended the slope from the surface and greeted us. Recall that this is an island thousands of miles from anywhere, so this was unexpected, but I felt the same power flowing off him in waves that I felt when I held the book. He offered to help. He claimed to know something of the ritual.

"Sadly, tragedy struck. The excavation collapsed in heavy rains, killing many of the men and women I had recruited to help, and trapping me. The strange man found me, spoke words of comfort to me, then he departed. Sometime later – it may have been moments or days – I saw this train."

"Wow, I'm sorry," I say. "Why do you think the train came for you?"

She glances at Mitch, then returns her gaze to me and shakes her head. "I don't know."

I try to keep my expression neutral at the obvious lie and when it becomes clear nobody else is going to speak, I say, "Well, that's quite a story."

SEVEN

The Surprise

WE TALK SOME more, but Mitch and Rona eventually take their leave of me. I breathe a sigh of relief when I'm alone. Talking to them, trying to decipher their weird dynamic, was exhausting. I sit there quietly for some time trying to work it out. Mitch interrupted at least twice that I can remember, steering Rona away from a particular avenue of conversation. What was that about? How did Mitch know I was originally from California? Was that just a lucky guess?

What was Rona about to say when Mitch interrupted? We were talking about the food just appearing on the table, and she started to say she remembered a time when... what? When that didn't happen? When it was delivered normally, by some sort of waitstaff?

I wonder about the relationship they have. Do they like each other, or merely tolerate each other? Is that what I have to look forward to? A life of merely tolerating people I'd rather not associate with?

When I'm sure Mitch and Rona must have reached their respective rooms, I take off in the direction of my own. I need to figure out if there's a way through into carriage eleven. Maybe there's something in my room I can use to open the door. I search and I search, but there's nothing. Not even a paper clip I could use to pick the lock. Of course, not knowing the first thing about picking locks would be a bigger problem. I'm not even sure what type of lock it has. Maybe it's electronic. Instead, I decide to just head down to carriage ten and see what I can see. Perhaps I'll figure something out. On impulse, I grab the bottle of water I boarded the train with. It's good to stay hydrated, and I don't think I've completely recovered from my hike across Oregon.

I hurry past Mitch's room, aware that hurrying is unnecessary but not able to stop myself. I'm not doing anything I shouldn't. It's not Mitch's train. It's not Rona's train either. Just because they have no obvious interest in figuring out its secrets doesn't mean I'm not allowed to. I pause in car six, eying the crates. Most of the wooden ones have lids that are nailed shut. I could probably get into one given enough time, but it wouldn't be easy. I would need to find a crowbar or something.

Carriage seven has a green line running around its interior today. I walk through slowly, checking the walls for anything that might tell me the purpose of the space, or failing that, some way to access the light for maintenance. There's nothing. On closer inspection, I see that the green line is hovering a half an inch from the wall like the text on the noticeboards. I sigh and move on.

I hesitate as I pass Rona's room. I could knock. I could ask what she was about to say before Mitch interrupted her.

But I don't.

In the next carriage – a passenger carriage – I pause and turn back to face the way I've come. The blinds are up in here and I can see the swirling grays and whites and blacks on the other side of the windows, but I think it's become less awful. It's still unpleasant to look at, still evokes a visceral reaction, but it's starting not to bother me that it's there. I'm learning to ignore it. Or maybe it's letting me ignore it right now, I don't know.

In carriage ten, I get a few paces down the corridor then stop in my tracks. Something is different. Something I caught out of the corner of my eye. What was it?

I glance around slowly, trying to figure it out, then I take a few steps back.

The first door on the right now bears a name.

Kyle Jacob Kinney

I stand there dumbstruck for several seconds. Then I knock.

The man who opens the door is nearly a foot taller than me with a long angular face and an expression evoking melancholy. His eyes are dark chocolate and look haunted, his skin a rich shade of brown. His hair is mostly black, but the smattering of gray at his temples makes me think he's probably a couple of decades older than me. He wears a khaki shirt and matching pants and gazes at me disinterestedly.

"Uh, hi," I say. His height hurts my neck and I take a step back. He frowns fleetingly as I do.

"What do you want?" He has the deep booming voice I expected would go with a gentleman of his stature. It's hard not to be intimidated by him.

"I just noticed this room was occupied. It wasn't the last time I checked, and I just wanted to say hi and make sure you were okay."

He stares at me but says nothing.

"I'm Eden. Eden Lucas. I have a room a few carriages ahead." He continues to stare, and I can feel my cheeks starting to burn. I blink. "So, you're new. You weren't here yesterday."

"Hm," is all he says, and accompanies it with another frown.

I'm not sure how hard to push. I decide maybe he needs to be left alone to come to terms with his new surroundings having survived an apocalypse. "Okay, I get that you might be feeling disoriented or sad, any number of things. I'm going to leave you alone, but if you want to talk, my room's in the second carriage from the front." I smile tentatively, then turn to go.

"Wait."

I turn back.

He stares at me some more, but he looks uncertain now rather than disinterested. Suddenly, he steps aside holding the door open for me, and I enter a literal prison cell. The floor and walls are gunmetal gray, the ceiling white. There's a bed bolted to the floor in the same corner mine occupies and a window opposite with its blind pulled down. Diagonally opposite the bed are a toilet and a tiny washbasin.

"What the... what is this?"

"It's a prison cell."

"I... yeah, I can see that. Why, though?"

Kyle deflates, crosses the room in two massive strides and plops himself down on the uncomfortable looking metal-framed bed. "Yours isn't like this?"

I'm still looking around confusedly. "It's not, no."

Unexpectedly, Kyle begins to cry. My eyes go wide and I'm not sure what to do. I don't know if he wants comforting, or even if he'd accept comfort from a stranger, but it's not in my nature to ignore someone in pain. I go over and sit down on the bed next to him, putting my hand on his shoulder. "Hey," I whisper. "What's wrong?"

He sighs a deep, shuddering breath. "I thought I was free," he says. "It was almost my time. Then this train comes, and it seems like I can escape the... the..." He shakes his head. After a moment, he goes on. "For a while, I thought I had escaped. I sat in the passenger car ahead of this one and enjoyed the luxury. I couldn't believe my luck. Then I found a room with my name on it, opened the door and—" he gestures around the room, "—this."

I can't stand seeing the big guy crying. "What do you mean it was almost your time?"

"To die," he says. "I was on death row."

"Oh."

I'm opposed to the death penalty. I'm also firmly of the belief that people can change if they want to, even despite all the evidence I've seen to the contrary. I'm nothing if not stubborn. Kyle's revelation is a surprise, but I keep my hand on his shoulder and I don't make any kind of move to get away from him. I try not to think about the kind of things you have to do to end up on death row, but I find it's not that hard. This man doesn't seem dangerous, he seems beaten down.

"Most people would have run a mile at this point," he says. "Escaped death row inmate and all."

"Not most people."

He turns his head to the side and gazes down at me, then laughs a trifle uncertainly. "Maybe this is freedom after all."

"I wouldn't be so sure about that. It's... well, it's weird here," I say with a half-smile. Judging that my hand has been on his shoulder long enough, I withdraw my limbs back into my personal bubble.

"How do you mean?"

"Okay, so... life was basically normal for you?"

"As normal as death row gets, sure. Lots of sitting around and thinking."

"But everyone else was fine?"

"Fine how?" He rubs his chin.

"Alive."

A pause, then, "Everyone was alive. What aren't you telling me?"

I think about it for a second, twirling my hair around my finger. "I don't actually know. I'm here because I thought I was the only survivor of an... apocalypse, I guess. Everyone died. I'm pretty confident it was everyone, or nearly everyone, in America. But now you're here. So, that's another thing for my ever-increasing list of shit that doesn't make sense. Do you know how long you've been aboard?" I shake my head. "No, sorry, of course you don't."

He frowns. "What do you mean? It's only been... uh..." His eyes widen and dart around.

"Okay, so that's lesson number one. Time doesn't work here. I can't even tell you what year I was born. Any idea when the declaration of independence was signed?"

"No," he says, drawing out the word for a couple of seconds. He looks puzzled, but not worried. That's probably a good thing. "That's stupid."

I grin and nod. "It is. Second lesson: don't look outside when we're moving. Have you... have you looked already? It's kinda unsettling, but I don't think it's dangerous."

He looks confused. "I saw outside in the passenger car..."

"Ah. Yeah, this is different and only happens after we've been moving for a while. Do you want to see what I mean?"

"No, but show me anyway."

I like that response, so I get up and walk over to the window. "Ready?"

He nods and I pull the blinds up. I don't look out myself because I've seen it enough already. I try not to study Kyle's reaction, instead fixing my attention on his cell's door. I hear his sharp intake of breath and he gasps, "What the hell is that?

It's…" He pauses for some seconds before whispering, "It's like they're coming for me."

"The shapes outside? Yeah. I felt like they were trying to get my attention." I pull the blinds back down. "Still, we don't have to look at it, whatever it is. I may not know when I was born or when I boarded the train, but I do know I haven't been here that long. I haven't figured out the ins and outs yet, and the other two people on board don't seem interested in helping me."

"I'll help," he says immediately, and the look of child-like excitement on his face melts my heart. I assume it's because he's not used to being able to do things, any things. His grin suddenly falters and disappears, then he adds, "If you want me to."

"I absolutely want you to," I respond, then walk back to the bed and rest on the edge. "I'm guessing you got on when the train stopped earlier. What prison were you in?"

"Florida State, near Jacksonville. Why?"

"I was hoping you'd say somewhere covered in marshland. That's what I saw out of the window when we stopped, plus a bunch of ruined red brick buildings and maybe an alligator. Not where you were?"

"Nope. It was pretty where I was. A lot of trees. Florida does have gators, though."

"Just another mystery for the list. I can give you a tour if you'd like."

"In a minute. I'm kind of enjoying talking to someone real. It's been a long time."

"How long?" I ask before I can stop myself. "Sorry. Stupid question."

He smiles. "Yeah. No clue. The feeling of weight the memories carry, though... it must have been a long time. For what it's worth, I didn't do it. I guess that's what they all say, but I genuinely didn't."

I don't know what to say. I'd already accepted him, flaws and all. I don't need reassuring, but he seems to care what I think. I guess a prolonged period having your only human contact be with guards and other inmates must take a mental toll. Maybe he had visitors, but I don't want to ask. "I believe you."

He gives me a grateful look, then continues, "So... you mentioned something about an apocalypse?"

EIGHT

GOSSIP

AFTER A LITTLE squirming, I tell Kyle I'm going to grab some food and that I'll be right back, then I excuse myself. I'm not eager to relive the end of the world, and I have some reservations about my story now that someone else has boarded. From the little I've heard of Kyle's story, the world seemed to be functioning pretty much fine when the train found him.

Once I'm outside Kyle's room, I lean against the opposite cabin's door and exhale.

There are a few possibilities to explain his presence, but I don't like any of them. First is that I simply didn't notice his door had a plaque on it and Kyle has been on board longer than I have. That would directly contradict Mitch telling me that there was only one other passenger, though. I also remember checking the doors as Mitch and I walked through this car. I don't believe Kyle could have been on board and we just missed bumping into him, which was another of my ideas. That just leaves the outlandish ones. Can the train travel through time? That's a nice, neat thought, at least until I think too hard about it. It might explain why time on board doesn't work. Maybe it explains everything. The train simply picked Kyle up earlier in time than it picked me up; before the world ended.

My other theories require mental leaps I'm not willing to make right now.

Time travel, though... if it's possible, I could see my family again. All I need to do is take control of the train, and from everything I've seen, it's fully autonomous.

Another problem for later, then.

I walk to the dining car intending to order Kyle the steak dish I had the previous night, belatedly hoping he isn't vegetarian, and find Mitch alone reading a newspaper.

"Whatcha reading?" I ask brightly in lieu of a greeting.

He looks up. "Hi, Eden. Just an old newspaper." He folds it and holds it out to show me. I take it and look at the date. It says March 19th, 1907, but I have no frame of reference. Is that when Mitch is from? Maybe it's when I'm from too. I just have no way of knowing. I guess I could rule it out by looking at some of the grainy pictures or reading some of the stories. Maybe I'll try it later.

"Cool," I say, handing it back. "Where did it come from?"

He takes it back and places it on the table in front of him. "Another passenger, I think. Long gone now. What are you up to?"

"I'm just getting some food. There's a new guy in carriage ten."

Mitch looks at me a beat too long. "Ah, yes. Kyle, is it? I haven't had the pleasure." He sounds vaguely disappointed by this. Or... something else? Displeased, perhaps. Maybe he considers himself the train's welcome party and is annoyed that I got there first.

"How did you know he was here?"

"It's remarkable what you can see on board if you spend some time looking," he says with a wry grin.

I nod as if I know what he's talking about, then try to fill my mind with thoughts of steak, mashed potatoes and carrots, as well as a bagel with smoked salmon and cream cheese for me, since I only had coffee earlier. As an afterthought, I conjure up an image of two cups of coffee as well.

Then I wonder if Mitch is trying to drop a hint of some kind. Maybe I should be doing more poking around. I haven't done any, not really. There are twenty-seven other sleeper compartments that I haven't even considered looking in. There's the kitchen in here. There are more bathrooms than the one I used.

There's whatever's beyond carriage ten, too. Maybe something about carriage seven needs puzzling out? It's a lot of open space that seems like it might have a purpose, but no way to tell what that might be.

For a second, I consider asking if Mitch knows how long the train really is, but something stops me. Instead, I offer him my best smile. "I'll keep that in mind."

"About earlier," he says. "Rona can be... I guess a little blunt. She doesn't mean anything by it."

I raise one eyebrow. "I'll keep that in mind, too."

"You do that," he says with a smile, then stands with obvious effort. "Right. I think it's about time for my nap."

"Enjoy." I watch him shuffle out of the room. Shortly after, my food and coffee appear in front of me. I hunt around for a tray, finding one behind the bar, then carry everything back to Kyle's compartment.

"This is great!" Kyle remarks sometime later.

I smile. My bagel is ancient history and I've nearly drained my coffee, too. "Food's no good on death row, huh?"

"My last meal was pretty good."

My mouth drops open. "Wait. You had your last meal? Like your *last* last meal? The one you get before they..." I trail off.

"Yeah. Well, it's usually a couple of days before. Not immediately. I had pizza. That was nice. Do they have pizza here? I could really go for a Chicago-style deep dish pizza right about now."

"You're cheating on your steak. Don't be that guy."

He laughs and it's deep and pleasant and slow. I wonder when he last had cause to laugh about anything. "Don't think it's cheating if it's just in my head," he says.

I know he's eager to hear about the end of the world. Just as eager as I am to never have to relive that experience, but I guess he has a right to know about the fate of his species, at least as I understand it.

"So, the end of the world went something like this..."

And I tell him.

When I'm finished, I'm crying.

"Hey," Kyle says. "It's okay. Wherever they are now, they're in a better place." He's referring, of course, to Alice, and my mom and Nana. I screw up my face and cry more at his kindness, but I don't tell him that I think he's wrong. I think they're just dead. Maybe they're still out there somewhere in time, but I don't know.

"Thanks," I say, then spend some time sniffling before deciding to change the subject. "So, how about that tour?"

"Maybe later. First, tell me about the other people on board." His expression speaks of eagerness, but some apprehension.

I grin and wipe at my eyes. "All right. Well, Mitch is an old guy and he seems pretty nice, but he's convinced the train is taking us to see God."

Kyle's eyes widen. "Seriously?"

"Seriously. He was involved in a car accident. He thinks he died, and this is how he gets to heaven. Trouble is, it doesn't fit with our stories. I didn't die. You didn't die. Mitch's wife *did* die, but she's not on the train with him. Maybe she was destined for... the other place."

Kyle snorts. "You're not supposed to say things like that about the dead."

I feel my traitorous cheeks turn red and I force a smile. "Yeah, well. The other person is Rona. She's... weird. Like a sweet old lady who doesn't realize what she's saying or how it could be perceived as irritating."

"Not a fan?"

I shrug. "Eh. She's okay, I guess. In small doses." Thinking about it, Kyle is the only person on board I can see myself becoming genuine friends with. Mitch is nice enough, but I don't feel much of a connection, and something about him feels a little off. I'm not sure what to make of Rona.

The train jolts and lurches suddenly. I fall to the side, bracing myself with my arm. Kyle hits the wall, but not hard. He looks bewildered when he recovers, but I think I know what's happening.

The train is stopping again.

NINE

THE OUTSIDE (1)

"SHIT," I HISS, standing up.

Kyle stands, too, but seems to be looking frantically around the room for some kind of threat. "What's happening?"

"You said you wanted to help, right? Want to start right now?" I flash him a desperate, hopeful smile.

He looks confused, but nods. "Sure, of course."

"There's a lot I haven't had a chance to tell you. Did you try the door at the rear of this car?"

He nods again. "Yeah, it's locked."

"Right. But there are carriages behind us. I saw them out of the window when the train was rounding a corner. I was going to try to get into carriage eleven – that's the one behind us – the next time the train stopped. So... want to come with?"

He hesitates for a fraction of a second, but then beams and says, "Sure."

"We might get trapped outside. I don't know what's out there, but you're a wanted man."

He bobs his head. "Let's not get trapped then."

I laugh. "Which doors did you use to get on?"

"The ones at the front of the passenger car ahead of us."

We hurry out of his room and I grab my water bottle as we leave, then we make our way quickly to the front of carriage nine. Once in the vestibule, we begin the agonizing wait. I can see a city in the distance, but it's not one I can identify from its stunted skyline. The land around it is almost unfeasibly flat and tinted orange. The road system forms a grid, which I think means this is the Americas somewhere, possibly Utah or Arizona. I don't see any traffic on the roads.

"We're still a long way up," Kyle remarks. He's standing right next to the door, peering out the window.

I stay where I am, back to the wall between the noticeboard and the door into car eight. "Can you see what's below us?"

"Whole lotta nothin', looks like."

"I guess that's a good thing."

We've almost stopped moving forward and haven't started descending, and I'm wondering if we're just going to hover here then move on, like we're waiting at some nonsensical signal. I will the train to descend. It hangs stubbornly in the air for a long moment, but finally starts to sink to the ground and I silently rejoice. Maybe I'm one step closer to figuring out something real about the train.

"We need to be quick," I say, moving next to Kyle. "I don't know how long the train will stay put once it's stopped."

Finally, we reach ground level. Kyle and I share a nervous glance and I turn my attention to the buttons that control the doors.

Come on, light up!

I'm about to give up hope when the Open button illuminates and I smash my palm into it, eager not to lose the opportunity. The doors slide open in front of me. I take a deep breath and I'm overwhelmed by the smells of life. Flowers and trees and pollution and soil and everything else. It's like I've never smelled anything except the inside of this fucking train. I can feel the breeze on my skin, taste the fresh air. Kyle looks over at me, grins uncertainly, and we climb the short ladder to the ground.

Then we're running alongside the train. I'm vaguely aware that the line on the outside is teal, but I can't comment on it. I'm panting. Kyle is several strides ahead of me, but neither of us stops.

We reach the start of carriage ten.

I suddenly realize I can think about time again. I want to call out to Kyle, to ask him what year he boarded, and to tell him when I did. But if I call out, he's going to stop. If he stops, we may miss our opportunity.

We reach carriage eleven.

I've been terrified that we'll have to turn back, that the buttons on the outside of the train won't be illuminated, or that the doors will be locked, but I'm relieved when Kyle reaches the entrance, slaps the open button and the doors slide apart. He climbs aboard, turns, then helps me up. The doors slide shut immediately, the open button dimming to black.

"That was lucky," Kyle says breathlessly.

I nod, but it almost feels like the train was waiting for us to get back on. As if confirming this, it starts to move as I stand there panting. We take some time to recover as we watch the world outside become gradually more distant.

"Do you remember what color that line on the outside of the train was when you boarded?" I ask when I can speak.

"Kind of reddish-brown. It was blueish just now. What does that mean?"

"I'm not sure. It was white when it came for me."

"Maybe it's, like, each color is a different stop along the route."

My eyebrows shoot up. "That's... I hadn't thought of that." I start to wonder if it might be possible to catalog the locations, try to get some idea about each one, then if we revisit one that we like the look of, maybe we can get off.

"Come on," Kyle says. "I'm dying to see what's through that door."

I grin. Me too.

TEN

Lara

WHAT'S THROUGH THE door is not nearly as nice as the front half of the train. It's not exactly Kyle's prison cell, but it's also not what I'd call luxurious. The passenger compartment has the same basic configuration – sixteen chairs in total, four tables, all spaced far apart – but everything feels cheaper and looks less comfortable. The walls are plain white, the lights provided by fluorescent tubing recessed into the ceiling behind plastic panels. The carpet is black edged with gray, basically the same as the fabric covering the meager cushioning on the chairs. Something about it feels more correct than the furnishings up front, though. The black of the carpet and other fabric, the grays, the whites. It reflects the train's own external color scheme, and that of the scary shit it travels through most of the time. A world in monochrome. Right on cue, the daylight outside is replaced with said scary shit, and I realize that there are no curtains in here.

"Oh, fuck that," I say, wondering if I could pull the carpet up and fasten it over the windows somehow.

Kyle is staring out of the window closest to him. "God, it's... it's..."

"Try not to look at it."

It takes him some effort to meet my gaze, but when he does, he nods. "Come on, let's look around." He strides past me in the direction of the rear vestibule. When he's five feet from the door, it opens, and he stumbles back against one of the chairs. A woman steps into the carriage. She has long reddish-brown hair parted to one side and tucked behind her ears. She stops when she sees us and her expression morphs from one of hopeless resignation to one of frantic wide-eyed wonder in a split second. She darts forward, stopping in front of Kyle. "Oh, my God!" she yells.

As she looks Kyle over, I realize she isn't a woman. She can't be older than sixteen. She looks past Kyle at me, then hurries over. "Oh, my God! Are you... you're real, right? I'm not imagining you?"

I'm startled into a smile. "We're real. Who are you?"

She casts a glance back at Kyle, who is looking perplexed. Shyly, she tells us, "My name is Lara."

"Hi, Lara," I say. "I'm Eden. That's Kyle."

She laughs as if this is the funniest thing she's ever heard, then claps a hand over her mouth, eyes bulging. "Sorry. I thought I was alone. Except for the ghosts. You're really real?"

Kyle walks closer. "The what now?"

The girl spins to face him. "The ghosts. I don't know if that's what they are really, but it's what I call them. They make noises when I'm trying to sleep. And when I'm not. But mostly when I am. Actually, I don't seem to do much else."

I blink at this, wondering how long this girl has been on board with nothing but spooky noises for company. "You have a room?"

She nods. "Where did you come from?"

I consider how best to answer that while I look her up and down. She's painfully thin, but beautiful. Her heart shaped face carries a faint spray of freckles. I always wanted freckles as a kid. She stares at me with earnest dark eyes. "We're from the front half of the train. This is carriage eleven. The door into ten is locked." I point toward the front of the carriage unnecessarily.

She looks around, as if searching for someone or something to verify this version of reality. When she finds nothing, she eyes me skeptically. "So how did you get here?"

"We went outside when the train stopped just now," Kyle says in his deep, calming voice.

Lara frowns, appearing to consider this, then nods, satisfied. "Do you guys have rooms?"

I nod. "We do, but they're in the front of the train." I hadn't considered that we'd lose access to our rooms, but hopefully one of the empty ones might be habitable. I wish I'd brought my violin, but the only thing I have from my room is my bottle of water.

"Well, I can show you around back here if you like. It'll be nice to have some company. Come on, I'll show you my room. It's ridiculous!" She leads us through carriage twelve, which is another dining car, but one which would look at home next to Kyle's prison cell. It's sparsely decorated with metal tables and chairs and not a lot else. There's no bar here, and no sign of a kitchen. I wonder if it works the same way as the other one, but Lara is at the far end before Kyle and I are even halfway across.

Carriage thirteen is a clone of eleven.

Fourteen is interesting, and I initially assume it's our destination. It's a sleeper car in the same tradition as mine, but the decor is all white. The walls are clad in white plastic, the floor in white carpet tiles. Each of the white doors carries a white plastic sign with bold, black letters. Every sign has a name, though I don't have time to read many before Lara is in the next car. The ones I do read are only first names, not full names like the ones at the front.

Fifteen is another car with crates, but this one is stacked floor to ceiling. There's barely any room to move and at a couple of points, we need to climb over a low wall of boxes. Lara does this with the ease of someone who's had a lot of practice, and I wonder again how long she's been on board.

The next carriage is our destination. Carriage sixteen.

It's another sleeper car, like the last one. Only one of the doors bears a name, and it's the first on the right.

Lara Mae Parker

She giggles as she slides a key into the lock and pushes the door open. "Come in, won't you?" she says excitedly, giving a theatrical sweep of her hand as if welcoming us to a party she's been planning for months.

"Thanks," I say as I pass her. I stop in my tracks when I'm inside.

It's a girl's bedroom. A very girly girl's bedroom. If I had to guess, it's decorated for a six-year-old who is obsessed with Disney princesses and *My Little Pony* and... pink. Everywhere I look is pink. Pink mesh fabric hangs down over her bed to form a canopy. I watch as she dives through an opening and lands on the mattress, then turns to face us.

"It's not quite right," she says. "There was different stuff at home, but it's a pretty good match."

I stop gazing around for long enough to look at her and ask, "How do you mean?"

"I had all this stuff in my room as a kid. Not anymore, of course."

I wonder again about Mitch and Rona's rooms. I wonder about the vacant sleeper compartments I haven't been inside yet. It seems like everyone's assigned room is at least based on their actual bedroom. I stare at a *Care Bears* poster on the wall behind the bed. Owing to my own obsession as a kid, this is the first thing that's allowed me to guess at something related to time. It's an original *Care Bears* poster, not from the reboots. I don't know the year, because that's a concept with no meaning, but I know the *Care Bears* ended shortly before I was born. I watched it on VHS. Does that mean Lara is from a similar time period, or is it simply that she was a retro child? Perhaps this isn't as helpful as I'd thought.

"Pretty cool though," I say. "I loved the *Care Bears* when I was younger. Who's your favorite?"

Lara looks down as she says, almost apologetically, "Funshine Bear." When nobody else speaks, she looks up, glances from me to Kyle and back to me, then apparently encouraged, adds, "I wanted to be him! He laughs and jokes all the time and I..." She trails off.

"I always liked Good Luck Bear. Pretty shade of green," I say. I notice Kyle in the corner and initially mistake his expression for bafflement. "Not a fan?" I ask him, and suddenly he looks like he's in pain. I turn back to Lara in a hurry. "Can you tell us how you got here, Lara?"

She sighs and adjusts her position on the bed. "My dad. I'm the youngest of three sisters. Our mom died when I was really young. I don't even remember her. Samantha – my oldest sister – left home as soon as she could. I was devastated because I didn't understand why she was leaving me. It was only when Paige did the same thing that I understood. Dad... he takes his... *frustrations* out on the oldest daughter. I had no idea he knocked them both around a lot, belittled them, bullied them, until I was the only one left and he started doing it to me."

"Oh, Lara," I say, but she continues as if I've not spoken.

"I grew to resent my sisters for their weakness. Why did they let it go on for so long? Why was their solution to leave and let the next sister deal with it? After a while of being the sister on the receiving end, I kind of understood. Whatever confidence or happiness I gained was systematically knocked out of me whenever my dad had a bad day, or when he drank too much, or whatever it was. If you can't summon the will to fight for yourself, how can you be expected to fight for your sisters?" She stops talking and shakes her head. "I still resent them, though. Maybe I shouldn't, but I do. I tried to ask them for help, but they wouldn't. As much as they hated him for what he'd done to them, they weren't willing to see him in prison or whatever. They thought my mom's death was the reason he was so screwed up and he didn't deserve to be punished for what it had done to him. I was scared they wouldn't back me up if I went to the cops on my own, though, so I didn't. I figured I'd just deal with it until I could leave home, too. I think I wasn't far off... I can't remember how old I am. Is that weird?"

I shake my head. "No, honey. It's something about the train."

Lara nods, apparently satisfied with that half-assed explanation. She goes on, "The day I got on the train was the day I finally got sick of it. I was supposed to be going out with a friend, but dad had dumped a stack of dirty dishes in the sink and expected me to wash them. I refused. He hit me, so I hit him back. Hard enough to knock him over. I didn't mean to, though I'm not exactly sorry. He's getting old and I'm probably as strong as he is now. I realized quickly that the day when I could finally leave home had arrived without warning. I ran. I got to the street and this train was waiting. I got on. I didn't even think it was strange until it started flying."

When she's finished, she looks down at her hands and fidgets. I walk over to the bed and perch on the edge. "I'm so sorry that happened to you."

She looks at me. "It is what it is. I didn't have to take it nearly as long as Sam did. For a while, after Paige left, I thought I deserved whatever I got. I think I realized something my sisters never did, though."

"What's that?"

"I didn't deserve any of it. They both got out, sure, but neither of them is doing great on their own. I think he broke them. But everything my dad did says nothing about me, and everything about him. So, fuck him. I'm glad I got away."

I nod emphatically. "You're a smart kid." On impulse, I put an arm around Lara and pull her close for a second. She tenses initially, but relaxes into it quickly. I glance over at Kyle, who's looking like he wants to smash something. I can't blame him.

Lara pulls away from me. "So, how did you both end up here?"

ELEVEN

KYLE

To my surprise, Kyle begins to speak, and he visibly struggles with the words.

"I was on death row," he says. I feel Lara shift next to me, and Kyle goes on, "Eden already knew that, and she's already shown me more compassion than, well, pretty much everyone I ever met." I blink at this, but hold Kyle's gaze. "What she doesn't know is why I was there."

"It's going to sound like a cliché, but I never had much. I dropped out of high school and took whatever dead-end job I could find. My family never had any money, and I was determined to stop leeching off of them as soon as I was able. Eventually I got a job in a supermarket and started to work my way up. I was doing okay. It wasn't a glamorous job and it didn't pay that well, but it was steady money, and more than any of my family had when I was growing up. I could finally help them out, you know? It felt good.

"I met Leanna while I was assistant manager. She was a cashier and we hit it off immediately. She had her own problems and knew the same poverty as I had growing up. I didn't know how deep her problems ran back then. It was a couple of years later when she got pregnant. I was still assistant manager, and she was still a cashier and I wasn't sure how we'd make it work, but I was still over the moon. I thought maybe I could try for another job somewhere else. I had experience now, and that seemed like it was valuable. We had a tiny apartment in a shitty part of town, and I hoped maybe we could move into something better, you know? Well, I got that better job, and we got a better apartment. It had a room for the baby, and I put money aside every paycheck for things to put in there. When the baby - Jade - finally came, I reckoned I must be about as happy as anyone has ever been.

"Leanna was different, though. My new job had longer hours and I wasn't around as much. I never knew if she resented me or not because she wouldn't talk to me. Finally, when Jade was in kindergarten, Leanna was able to get part time work. We relaxed into a routine.

"I should have known something was wrong the first time I found bruises on Jade."

Lara's sharp intake of breath next to me pulls me out of Kyle's story, but he starts talking again quickly.

"I asked Lee about it, but she said it must have happened at kindergarten, and I believed her. I didn't even consider that she might have been lying. It happened a few more times over the next year and I started to notice Jade becoming more and more withdrawn, especially around her mother. I still didn't put two and two together. Jade kept asking to spend more time with me, but I had work."

Lara shuffles closer to me and grips my right arm as she listens. I figure we both know that a story that ends in death row means that one or both people in it are going to wind up dead. The fizzing in my stomach is almost too much to bear.

"Our new apartment wasn't in a much better neighborhood than our first. I still had a gun for self-defense, and I had a baseball bat I kept behind the door to the place. I came home one time, six months later, and found Jade motionless on the floor of her room, surrounded by blood, the baseball bat lying six feet from her. I ran to her. Tried to pick her up, to revive her. Then I noticed Leanna standing in the corner with my gun held up under her chin. I shouted, pleaded with her not to do anything stupid. She didn't offer any last words or any explanation. I think she... she just wanted me to watch."

Lara moves even closer to me. I put my arm around her. Tears streak down Kyle's face as he continues to speak.

"Of course, they pinned it on me. I didn't know at the time, but she'd been talking at work about the bruises Jade kept getting and wondering aloud if I might be hurting her. When the cops interviewed Leanna's friends, they were all convinced I did it and they'd never even met me. I swear to you both that

I didn't do it. I'm telling the truth. I can't imagine how any mother could do what Leanna did. I can't imagine how any father could do what yours did to you and your sisters, Lara. I just—"

He stops and starts to sob.

"You okay, kiddo?" I whisper to Lara.

She nods and I extricate myself from her and go to Kyle, kneeling before him. "I believe you," I say. "I'm so unbelievably sorry for your loss, but I believe you." I wonder if it's a coincidence that everyone on this train has such sad stories. I feel like I've been commiserating with people almost non-stop since I got on.

"Me too," Lara calls from her bed.

I stand and walk to the side of the room, stopping next to a *Rainbow Brite* poster. It seems like an appropriate counterpoint to what I'm about to say.

"I suppose this is as good a time as any to tell Lara about the end of the world." I recap that particular nightmare for Lara.

"So, my daddy's dead," Lara says, breaking the silence that has descended. She doesn't look particularly broken up about this possibility.

I tip my head to the side. "It's difficult to say for sure. I'm confident Kyle wasn't on the train when I got on, which means he came from some place the world hadn't ended. I've been starting to wonder just how localized it was. We all know time doesn't work on board, but we can puzzle certain things out. That *Care Bears* poster is from the original television series. That was over before I was born, but I watched it obsessively on

VHS. I also know there were a lot of reboots after the original series. I think they did a reboot of *Rainbow Brite*, too, but it didn't go so well."

"What's a reboot?" Lara asks, which lends further credence to my time travel theory.

"It's where they take something that was perfect the first time and they make it worse."

Kyle is surprised into a laugh, which I guess means he knows what I'm talking about. He wipes at his eyes.

Lara smiles as if she gets the joke, but I can tell that she doesn't. "It's where they remake something from the start and pretend the original never happened. Some stuff gets rebooted over and over again. I never understood why they just couldn't leave things alone."

"Money," Kyle says.

I nod. "Probably. Okay, so, what's the most recent movie you guys remember being out before you came here?"

"*The Lion King*!" Lara squeals immediately, and I can't help but laugh.

I've seen it, of course, but I think I was too young when it first came out to see it on the big screen.

"*Forgotten Flame*," Kyle says.

"I don't recognize the name. Any others?"

"Hmm. I didn't get to see much of popular culture. *Scent of Memory*? I think that's what it was called."

I ponder, but I don't recognize that either. I'm kind of half-assing my way through a theory that has us all on the same timeline, but from different points along it. A scene from *Back to the Future 2* pops into my head as I consider that maybe Kyle came from an alternate timeline, and that maybe there are many alternate timelines. It isn't lost on me that the third film in that franchise features a time traveling train, either. If the multiple timeline hypothesis holds, that makes everything about this situation far more complicated. If I intend to see my mom and Nana and Alice again, I need to not only find the right time, but the right timeline. "Nope. Don't know that one either. But here's what I'm thinking: I think we're all from different times. I think this train can time travel. Lara, it seems obvious that you're from a time a few years before I was born. Kyle, well, I'm not sure. Can you think of anything else that might let us pinpoint you?"

"What if I'm from so far in the future that neither of you is able to corroborate anything I say?"

"That... I hadn't thought of that. Is the stuff in here familiar?" I ask, gesturing at the posters.

"*Care Bears*, yeah. I don't know that, though," he says, pointing at the *Rainbow Brite* poster. "But it's possible I just wasn't paying attention."

"God, I wish we could go outside for a minute."

"Why?" Lara asks.

"Time works out there. We went outside to get to carriage eleven where we found you. We were in a hurry though. We should have had this conversation, but we didn't."

"Then I think that needs to be our plan," Kyle says. "The next time the train stops, we go outside. We take a piece of paper and a pen — if we can find those things — and we write down as much as we can remember about ourselves. When we're back on board, we can compare notes."

I nod along as he talks, growing more excited with every word. "That," I say, "is a wonderful idea."

TWELVE

THE SEARCH

I'M STARTING TO get tired but, of course, I have no idea what time it is. This feels like a mid-afternoon slump. It can't possibly be bedtime, can it? I decide maybe food is the answer. "Who's hungry?"

Lara looks timid. "There's some stuff in my refrigerator, but not much..."

"Hey, you don't have to give us your food. I know a much better way to get it. Kyle, I don't think you know this either."

"I figured when you brought me food that you just got it from the dining car."

I nod. "I did. But it's... a little weird."

On our way to the dining room in car twelve, we stop in fourteen, the sleeper car with the names on all the doors.

"Do you know who these rooms belong to?" I ask Lara.

She shakes her head. "I've knocked on the doors more than once. Nobody ever answers, and they're all locked except the bathroom."

I can't resist trying for myself. I pick the closest door – the name on the sign reads simply 'Jane' – and knock gently. When there's no response, I hammer with the side of my fist.

"What, you didn't believe me?" Lara asks.

"I did. I just... I don't know. I want there to be someone home."

She gives me a knowing smile. Kyle looks like he wants to give it a try, too, but after a moment of indecisiveness, we decide to move on.

The dining room is even more depressing than I remember. Vinyl tiles adorn the floor, mostly a dirty shade of off-white, but some are black. There's no pattern to it, but I guess maybe someone wanted to liven the place up a bit. It didn't work. The walls are beige and, surprisingly for a carriage meant for passengers, there are no windows. The crate cars and the one with the colored line don't have windows either, but I wouldn't expect them to. It seems odd in here, but also welcome as we don't have to look at the outside world. Harsh fluorescent lights flood the space with a pallid glow that reminds me of lemonade. We plop down at the first table we come to.

"Okay, let's do a magic trick," I say. "Think about your favorite meal, but don't tell me what it is."

"Eden, I'm hungry," Lara whines.

Kyle glances uncertainly around the room, then gives me a look like he thinks I might be insane.

I grin. "Trust me, guys."

"Okay, okay," Lara says. "I'm thinking of it."

After a moment of hesitation, Kyle chimes in, "Me too."

I picture a burger and fries, melted cheese oozing out of the bun, with an orange Fanta. I wonder if we can get brand names here. I didn't see any familiar brands behind the bar in the dining car where I met Mitch, but that doesn't necessarily mean anything.

"Now what?" Lara asks.

"Now we wait."

"Seriously?" Kyle asks.

"Seriously. It works in the other dining car, anyway. At some point in the next few minutes, whatever you imagined will appear on the table in front of you. I can't guarantee it'll work here, but I'm hoping it does, or we're going to start having problems. Especially if we can't get back to the front half of the train."

"What's it like?" Lara asks. "Up front, I mean."

"It's pretty nice. Luxurious—"

"Apart from my room," Kyle adds.

"—yeah, apart from that. It's very functional back here, not very pretty, not that comfortable. But it's nice up front. We'll take you to see it when we can."

She seems inordinately pleased by this and smiles down at the table. "Thanks."

"No worries, kiddo. So, you haven't seen anyone else since you got on?"

"Nope."

I wonder again how long she's been roaming the carriages with nobody but her ghosts for company. I wonder why she's locked back here when Kyle and I weren't. Because she's a child? Some other reason?

Kyle and Lara both recoil in surprise as plates of food appear on the table in front of them. I laugh.

"Jesus!" Kyle says.

"Pretty cool, right?"

The first thing I notice is that brand names are allowed. Kyle has a can of Dr Pepper, Lara has Coke, and I have my Fanta. Perfect. It does beg the question: how the hell? But I'll think about that later. For his meal, Kyle orders the Chicago-style deep dish pizza he told me about. Lara has gone for sushi, which I spend a moment staring at, wondering where the hell the train sources its fish. My burger and fries glisten with grease, the cheese just starting to become melted enough to begin making its escape from its bready confinement. Oh, God, I need this.

I take a bite, trying not to moan with pleasure this time, and I think of Alice. This is basically what I ordered for lunch on the day the world ended. That's why I ordered it. It's hard, knowing I'll never see her again. It's hard knowing that about everyone I loved, everyone I *knew*.

The more I think about ways to get back to them, the more convoluted they start to seem. Timelines and causality and confusing shit like that. Anywhere I choose to go, they wouldn't be *my* family, *my* friends. They wouldn't know who I am, unless I already existed, and that would be so weird, and... completely unfair of me. What if I happened upon a timeline where I'd died as a child? What would re-inserting myself back into my family's lives do to them? Maybe they'd accept me and maybe they wouldn't, but... I don't think I can do that to them.

I'm sobbing and the tears are landing on my fries. "Eden?" Lara asks. "Are you..."

I shake my head before she's finished.

"What's wrong?"

I can't seem to control my voice, but I manage to choke out, "I'm just realizing I'm never going to see my family again." I'm annoyed that I let myself believe there might be a way to get back to them. I got my hopes up.

Lara gives me a sympathetic look, as does Kyle. I take a deep breath and try for something coherent. "I've been thinking ever since I formed my time travel theory that I could maybe take charge of the train and somehow make it take me back to my family. Until now, I didn't consider how weird that might be. It either wouldn't be my exact family, or they'd not be able to deal with the fact that there are two of me, you know?"

Kyle nods, his head lowered.

"But..." Lara says, and I meet her gaze.

"But what?" I ask when she hasn't spoken for a while.

"Sorry, I'm thinking. Are we saying that we're going to spend the rest of our lives on the train?"

"We could get off, I guess. But who knows where we'd end up, or when?"

"So that's what we're saying. We're stuck on the train because it's familiar?"

"Lara, I don't think that's what Eden's saying," Kyle says.

It's not what I'm trying to say. Not exactly, but maybe it's close enough. I have everything I need to live here except everything that makes life worth living. Maybe if I leave, I can find people to share life with. Or maybe I'll walk for years and never find another living soul. It's not a bet I'm willing to make. "I guess it is what I'm saying. You're free to do whatever you want, though."

"Right," Lara says, and returns to her food. I think I've upset her.

Kyle says, "We need to find out what the train is and where it's going. We can't say anything for sure without knowing that. We might reach the end of the line and be forced off into some unimaginable hell. Maybe into that gray shit that's out there. We need to know what other stops are along the way."

He's exactly right. He has this knack of cutting through the problem and getting to the crux of the matter. "How do we do that?"

"We start by searching every inch of the place."

I nod, thinking about the crates, and about the empty sleeper compartments. Even if the doors are locked, maybe we could break them down. "Yeah. Yes, okay. Let's do that."

"Can I finish my sushi first?" Lara asks, apparently electing to not be pissed at me. Good. I didn't have that skill at her age. "It's really good."

I smile. "Sure thing."

We stand outside Lara's room some time later. My hand is on the handle of the door across the hall.

"It'll be locked," I say.

"The only way to know is to try it," Kyle says.

He's right, but I still find myself apprehensive and I'm not sure why. It's not the potential invasion of privacy, though I don't honestly believe there'll be anyone behind the door. It's more like simple knowledge that we're doing something we shouldn't be on a train that seems to ignore a myriad of concepts I assumed were immutable.

"Do you want me to do it?" Lara asks.

"No, I can do it." Screw it. I depress the handle as far as it'll go and wait to see if anyone inside objects to our imminent intrusion. Nothing happens, so I push the door inward. There's a deafening sound of air rushing past and then I see what's inside.

"Fuck!" I shout and step back into Lara, who goes sprawling on the floor. I land between her splayed legs, grabbing at Kyle's hand on the way down and causing him to stumble into the wall behind me. There's a mind-numbing sound like when you rub your finger around the rim of a wine glass, but it's loud and it's all-encompassing and it feels like if it goes on any longer, it'll turn my brain off.

Inside the room is nothing. I don't mean that it's an empty room, I mean that there's nothing there. There is no floor, no walls, and no ceiling. It's like standing in the open door of a spaceship and looking out into a completely empty universe, all dark, forever.

Kyle has recovered and hurriedly pulls the door closed. The sound stops immediately.

"Jesus Christ, what was that!?" he shouts.

"I... I don't know."

"Nothing," Lara says from her position on the floor behind me. "It was nothing. The absence of anything."

"Was it a vacuum in there until we opened the door?" I ask. "The sound when I pushed the door open, was that air flowing in?"

There are blank looks all around, then Kyle says, "I don't know about that, but I guess I don't have the worst room in the place after all!"

My laugh is a little manic, but it's genuine. Lara giggles behind me. Kyle offers me his hand and pulls me to my feet, then does the same for Lara. "Do you think the others are like that?"

"One way to find out," Kyle says, then walks casually down the corridor pushing every door on his left open. I cover my ears against the noise. He turns around at the end of the carriage and walks back, closing them. "Yup."

"I don't know if I'm relieved or not. I mean, better that it's more of the same rather than... I dunno, a fucking minotaur jumping out of one."

Kyle's eyes suddenly seem to double in size. "You tellin' me that was a possibility?"

I grin. "Not a clue, big guy. I'll tell you what, though. I'm a little scared about going in any of the compartments now. Knowing what's next door, I mean. Or, I guess, what isn't next door."

Lara's voice comes from behind me, squeaky and afraid. "Do you... do you think our rooms might do that? Like, turn off? Disappear?"

"I don't know, honey, but if it makes you feel better, we'll all sleep in your room tonight. Then at least we're together if something happens." I leave out the fact that there's likely nothing we could do about it if something *did* happen.

She beams and tucks her hair behind her ears. "Cool. Slumber party."

Lara's words have set my mind racing though. Turning off the room, meaning that everything inside just disappears, and the room becomes a whole lot of nothing. Is that how they are until someone or something turns them on? It makes a certain kind of sense. These rooms are clearly constructed to mirror the occupants' previous life in some way, so there's no point having anything in the rooms until there's an occupant. I don't know why it can't just be an empty room instead of the complete absence of matter, but I guess I don't know why this train exists or what it's for, either.

Lara yawns, which makes me yawn. The stress of opening the doors has certainly taken a toll. I feel drained. Lara looks exhausted, though Kyle is feigning nonchalance. Idly, I wonder if Mitch and Rona have noticed I'm missing yet, or if they'll come looking for me. "Okay. More searching, or do we hit the sack?"

"I'm tired," Lara says immediately. "We can look more in the morning. Maybe start with all those crates."

I nod. "Good idea. Kyle?"

He sighs as if he's not happy to admit it, but says, "Pretty sure I could sleep for a month at this point."

That settled, we pile into Lara's room and start figuring out sleeping arrangements.

THIRTEEN

Slumber Party

IT TURNS OUT that Lara's room has a preponderance of soft things on which to sleep. There's only one bed, but it's a double and, unexpectedly, she offered me the other side. I declined when she showed me what else she had. In one of the cupboards that I hadn't noticed was a huge array of enormous fluffy cushions. I'd always wanted to know what it's like to sleep on a mountain of cushions. It seemed like it would be beyond comfortable, the epitome of luxury. Well, I'm here to tell you that it's not. It's lumpy and I can't find a position that I can stay in for more than ten minutes. It makes sleeping nearly impossible, which gives me a chance to hear the ghosts Lara talked about when we first met.

When I first hear the shuffling in the corridor outside, I glance over at Kyle to see if he's noticed, and as if he can sense that I'm looking his way, he sits up. Perhaps his short stack of blankets isn't as comfortable as it looks.

"What was that?" I whisper.

"Someone walking past, I think. The door's locked, right?"

"Yeah."

I get up anyway, trying not to collapse to the floor every time one of my muscles twinges to exact revenge on me for my stupid sleeping arrangement. "*Fuck,*" I whisper as I hobble the eight feet to the door. Some other words of a similar length, too.

"What's going on?" Lara suddenly asks, much louder than I'd have liked. The shuffling in the hall stops. Maybe it was going to stop anyway, but I don't think so. I wonder what would happen if I poked my head outside now. Would I see anything out of the ordinary at all?

"Nothing, sweetie, go back to sleep," I say. I wonder if I'm mothering the girl too much. She's got to be nearly an adult, but she hasn't objected to my pet names so far. Maybe she finds it comforting. I know I would if I had my mom here right now.

"I can't sleep. I haven't had a full night's sleep since I got here. Those noises... I can't help but think someone's going to come in."

"I get that," I say. "Aren't you exhausted?"

"All the time."

"You hide it well." I shuffle awkwardly to the bed and sit on the edge.

She yawns. "I'm sick of it. We should just go out there and prove to ourselves that there's nothing to worry about. Or that there is, I just want to know. I just want to be able to sleep."

Kyle hauls himself to his feet like a mountain forming along tectonic plate boundaries. "I'm all for that," he says, then begins to lurch unsteadily to the door. I guess his stack of blankets isn't any better than my cushions.

"*Wait!*" I hiss. "What are you going to do?"

"I'm going to do as the little lady says," he drawls. I can hear the smile in his words even though he's facing the door. I'm suddenly struck by how much I like these people. While it's true that what I know about them only really stretches to the saddest and most appalling parts of their lives, I really couldn't have asked for a better couple of people to spend this time with.

I watch as Kyle stands by the door, listening intently. I get up and trot over to him, my muscles now far more cooperative. "Coming?" I ask Lara.

"Absolutely."

Kyle opens the door, and we step out. It's just a corridor. There's nobody there, no obvious source of the shuffling noise. "Could the noise have been the train itself?" I ask.

"No, somebody's been here, look." Kyle bends down and picks up my empty Fanta can from dinner. I know it's mine because the ring-pull has been rotated around so it covers the hole, something I've done since I was a kid.

"My first night here, I shredded a napkin and sprinkled it on the carpet outside my room to see what would happen. It was gone when I woke up. I thought maybe the train was controlled by some all-powerful AI, but I'm just remembering the carriage with all the names on the doors."

"You think there are cleaners?" Lara asks, looking surprised, but also relieved.

"Yeah, I think those rooms are the crew quarters."

Kyle stares at me with a contemplative expression. He raises one eyebrow. "You know, that's not actually a terrible theory."

"Hey! There's no need to sound so surprised." He jabs his elbow lightly into my arm, and I poke him in the ribs. "It's weird that we haven't seen them, though. And the way food appears in the dining car..."

"Yeah," Kyle agrees. Lara just nods. Her eyes are red and puffy, and she looks exhausted.

"What are we doing now?" she asks. "Do you think they've finished for the night, whoever they are? I'm so tired."

"I'm pretty wired," I admit. "But if you want to go back to bed, then to bed we shall go. I'll fall asleep eventually. Gonna need to demolish pillow mountain though if I ever want to be able to walk again."

Lara giggles and we head back to bed.

I wake up before Kyle and Lara and I leave the room, intending to see how close to the rear of the train I can get. Not very is the answer. After Lara's sleeper car is another passenger car, and that seems to be it. The door on the far end is of a kind I haven't seen anywhere else on the train. It has a keypad and is made of some dark metallic substance. I'm still pretty sure there are things beyond it, but without something seriously heavy duty, I'm not getting any farther unless the train stops again.

Instead, I head back to the dining car and imagine up some coffees. I don't know if Lara drinks coffee, but it's never too early to start. While I wait, I wonder how the dining experience works. I'm liking my theory about an actual crew on board because it's one thing that finally feels a little bit normal about the train, but I just can't think of a compelling reason why I wouldn't be able to see them, or why there's such a weird delivery mechanism for the food and drink. The coffees appear on a tray which I carry back to Lara's room.

Kyle and Lara are both awake when I enter.

"Good morning!" I'm not sure why I'm feeling so chipper this morning. All the bad shit seems a little more distant, a little less potent. I think it's because I'm starting to feel like I'm among friends. And perhaps that I'm starting to accept that I can't do anything about the situation we're all in.

"Hey," Lara says. "What's in the cup?"

"Coffee. You like?"

She screws her face up, which I guess means no, but then she says, "I don't actually know. I never tried."

"What? How is that…" I trail off. "Huh. I was about to say I thought kids today spent all their time in Starbucks, but I'm guessing that may not be true for you."

"What's Starbucks?" Lara asks.

"Exactly. You know what I'm talking about, right Kyle?"

"I am familiar with that particular establishment, sure."

I grin at him. To Lara, I say, "It's a big coffee chain. They're all over the world."

"Coffee? Seriously?"

"Yep," I proclaim proudly. "Anyway, you wanna try some or what? I'll warn you now, once you're hooked, you'll never get off the stuff."

"Maybe you shouldn't be corrupting the youth," Kyle suggests. I raise an eyebrow at him, and he offers a goofy grin in return. He shrugs. "Fine, go ahead."

I offer Lara a cup and she sniffs it tentatively, then takes the tiniest sip. "That mostly just tasted hot."

"You need to get more. Like this," I say, then gulp down a mouthful. It burns a little, but it's a pleasant burn. I think the nerves in my mouth long since atrophied due to my hot coffee abuse.

She takes another, longer sip, then her mouth turns down at the edges. "I'm so confused," she says, shaking her head and grinning. "It's sweet, which I like, but it's also gross, which I don't. You want the rest of this?"

I take the mug back. "One day, you'll understand," I say in my most patronizing voice. She shakes her head.

I hand Kyle his cup and he starts downing it with a commitment I rarely see in other coffee drinkers. It's almost gone before I finish asking, "So, what's on the agenda today? Are we planning to open any more doors into crazy non-existent spaces?"

"God, I hope not," Lara says. She walks to the refrigerator and pulls out a bottle of water and starts drinking from it. It reminds me of my own bottle of water which is just standing there on the counter at the back of the room. I walk over, grab it and put it in the fridge for later.

Kyle puts his somehow already empty mug down on top of the fridge then says, "I think we should look through the crates, like Lara said last night. Then maybe we can check on the crew car again, see if anyone's home?"

"Suits me," I say.

"I'm going to shower," Lara says. "I'll be back in five."

I raise an eyebrow. "Five what? Hours? Days?"

"Ha-ha."

"What? Teenage girls are renowned for the length of their showers. Maybe that was just me."

She rolls her eyes and leaves.

"I do wonder if we can get more clothes from somewhere, though. I had a shower my first night, but I'm still wearing my end of the world outfit."

"I guess we need to find one of the crew and ask," Kyle says.

FOURTEEN

THE NIGHT TO REMEMBER

THE FIRST THING I learned today is that clothes can be ordered up the same way we order food. Lara figured that out. She thought about clothes, and clothes were delivered. We don't appear to get any choice in design, but everything is clean and the right size. The next thing I learned is that the crates are filled with supplies. We found brand name drinks, chips, other snacks, a whole lot of rice and pasta and a bunch of other stuff. Nothing to explain the train or why we're on it, and nothing to hint at a way off. Kyle spent the afternoon taking things apart with a screwdriver he also conjured up in the dining room. He calls it "being thorough." He even took one of the noticeboards off the wall in car seventeen, but he didn't find much behind it. Apparently, any power on board is not something we can hijack, which is a shame as I'd really like to charge my phone. I have photos of Mom and Nana and Alice on there.

When it gets close to what I judge to be evening, I sit in the horrible dining car, waiting for Kyle and Lara. I told them to meet me in ten minutes before realizing none of us has any idea how to measure that. Hopefully, they understood the gist. There are some things I found in one of the crates that I haven't told the others about yet: a bottle of vodka, one of cranberry juice, another of Cointreau. I'm hoping the crew can provide some limes.

It's time we had some fun.

Also on the table are one of Lara's big bottles of water from her refrigerator, plus the one I boarded the train with. If we can maybe avoid a hangover, then great.

Lara walks in first and shoots a puzzled look my way.

"What?" I ask, grinning.

"What's all this?"

"Party time."

Kyle appears behind her, already rolling his eyes so hard I can almost hear it. "Lara's underage. And what if I'm an alcoholic or something?"

I'll admit, these things did occur to me. About the first one, I decided I don't care. Lara must be old enough to have had some experience with alcohol, and she'll be in the company of semi-responsible adults. That Kyle might be a recovering alcoholic, or simply teetotal... well, I'm just hoping he isn't.

The smile that gradually makes its way over Kyle's features as I hold his gaze tells me he's just fucking with me, and that's good. I think we need this.

Lara sits next to me and picks up the bottle of vodka. Kyle sits opposite, and asks, "You couldn't just order a ready mixed drink?"

I smile. "Feel free. But I'd kind of like to forget I'm on this damned train for a while, and putting us in control of the drinks seems the best way to do that."

"Fair point."

Lara puts down the vodka and picks up the triple sec. "What can you make with this stuff?"

"Cosmos, baby!"

Kyle rolls his eyes again. Lara remarks, "I don't think I've had one."

"There were other options, but a cosmopolitan is something I know how to make."

"So, get with the making," Kyle says. "Are we allowed to order food at this here shindig, or what?"

"Go right ahead," I say. "But maybe try to get everything now so we don't have to keep being reminded where we are?"

Kyle nods once, then his eyes glaze over as, I assume, he starts to fantasize about food. The stuff I ordered before Kyle and Lara got here suddenly appears on the table. Cocktail glasses and a bowl of limes. There's a cocktail shaker, too, and a little plastic bucket of ice.

"Guys, I think this proves it," I say, picking up the shaker.

"What?" Lara asks.

"The crew is human. Or sentient, at least. Not an AI. I didn't ask for this, or the ice. I was just going to stir everything."

Kyle's eyebrows raise as he considers this. "Interesting. You think whoever they are figured out we're having ourselves a party, and what you were planning?"

"I'm guessing so. Though maybe they're just listening."

Lara's head jerks up and she glances around the room. "Like, right now? Why wouldn't we be able to see them?"

"Hey, I didn't say I had the whole thing figured out," I say, and Lara laughs. I wish there were more to laugh about on board.

I start adding stuff to the cocktail shaker under the all-too-intense gazes of both Lara and Kyle. When I'm done, I pick up the shaker and wobble it gently.

"Oh, come on," Kyle says. "That's really how you're going to do that?"

"Economy of movement," I say. "It does the job, and I don't have to look like an idiot when I throw the damn thing across the room."

"Give it to me," he says, and when I do, he proceeds to dance around the room with it, passing it from hand to hand, behind his back, between his legs. Lara is in hysterics, and I guess that's the point. I start to laugh, too. It feels good, though it also makes me feel a little guilty.

"You're going to do that for every drink I make, I assume?"

"Sure."

"All right, but don't blame me when your arms don't work in the morning."

He grins and I pour the first drink into Lara's glass. She takes a tentative sip, screws up her face, then considers, "Not bad. Thanks, Eden."

I smile. "No problem, kid."

I make drinks for Kyle and myself next, and then the food arrives.

Later, we're all a little bit drunk. We abandoned the plan to limit our use of the train's dining facilities when Kyle started talking about whiskey. Thus, the table is now covered in drinks I didn't make, and the more we drank, the more food we ordered. Then we started to try to outdo each other with the outlandishness of the food orders.

Kyle started it when he decided he was craving fresh bread and butter. I reasoned that I haven't smelled baking bread since before getting on, but wonderful smelling fresh bread and butter turned up moments later, and it went on from there. I ordered my Nana's lasagna, and it was indistinguishable from the real thing. Lara won the contest when a two-tier cake covered in pink frosting appeared on the table with 'Happy Birthday, Lara' written on it and a single candle burning in its center.

I crack up when it appears, and laugh for quite some time. Lara, rather than looking pleased with herself, looks sad.

"What's up? That's awesome," I say.

"It's nothing. It's... it just reminds me of the cake Sam and Paige made me once for my birthday when my dad couldn't even be bothered to buy a ready-made one."

I nod. I consider raising my glass and toasting her sisters, but I know she feels conflicted about them leaving her at the mercy of their father, so I don't. Instead, I say, "I'm sorry."

"Thanks. Kinda wish I hadn't thought of it now."

I hesitate. "I don't get it, though. It didn't take any longer than any of the other stuff. You can't make a cake like that in the time it took to arrive." I'm slurring my words, but I don't care.

"Is there anything you've seen since getting on the train that has made any sense?" Lara asks.

"Well, no."

Lara raises an eyebrow at me. "There you go, then. We live in total inexplicability."

I frown. "Inexpic... inexclipable... what?"

"Inexplicability. I'm cutting you off, Eden." She grins.

"Can't do that."

Kyle laughs and says, "You actually can't. She can just imagine up anything she feels like." He pushes the two bottles of water I brought from Lara's room to the middle of the table. "Maybe drink some of this, though?"

I grab the bottle I brought with me from the supermarket where I got the Oxycodone and twist the cap off, then gulp down half the bottle. "Happy?" I ask.

"Inordinately."

Lara grabs the bigger bottle and drinks some, then passes it to Kyle.

"I went drinking with my dad once when I was underage," I say suddenly. I wasn't intending to say this, but the words keep coming and I seem powerless to stop them. Kyle and Lara look intrigued. "It was a scam. A bad one. It always was with him. He was intending to get me drunk, then reveal that I was underage to the bar's owner. He thought he could use it to get free drinks, or something like that. He didn't expect them to card me."

Lara giggles. "Wow, that's..."

I feel myself sobering up, talking about this. "Yeah. My dad was an asshole. Nothing like yours, Lara, but he had his spectacularly shitty moments."

"Like what?" Kyle asks.

"Like the time he pulled me out of class on the pretense of a family emergency. I thought Mom or Nana had died or something, but no. He just wanted my lunch money so he could get drunk. Or high."

"Wow," Lara says again. "What a dick!"

"Or the time he drained my college fund a few months before my high school graduation. I don't want to sound entitled or anything, but Mom and Nana had been saving that money since I was born. I had to work a lot of shitty, demeaning jobs because of him." I find I'm getting worked up about this. I know I shouldn't be. I know it's nothing in the grand scheme of things, especially compared to Lara's father, but it's also exhausting being so thoroughly and repeatedly disappointed in somebody who is supposed to love you. That exhaustion and disappointment stays with you.

"My mom kicked him out when I was young, just before we moved to Oregon, but he stuck around like a bad smell. Only ever contacted me if he wanted something. I wasn't old enough to understand that he had no interest in me beyond how he could profit from my existence. I always hoped he'd come to see *me*. For a while, he even tried to pretend that was the case, you know? He'd spend some time talking to me about school or whatever, but then he'd get to the point. He needed some money. It was nearly always money. He told me once that some gang was going to break his arms and legs if he didn't pay them what he owed, and he's still my dad, so I felt like I should help. There was no gang, though. He just wanted the money."

Kyle and Lara are just watching me talk now, and I'm okay with that. This is cathartic. "The last straw was when he had to go to the hospital and tried to commit insurance fraud. He lied on the form about who he was, where he lived. Stole some poor sucker's identity. He was unlucky to get my friend Alice as his doctor. She called me rather than the police. Sometimes I wish she'd just called the cops, but if she had, he might still be in my life. I exploded at him. Involving my best friend in his shit... it made me feel stupid for letting him do this to me for so long. We had it out, and I didn't see him again after that."

"It sounds like you're better off," Kyle says, his words hesitant.

Lara nods her agreement. "Yeah. He had that coming."

"Just like your dad," I say, and she nods again, slowly and sadly this time, her lips pressed tightly together.

She starts to add, "It's a shame—" when I interrupt.

"Wait, wait! Guys! Shut up!" I blink repeatedly until I'm sure the person who just appeared in the corner of the room isn't a figment of my imagination. "Do either of you see him?"

Lara whips her head around to see what I'm talking about. Kyle does the same. "Uh. Who?"

"I don't see anything," Lara says.

The man has apparently become aware he is being watched. He turns to me slowly and I can practically hear his bones creaking. His face sags and the uniform he wears is threadbare and gray. He stares at me for a moment, dumbfounded. When he speaks, his voice sounds like an ancient, forgotten thing waking up for the first time in centuries. "You can see me?"

PART THREE

FIFTEEN

THE HELP

"I..." I BEGIN, but I'm lost for words. I was *right!* Well, maybe not at first. "You're real? I mean... sorry. Yes, I can see you. But you're real, right? I'm not hallucinating?" I remember Lara asking us the same thing when we met her.

The man's features rise in what I think might be the approximation of a smile. It's hard to tell. "Real as you." He speaks slowly and draws his words out some, but it's hard to place his accent because it's so dusty and worn.

"But... why?" I'm not articulating myself very well.

This time, he laughs. It's a low, throaty sound and doesn't seem to come easily. "Why what?"

"Eden, what the hell is going on?" Kyle asks.

"Wait..." I'm so confused. "Hang on. Stay right there, okay?" I say to the man.

He inclines his head in what I hope is a gesture of acquiescence. I turn to Kyle and Lara and say, "There's an old man in the corner. Shit." I turn back and call, "No offense!"

Kyle's eyebrows are knitted together as he watches me closely. I think he's inspecting me for signs of psychosis or something. Lara's head is cocked to one side. "Where exactly?"

"Right there," I point, and they both look. "You can't see him?"

She shakes her head.

"Why can't they see you?" I ask the man.

"You'd have to take that up with Rona."

I blink, then shudder as if something unpleasant just happened, but I'm not exactly sure what. "Rona? Why?"

"She's the one supposed to be in charge of the train while The Creator's away."

"Wait, what?" If I sound incredulous, it's only because I am. "Rona runs the train?" Lara and Kyle gape at me.

The man considers. "No, not exactly. She was left in charge. The train mostly runs itself, but she was left in charge of some functions."

"Like make it so we can't see you?"

He tips his head. "Right. Feels strange, talking to someone else. It's been a long time since anyone saw us."

"Us?" I ask, reeling from the news that Rona might oversee some aspects of this journey. Why didn't she tell me?

"Eden," Lara says, but I ignore her.

The man nods. "The crew."

"I knew it!" I say, louder than I intended.

The man raises one eyebrow comically high. "You thought we were an artificial intelligence, as I recall."

My eyes go wide, and he laughs again. I smile, but I'm not sure if I should. Part of me thinks that laugh might be sinister, but his expression is kind enough. "How do you know that?"

He gives me a look that says he shouldn't have to explain this. "You want the truth, or the version that sits better with most folk?"

"The... truth?"

"I heard you thinking about it."

"Jeez. You can read minds? What's the nicer version?"

"I overheard you talking with your friends about it. 'Course I can read minds. We all can. How else do you think you can order food and get those nice clothes you're all wearing?"

"Oh... okay." I can't think of anything else to say.

"Eden, why can't we see him?" Lara asks. "What's going on?"

"In a minute, Lara, honey." To the man, I say, "I'm sorry, I'm Eden. This is Lara and Kyle. Can I ask your name?"

The man appears confused for a second, then shakes his head sadly. "Can't say I remember my actual name, but we borrowed names from some of the other passengers we've had. The other crew call me James."

"Nice to meet you," I say automatically. He tilts his head and raises both eyebrows. "So, Rona made you invisible? Why would she do that?"

"I... don't know. It's possible I'm wrong. I never interacted with her much, and I only know what the others told me. It's been a long time."

"How long is a long time?"

He wheezes out something that may be a cough. "Time doesn't really mean anything on the scale I'm talking about, and as I'm sure you're aware, there is no time on board. Lifetimes, I guess." He waves a hand as if this information means nothing.

This is too much, too fast, but I'm scared that whatever is allowing me to see this frail old man will stop as suddenly as it started, and I want to try to get as much information as I can. Being drunk isn't helping. I shake my head to try to clear it. I wanted things to become less confusing, not more, and trying to come up with meaningful questions under this much pressure is impossible, and it's almost as if some cosmic force senses my stress, because James disappears.

I jump to my feet immediately, galumph my way to where he stood, then realize I might be standing in the exact spot he's occupying, and I retreat. "Shit!"

"Eden, what the hell?" Lara yells. She's standing, too, and looking at me with what I realize is terror in her eyes.

"Oh, Jeez, I'm sorry. That must have looked a bit... well, nuts."

"Little bit," Kyle says. "What did we miss?"

I fill them in.

We're all back in Lara's room, sitting on the floor in a triangle. The door is locked. My head hurts, and it's not from the alcohol. Kyle scratches his own head. "It doesn't make any sense," he says, not for the first time. I've stopped even acknowledging his confusion because it doesn't help anything.

"You're sure that's all he said?" Lara asks.

I've just been over the story for the third time. Lara has written down some notes, which is good thinking, but I'm struggling to make sense of what James told me. He said very little, but what he did say was astonishing. Can we trust him? "Yes, I'm pretty sure that's everything."

She cracks her knuckles. "I wonder how many more of them there are."

"Eight, I'd guess. There are nine crew compartments." I looked at the plaques on some of their doors, but I'm not sure I remember seeing a James. It's easy enough to check, but I'm finding that I'm a little creeped out that there are people we can't see sharing this limited space with us. People who can apparently read our minds.

Kyle suddenly blurts, "What if we stand where they are?" I shake my head. I don't have any answers for him, though I did have that same thought in the dining car.

Lara says, "They probably get out of the way. They know we can't see them, but I guess they can see us. The more interesting question is whether it's possible to collide with them at all. What if they're insubstantial when they're invisible or something?"

"Like they really are ghosts?" I ask.

"Yeah." She looks pensive. Ghost was the word she used to describe the things making noises in the night, she might have been right all along.

A thought occurs to me. "How would they cook the food if they can't touch anything?"

Lara's face registers surprise, then she smiles. "We're on a flying train, I think we can throw out whatever rulebook we used to live by."

"Yeah, okay," I shake my head and sigh.

Kyle interjects, "Jesus. This is *insane*." There's real anguish in his voice and I wonder if I should be worried about him. I'm not sure I'm doing any better, though. Lara's the one making sense right now. She's the one writing down what I can remember. She's the one in charge, because both the adults are struggling with this. I feel a vague sense of guilt about that, but mostly I'm just glad one of us is able to keep a cool head.

"The most important part of the conversation was the stuff about Rona, I think. Maybe the stuff about time. And he mentioned The Creator. If we could find out who that is and *find* them..." Lara says.

"Creator of what?" Kyle asks.

"The train, I assume," Lara replies.

I nod slowly, replaying what James said in my head. "I find it hard to believe Rona has access to some of the train's controls. She seems like she'd struggle to use an iPad."

Lara looks confused. "A what?"

"Uh... It's a handheld computer thing."

"Right. Well, we need to know more about that. Either we need to talk to the crew again – someone who knows more – or we need to ask Rona about it directly."

I start nodding. "That's a good idea. Maybe we can force the lock on the door to carriage ten."

"It's worth a try. Maybe in the morning."

"Why do we think I'm the only one who could see him?"

Kyle sits there, massaging his temples slowly. Lara appears to consider my question, then gets up and walks over to the stuff we brought back from the dining car. She picks the bottles up in turn and examines them. "What's this?" She holds up the water bottle I boarded the train with.

I stare at the bottle, it's half empty. "It's... my water."

"You brought it from home?"

"More or less. It's not from the train's stocks. You think that could be it?"

Lara bobs her head from side to side. She picks up another bottle, this one much bigger. "My water's from the train. You're the only one to drink your water, right? We all had some of the other drinks, and I'm pretty sure we all shared the food."

"I think so. So, we can only talk to the crew until that bottle is empty?"

"I don't know, Eden. But that would be my guess. It kind of makes sense, right?"

The thought is disquieting. What if we need the crew's help to get off the train? How much of the water do I need to drink to start seeing them? The other half? Do we only have one more shot at this? I get up and take my bottle from Lara and turn it over in my hands. There's absolutely nothing noteworthy about it. "We need to keep this safe," I say, then open Lara's fridge and place it inside after making sure the cap is screwed on tightly.

Lara nods once.

"Why the fuck are they invisible anyway? This is bullshit!" Kyle exclaims suddenly.

"I don't know, big guy."

Lara says, "It's the ultimate wet dream of the rich and powerful, isn't it?"

I sit on the counter next to the refrigerator. "What do you mean?"

"If you can see your servants, if you can interact with them, you're forced to consider their humanity. If you can't see them, you can ignore their needs, their desires. You can treat them as badly as you want because you can't see how much you're hurting or demeaning them."

I raise my eyebrows. "I had no idea you were so cynical."

"I'm a product of my environment." She smiles sadly.

Kyle runs a hand over his stubble, making a scratchy sound. "Are we saying that this creator James talked about installed a feature to... hide the crew?"

I guess he must be starting to come to terms with things, because that's a good question. Lara presses on, "Why not? They also installed rooms filled with nothing and made the train fly." She walks over to her bed and plops down, deep in thought. I get up and follow her over and sit on the edge. Kyle remains in the middle of the floor. "I think we need to do two things. First, we need to come up with a list of questions for the crew, just in case we're wrong about the water and one of us sees them again. Three copies of the questions. We each keep a copy on us, and a pencil. There are some in one of the drawers."

I nod. "What about just leaving a page with some questions on it in the dining room? Do you think they'd write the answers down for us?"

Lara chuckles. "I guess they might! Although... what if everything they write is invisible, too?"

"Huh. Worth a shot, though, right? What's the other thing?"

"Figure out how to get to the front half of the train and have a conversation with Rona."

Kyle looks up at this, finally seeming interested. "Yes. Yes, that's... that's good. If anyone has answers, she will, right? The *invisible man* said she was in charge." He looks incredulous, like he can't believe he's allowing himself to buy into any of this.

James said Rona wasn't in charge, she was more of a caretaker, though I'm not about to correct Kyle. He seems to have taken some comfort in having a way forward. I'll let him have that for tonight.

Lara says, "I'm exhausted. You want to share the bed, Eden?"

"You're sure you don't mind?" The pile of blankets I exchanged my pile of cushions for was better, but only slightly. A night in a bed would be wonderful.

She yawns. "Wouldn't have offered if I minded."

I smile. "Then I accept."

SIXTEEN

THE HANGOVER

A NIGHT IN a bed was wonderful, and not just in terms of comfort. I felt about as secure as I've felt since all this began. I glance over at Lara and wonder if I can get up without disturbing her, decide I probably can't, and resign myself to lying there until she wakes. Kyle appears to have left at some point, presumably to get something to eat, or shower, or take the train apart some more. As I lie there, I find myself thinking about things I thought I'd long since put to bed.

I never wanted children. Part of that was thanks to my dad. I was always terrified by the idea that I might turn out to be just as lousy at raising kids as he was. I thought maybe something about that was genetic. That wasn't all of it, though. It just never seemed like something that was right for me. I came out to my family when I was eighteen, and it was a relief in so many ways, but one of those ways was that people stopped blithely assuming I was going to procreate. Of course, things have changed since then and maybe people wouldn't assume that now, but I was glad of it at the time.

Lara seems to have changed something in me. She's a lost kid running from her own shitty father, and she found me. That seems to have been good for her, but until now I hadn't considered how much it's affected me. Mathematically, I am probably old enough to be her mother, but I don't know that she's looking for a surrogate. Maybe she hasn't considered it, or maybe she thinks we fit the roles of mother and daughter so well that it should be obvious what our relationship is. I never expected to feel anything like this, and I wonder if I should ask her about it, or if that would make things awkward.

She stirs next to me, then makes a sound like some cave dwelling monster. She sits up and looks around blearily.

"Good morning!"

She rubs her eyes. "Hey. Sleep better?"

"Much, thanks." I pause, then find myself saying the rest of what I'm thinking. "I think... well, I think since Alice and Greg died, I've been worried that letting myself get too close to someone is going to end badly. Like, they survived, but then they were taken anyway, you know?"

She turns to face me and smiles warmly, then leans over for a hug. I oblige. When we part, she says, "The spot's yours if you want it."

I smile and nod. "How's your head?"

She touches her temple with two fingers, then lifts her eyebrows. "Fine, actually."

"Good. Water cures all ills."

"And lets you see invisible people," she says, and I grin. "Where's Kyle?"

"Not sure. He was gone when I woke up. Dining car, maybe." I start to drag myself out of bed.

We get up and I start to straighten up the room. Lara gathers pencils and paper and places them on the desk next to her bed. "For the crew questions," she explains. "We should also keep a blank sheet of paper on us in case we get to go outside. Write down our ages and dates of birth and anything else the train might be blocking." She looks at me for agreement.

"You're full of good ideas lately."

Lara beams. "I actually feel pretty guilty about last night. Making them bake that birthday cake. If we can start to figure out a way to make them visible again, it seems like the least we can do."

"Oh shit. I hadn't even thought about that."

She grins. "And now that I've dumped my guilt on you, I'm going to shower. Back in a few."

When she's gone, I sit back down on the bed and sigh. Every feeling I have right now is tinged with something else. It's very confusing. Lara and Kyle are fast becoming friends, and Lara invokes a completely alien but entirely pleasant maternal feeling in me, but I still can't escape the idea that we're trapped and everything about this life is somehow fake. I still haven't completely let go of the idea that this is just my brain's final nonsense dream before death. Occasionally I find myself just expecting this whole fantastic endeavor to stop.

Rather than receding into that muddled place in my mind where I overthink everything, I decide to go for a walk. I leave Lara's room and head to car seventeen. The place is a mess since we dragged some of the crates out here to have more room to work on them and neglected to tidy up after ourselves. Thankfully, the crew haven't done it either. I don't want them to feel obliged. There's a pile of blankets along one wall that I don't remember seeing before, and I wonder if Kyle has decided he doesn't want to room with the girls anymore. I wouldn't necessarily blame him, though I would miss him. I enjoy the constant sleepover atmosphere we have. I gaze for a while at the heavy-duty door that blocks access to whatever else of the train exists. Surely there's something back there, but what? Controls? Does Rona come back here? Can I make the crew visible again back there?

When I've made myself anxious with my thoughts, I head back the way I came, past Lara's room and through car fifteen, the crate car, through the crew car, the passenger car and to our dining car where I expect to see Kyle. When I don't, I keep going. He's not in eleven either. I guess I missed him, so I head back to Lara's room.

We can't find Kyle.

When I got back to the room, Lara was sitting on the edge of her bed drying her hair. I was expecting to see Kyle with her, but she said she hadn't seen him either. Given how little we know about pretty much everything, it seemed like a good idea to find him, so we started our search in the dining room in car twelve. We checked both bathrooms and we knocked on all the crew cabin doors, though none of them opened. We even went down all the compartments in car sixteen, where Lara's room is, and pushed their doors open to reveal the howling voids behind. It's possible Kyle could be in one of them, but we'd never know it, and I can't imagine what would have happened to make him enter one of those rooms. We checked all the passenger cars and spent some time moving crates, just in case he'd gotten himself stuck behind a particularly big one. We checked Lara's room repeatedly in case we just kept missing him.

He has disappeared, and I'm starting to become frantic about it. Lara sits at her desk while I sit on her bed. I don't want to be sitting here, though it was my idea for us to stop moving around and see if Kyle returned of his own accord.

I can't get the worst-case scenarios to stop swirling around in my head, though, so I blurt, "What if he'd had enough? What if he threw himself outside, or into one of those rooms with nothing in it?"

Lara looks up. "Eden, I don't think he'd do that. He came here to escape death; do you think he'd give up on life so easily now?"

She has a point. He did escape death row for this. I doubt his will to live would reverse so quickly. I take a few deep breaths and try to calm down. "Yeah, okay. You're probably right. But... where is he?"

Lara stands and paces. "There's only one place we haven't looked." She holds my gaze until I get it.

"Shit. The front half of the train." I hadn't even considered it. I'd even been in carriage eleven and hadn't thought to try the door. I stand up and experience a momentary appreciation for the fact that this teenager is managing to keep it together far better than I am. I'm just done with losing people. I don't want to lose Kyle as well as everyone else.

We leave Lara's room and head through the crate room. Since we searched for Kyle in here, it's now just as difficult to get through as it was when we first met Lara. Even though we've already checked, I push open the bathroom door in the crew car and peer inside. Kyle isn't there. I have to fight the urge to knock again on every crew door we pass on the way to the next carriage, which we just run through. The dining car is next and I'm disappointed to find he's not here either. I wish I could stop torturing myself like this. Then we're in carriage eleven. This is where we met Lara. This was where I spent so long fantasizing about getting to. The way back to the front half of the train.

I'm apprehensive as I push the button next to the door, then I'm shocked when it opens.

"Shit," I whisper. "How long has it been unlocked? Why isn't the button lit up?" What if it was never locked in this direction?

"Don't know. Come on," Lara says. She's right; it doesn't matter.

We walk cautiously through and I say, "This is Kyle's car. His room is here. Last door on the left." We head there and I hesitate when we reach it. It still bears his name, which I hope is a good sign. Lara depresses the handle, pushes the door open and visibly deflates when she sees Kyle isn't inside, or maybe it's because of the awful interior design choices. The place is a prison cell, after all.

We find Kyle in the rear vestibule of the next carriage along. The door to the outside is open and there are tendrils of that awful gray stuff clinging to the edges of the frame, appearing for all the world like they are touching or tasting this new and interesting place, wondering about coming further inside. I struggle to understand what I'm seeing at first, because the sight of a two-hundred-and-fifty-pound guy being dangled out of the train by the elderly hundred-and ten-pound Mitch simply does not compute.

"What the fuck are you doing!?" I yell.

"Get back, Eden!" Mitch says, looking around and noticing us for the first time. The only thing holding Kyle inside the train is the balled-up fistful of Kyle's shirt that Mitch clutches.

"Eden!" Kyle yells. His eyes plead. He's closer to the gray stuff than anyone has been, and I don't like it. It looks alive. It looks like it might decide to grab him.

"Stop it!" I shout, striding forward, intending to grab Kyle's flailing arms and haul him back inside. Lara, after a brief hesitation, does the same. Mitch thrusts his left hand against the wall, blocking us both with his arm. I come close to just punching him, but if I do, we could lose Kyle. I take a step back. "Why are you doing this?"

"He's a killer, Eden! He was on death row. He killed his entire family!"

We have to shout to be heard. The sound from the outside is deafening, but I can't tell exactly what's making it. It's not the sound of air rushing past, it's more guttural than that. Maybe it's the gray stuff itself.

"You're wrong!" I shout back. "He told us the story."

Mitch laughs, though I don't hear the sound. "And you just believe him? I knew I should never have..." I lose the rest of whatever he says to a particularly loud cry from Kyle. I watch helplessly as Mitch starts to lose his grip on Kyle's shirt.

"Oh, Jesus, I don't want to die like this!" Kyle babbles. The gray tendrils snake closer to him, bridging the gap between him and the door frame. I don't know what to do.

"You should have thought of that before killing your wife and daughter," Mitch shouts into Kyle's face.

"So, you're judge, jury and executioner?" I shout. "You get to decide? I thought God was the only judge." I'm trying to appeal to his spiritual side, but his sneer tells me it doesn't work.

"There is no G—" he begins.

Lara literally screams over him, her voice strained and manic, "If you let him go, you're going straight after him!"

Mitch's face registers a flicker of uncertainty. I try, "Come on, Mitch, let's talk about this."

He looks at me with disgust, then at Lara with something approaching hate, his eyes narrowing to slits. I don't know this man at all. I can't believe I ever thought he was nice. He shakes his head and Kyle jolts backwards half a foot.

"No!" I dart around behind Mitch, wrapping both arms around his neck as I go and pulling backwards, throwing him and myself to the floor. Lara darts forward to grab Kyle's hand just as Mitch lets go of his shirt. She struggles for several seconds before I scramble to my feet and run to help her. Together, we get Kyle back inside the car and I hit the close button on the door.

SEVENTEEN

The Threat

I TRY TO force my brain to slow down as I assess the scene in front of me. It seems the immediate danger has passed. Kyle gasps on the floor just inside the door to gray hell, interfering with Lara's attempts to fuss over him, batting her hands away seemingly unaware of doing so. His hands shake and I watch as Lara grabs hold of them, gripping them hard. She whispers something to Kyle. She's got this. She may have had what little sense of safety she'd gained snatched away from her – something I am mightily pissed off about – but she's still able to give comfort, to remain calm enough to help others. It's impressive to watch. I cast a glance Mitch's way, just to make sure he's not going to try anything, then I crouch next to Lara and Kyle. His haunted eyes meet my own.

"You okay, big guy?" I whisper.

He nods, closes his eyes, then says, "I think so. Thank you—
"

I cut him off. "You'd have done the same."

He nods again and I turn to Lara who is wiping at her eyes. "How about you, short stuff?" I'm amazed I can do the rounds so serenely. Underneath this facade of calm is a rough sea of murderous rage I have no idea how I'm controlling. Maybe I'm just too shocked to feel anything properly.

Lara nods shakily. "What are—"

I interrupt, pitching my voice low so that Mitch can't hear. "Listen, can you take Kyle back to your room for me? Lock the door, but don't let your guard down. Mitch may have keys to everything."

Her eyes widen and, just for a second, I see a look of utter defeat before she reins it in, draws her lips into a thin line and nods once.

"Good girl. I'll catch up shortly."

"Wait... what if the door's locked again?"

"Go to Kyle's room."

She nods. "What are you going to do with..." she tilts her head in Mitch's direction. He's still on the ground, looking confused.

"Just talk," I say. I hope that's all I'm about to do. I stand between my friends and Mitch, watching Lara struggle to help Kyle to his feet. I ignore the urge to assist because it would mean that nobody would be keeping an eye on Mitch. I watch them go, Lara trying her best to hold Kyle up as he leans on her. Then I turn to Mitch, and he visibly recoils.

I crouch down beside him and speak slowly and quietly.

"Would you like to explain that to me?" My tone makes it clear it's not really a question. I think it must be obvious what I want to do to him and how much effort it's taking to not just give in and do it. My fists are clenched, but I force them to relax.

"I... I'm sorry!" he starts to babble. It's not how I expected this to go. I thought he'd have some bullshit reason prepared. "I didn't think. I just found out that he was on... death row, you know? I jumped to conclusions. I can't believe... oh, God, I can't believe I was about to..." he shuffles back so he's sitting more upright, but he doesn't try to stand.

I stare at him, not sure if this is an act or if he's being genuine. It's a good act if that's what it is. "You're going to give me some answers."

He nods frantically, as if placating me is the only thing on his mind.

"First, how did you even know Kyle was on board?"

"It's like I said, word travels fast. Rona saw you board and told me, right? She keeps watch over the train pretty well." I don't ask if this is because she's in charge of it. I don't want to lose control of the conversation.

"Does she know about your murderous tendencies?"

"Oh, God. Oh, God, Eden. Promise me you won't tell her! She'll never talk to me again!"

I ignore his pleading. "Why was the door to carriage eleven locked?"

"I don't know."

I lean forward just a little farther. "I don't believe you, Mitch. You're going to want to make me believe you."

"Eden, I swear I'm telling you the—" he pauses for a second, seeming momentarily breathless, "—the truth! I swear it. I don't know what happened. I... I just saw red when I learned about Kyle's past and—"

I hold up a hand. "And how did you do that?"

His eyes widen a little. "Do what?"

"How did you learn about Kyle's past?"

"I... I don't remember. Rona, I... I think."

I shake my head and bite my lower lip. "Not good enough, Mitch."

He exhales a shaky breath. "I swear— I don't know what's happening to me. I can't... I don't know. Oh, God, Eden. I can't..."

I've seen my dad act like this. I remember confronting him about stealing my college fund, and his reaction to being caught and confronted reminds me of this. It's a good act, but I feel sure it is just an act. I just can't figure out what purpose it serves, and that's driving me crazy. Is he trying to make peace so that we let our guard down and he can try again? Or maybe Lara is next. Maybe he'll kill all of us.

"All right, Mitch. Calm down." I try to remove any sympathy from my tone, making it a demand, not a suggestion.

He nods and looks at me gratefully. "I'm so sorry," he says, and he does look sorry. He looks wretched, actually. He looks broken. A lot of people might even believe him. I do not, but I recognize how tenuous our situation onboard is. We are trapped. If Mitch has keys, he can kill us whenever he wants. We're never safe. If he's going to pretend to play nice, that gives us time to work out a counterattack for next time.

"Do you have keys to the doors on board?"

He shakes his head, and I sigh melodramatically. "I swear! I don't have keys!"

"So, the door to eleven just magically unlocked when you decided you wanted to murder someone?"

His face crumples, and I fight a fleeting moment of pity. I don't want to pity this man, I want to hate him.

"I..." he stops, shakes his head like he knows there's only so many ways he can say it and he's exhausted his repertoire. "I'm sorry. I don't know what happened."

I stare at him until he starts to look uncomfortable. "All right, Mitch. You promise you're not coming for Kyle again? For any of us?"

He gapes at me for a second. "I promise. I—"

"All right. I'll hold you to it." I scoot closer to him and lean in to whisper. "Because if you do, I am going to take great pleasure in making you scream."

I pull back, offer Mitch my biggest smile, and leave.

Lara gets up and hurries toward me as soon as I enter the dining room in car twelve. "Are you okay? What happened?" she asks. She's frantic and deeply upset. I can see a kind of wildness in her eyes that she's barely keeping concealed.

"I'm okay." I give her a quick hug. "How are you guys? Kyle, you doing all right?"

He nods slowly, while Lara says, "We're fine. Shaken."

"Good." I'm surprised I don't feel more shaken right now. Adrenaline, I guess. The comedown will be punishing. I sigh, then look around the room. I can't believe this is the same room where we had a party just the night before. Looking at it now, it seems everything has changed. "Okay, so, Mitch claims he's sorry. Says he doesn't know what came over him. Kyle, can you tell me what happened?"

Kyle gazes at me for a silent moment before saying, "I was in here having breakfast when the door through to the next car suddenly slides open, and there's this bald guy standing there. I think I greeted him, but he didn't say anything. Just walked over, grabbed my arms and twisted them behind my back, then started pushing me out of the room. We got to car nine and he threw me headfirst against the wall. I think I was unconscious for a while. When I came to, he was sitting there staring at me. When he opened the door, I started to plead. You walked in shortly after."

Lara looks concerned. "You... you didn't try to fight him off?"

Kyle seems momentarily offended. "Of course I did. I couldn't move once he had hold of me. That guy is extraordinarily strong. Like, inhumanly strong."

"That's another thing to worry about, then," I say. If Mitch were the frail old man he appears to be, I doubt any of us would have much of a problem incapacitating him, but if he overpowered Kyle, who is easily two of Mitch and all muscle, Lara and I have no chance at all. I wonder how I was able to pull him back from the door like I did. "Anyway, Mitch says he doesn't know why he did what he did, and he couldn't tell me where he even got the information that inspired him to do it. He claims he doesn't want to harm you — any of us — anymore, and he claims he won't try again."

Lara's eyes almost pop out of her head. "You believe him?"

"No. No, of course I don't. What do you take me for?" I elbow her gently, but she doesn't react. I guess the mood isn't ready to be lightened. "No. I don't believe him."

"So, you think he will come after Kyle again, or...?"

"It's difficult to say. I have an idea about that, but for now I think we have to consider the fact that it's better to be playing nice than to be at war. We're confined to this train. Mitch probably has keys, and who knows what else he has access to? If, as James says, Rona can control some aspects of the train, they could be working together. There are more of us, sure, but I think if either one of them wanted us dead, we would be dead. If he's pretending to play nice, even if he's working toward some other goal, that gives us time to plan a counterattack, or at least a decent defense."

Lara nods. Kyle just watches me intently, I'm not sure he's heard any of what I just said.

"Kyle, would you mind going to Lara's room and getting my bottle of water from the fridge, if you're up to it?"

Lara cocks her head, then a grin slowly spreads across her face. "You think the crew will help?"

"I don't know, but James seemed pretty unhappy about the fact that Rona had made them all invisible. I'm guessing they're not on great terms with either Mitch or Rona."

"Sure." Kyle says, and slowly stands, turns, and wobbles.

"You okay?" I ask.

He waves his hand to dismiss my concerns, then slowly plods toward the door. When he's gone, I take Lara's hands in mine and ask, "And you? You're sure you're okay? You said some things back there."

"About pushing Mitch out of the train? I meant every word."

"I know. But feelings like that can be... hard to deal with. Trust me. I had a lot of anger towards my dad once. It can consume you if you let it and I don't want that to happen to you."

She holds my gaze for quite some time, then she smiles. "I'm fine. Really." She pulls her hands from mine and hugs me tightly. I hope that's the end of it.

Kyle returns moments later holding the bottle of water in one hand, and one of the glass bottles of alcohol in the other. He walks over to us. "Listen, I wanted to thank you... both of you."

Lara assumes a faux stern expression. "Don't be stupid."

"You don't have to thank us. We look out for each other on this train," I say. "Right?"

Kyle nods emphatically. "Damn straight. So, what's this plan of yours?"

I take a deep breath. "Our immediate problem is closing off the back of the train in a way we can control. Mitch or Rona must have keys for the door in carriage eleven. Maybe the crew has something we can use to lock the door in here, a padlock or something. If not, well... I have another idea, but I would need to go back to my room."

Kyle immediately looks uncomfortable. "For what?"

"I have—" I begin, then I'm not sure if I want to admit the next part. After a moment, I figure this isn't the time to keep secrets. "I have a bottle of Oxycodone. I was considering downing the entire thing just before the train turned up."

Lara looks shocked by this. "Oh," she whispers, then louder, "You think the crew will consider slipping some into his food?"

"I don't know. It's a lot to ask, and I'm not sure we're there yet. There's always a tiny possibility that Mitch is telling the truth and he really doesn't know what happened. But I'd like to have the bottle in case things get worse. If the crew isn't willing to do it, maybe we can figure out a way to."

Kyle shakes his head. "This is messed up. We're talking about murdering someone."

I nod sadly, but there's nothing else to say. It *is* messed up, but what alternative do we have?

"Can I come? To your room, I mean?" Lara asks. "I'd still like to see the rest of the train, even if it's just a quick look."

I want to say no. I want to say that I'd be happier if someone stayed with Kyle, but Kyle is probably the size of three of her. Can she really protect him? The more I think about it, the more I think she might be better off with me. At least I can keep an eye on that wildness I still see in her eyes. "You okay with that?" I ask Kyle.

He nods reluctantly.

EIGHTEEN

Emma

RATHER THAN HEAD straight for the Oxy, we decide to see if we can achieve some peace of mind first. We sit around our usual table and I gulp a couple mouthfuls of water. "We should order some food, then we know there'll be crew in here."

Lara nods, but the churning in my stomach means I can't think about food. I want to drink as little water as possible just in case we need to do this again, but I'm also conscious of how little time I had with James before I stopped being able to see him, and I'd drunk half the bottle. I've had nothing to drink today, though, and maybe this will work better if the water is the only thing in my system.

I wonder again why Mitch allowed me to pull him back from the door if he's as strong as Kyle claims. Why did he just lie there on the floor while I threatened him? The fact that he didn't just kill all of us there and then seems to suggest he has something else in mind, but what?

Kyle is clutching the bottle of alcohol he brought back from Lara's room by the neck in shaking hands. I assume he intends to hit Mitch over the head with it if he makes an appearance, but he's starting to look a little unhinged. "Kyle? You're shaking. You're sure you're all right?"

He gives a little shake of his head. "I don't know. Being so close to that... that gray stuff. It feels like it's inside my head, crowding out my brain."

Shit. I'm really not ready for something else to go wrong. We have enough to deal with. Everything I can think to say is just a meaningless platitude. "You'll be okay. We just need to figure out a way to defend ourselves, to make ourselves safe." I'm far from certain safety is a concept that exists for us, and if any of that gray shit got into Kyle, well, who knows what it might do to him? We know literally nothing about it except that it seems to want to attract our attention when we look its way. What if some of it got into the train and is floating around, looking for someone else to infect?

Lara is uncharacteristically silent through all of this, and I wonder if she might be affected too. She was closer to the gray stuff than I was. In fact, she faced it head on while she pulled Kyle to safety. She hasn't said anything, but she was further away than Kyle was. Maybe it will affect her more slowly.

I fix my gaze on the door to carriage eleven. I don't expect Mitch to come for us now, but the more I think about it, the more paranoid I become. Maybe now is the perfect time to come for us. It'd certainly surprise the hell out of me. Suddenly, the back of my neck begins to tingle, and I turn around.

There's an old woman in the corner, standing behind a short countertop that juts out from the wall, watching me with sunken eyes. Her skin is pale and her hair white, and while she has made an attempt at gathering it up into a neat pile atop her head, she hasn't quite managed it. It's lopsided and messy. She wears a dirty uniform that once might have been blue. It's covered in patches and tears which have been stitched together.

"Hello," I say, and both Lara and Kyle start. They look at me and see that I'm staring into the corner. It's a good thing they believe I'm not insane, because this probably looks ridiculous.

"Hello," the old woman replies. "Eden, is it?"

"That's right. Can I ask your name?"

The woman smiles sadly. "You can call me Emma."

"James said he'd been on board for lifetimes and he didn't remember his real name. Is that the same for you?"

She shrugs. "As you know, it's... difficult to judge time while on board. But yes, lifetimes seems about right. Hundreds of lifetimes, maybe."

Hundreds of lifetimes? I'm starting to wish Lara had volunteered to do this. I feel like every new piece of information sends my brain reeling. "Do you know why I can see you?"

"I think you and your friends are correct about the water. It comes from outside the train, and I think that lets you bypass whatever renders us invisible. Some of us, maybe not all. I know that this train has a lot of capabilities that you have probably not guessed at. As you know, it can hide things. It can also turn off portions of reality aboard."

"The unoccupied rooms?"

Emma hunches over, resting her elbows on the countertop in front of her. "Yes. There were once whole carriages like that, and there may be again. The train can create matter. It can add and remove cars as needed. Each one begins as a shell and can be decorated in whatever way The Creator sees fit."

I hold up a finger, and Emma nods. I quickly relay everything she has said so far to Kyle and Lara.

Lara's eyes widen and she pulls her pencil and paper from her pants pocket and starts scribbling frantically. Kyle doesn't react at all.

"What about our age differences?" I ask. "Lara seems to have been born before I was, but I'm older than her. Can the train time travel?"

Emma's eyes crinkle as she smiles playfully. "No, of course not. Do you know how complicated that would be?"

I can't help but laugh at that, but almost at once I start to consider what it means for me. If I can't go back to a time before all this shit happened to me, I can't get back to my family. I stare at the floor for a second to compose myself before I say, "So, I can't go home? I can't see my family again?"

Emma shakes her head sadly. "Everything changes. The universe moves ever onward. Family is transient, especially to people like us; people on board the train, where time cannot penetrate."

I think about that for a moment. It seems profound. It seems like I should be able to take something from it, but mostly it leaves me feeling empty and a little bit scared. Eventually, I ask, "Are you saying people on the train don't age? Don't die?"

"Exactly."

My head spins. "But... I miss them."

Emma's expression is sympathetic. "Your family? Yes, nobody is immune from the feeling of loss. Not even us. There are those whom we miss, but they are gone and there is no changing that. Consider how you feel about the people you're with now."

I sigh. Immortality. Living forever. But only if we stay on the train with a man who has already tried to kill one of us, and a woman who may or may not be in league with him. I shake my head. "Eternity is too long."

She smiles, then stands up straight. "Be glad, then, that you are not a member of the crew. We are beholden to the train until there is no longer a train of which to speak."

"I'm sorry."

"Don't be. It is the hand we were dealt, and we live with it. You must figure out how to do the same."

"Do you know how we can get off?"

"The Creator put the train on a kind of autopilot. If you access the controls, you can affect the route."

"Is Rona The Creator?"

Emma voices a bitter laugh. "No. She was, at best, an assistant. The true creator left long ago to tend to matters elsewhere. One day, he will return."

I wish we knew for sure whether Rona was working with Mitch or not. If we could rule it out, we could find her, ask her to stop the train so we can get off and live our wonderfully finite lives. I start to imagine the moment when we might finally step from the train and not have to get back on. When I realize I'm wasting time, and water, I manage to pull myself back into the conversation. "James said Rona made you into ghosts."

"Indirectly, yes. Mitch is the one who enacted that particular form of hell. Rona merely showed him how."

My head is spinning. Does this confirm that Mitch and Rona really are working together? And to what end? "Can it be reversed?"

"Undoubtedly, but we do not know how. Mitch is dangerous, Eden. We have almost no interaction with anyone since we were hidden, but the interaction we do have is with Mitch, and it is usually abusive and violent. Sometimes it seems like he's not even present, like something else is in control."

"That's terrible," I say. I wish there were something that marked people out as evil, something you could detect at a distance. "He tried to kill Kyle. We're afraid he'll try again." I see Kyle move his head at the sound of his name, but I don't look his way.

Emma only nods as if this doesn't surprise her in the slightest.

"Do you have anything that might be able to help? Is there a way to lock the door in here from this side so he can't get in?"

She nods again. "We heard you talking. One of the others is going to bring you the lock you desire."

The relief I feel is immense and immediate. I take a deep breath, hold it for a second, then let it out. "Thank you."

Emma shakes her head. "Remember everything else I've said, Eden. The lock may keep you safe, or it may not. The train can change around you. Who's to say doors cannot cease to exist? Or walls?"

I open my mouth and inhale, then hold the breath. My eyes dart from Emma to the floor and back. My shoulders sag.

"What is it?" Lara whispers.

I shake my head. "What about my other plan? If you were listening, you must have heard it."

"The pills? Yes, that could work. If you can get them, we'll see what we can do."

"You can't... get them for us?"

"This is not our fight. We can help in limited ways, but—"

The old woman disappears. My shoulders slump and I turn back to Lara and Kyle and relay the rest of the conversation.

NINETEEN

Captive

THE PROMISED PADLOCK and key appear on the table moments later, startling all of us. I pick it up and test its weight in my hand. It's hefty; you could do some serious damage with this thing.

The doors between carriages are all controlled by the same open and close buttons that exist on the doors to the outside world, but it seems someone designed the internal doors to be manually lockable. There is a C-shaped handle on the door itself as well as a corresponding one on the frame. I position the lock so that it goes through both and click the shank home, and I wonder if this is what safety feels like. If it is, I'm not impressed.

I turn back to the others, a resigned smile on my face. "Better?" Lara asks.

"I hope so. I still need to go get the bottle of Oxy, but more than that, I need to let my brain catch up to everything that's happened. It feels like there's too much to think about."

Lara nods. "That's because there is."

I glance around the room looking for a clock before I realize that's pointless. "Does anyone have any idea what time of day it is?"

Kyle, who is sitting with his head almost between his legs, elbows on his knees, as if he's trying not to pass out, glances up briefly and shakes his head. Lara says, "Probably mid-morning."

"Fuck, really? It feels like it should be time for bed. Not that I could sleep. I'm not sure I'll ever sleep again." I intended the hyperbole as a joke, but it falls flat. Lara actually looks like not sleeping again might be a real possibility for her, and I regret saying it.

"I guess I should be grateful for the one decent night I had last night," Lara says. She's taken her ponytail in both hands and is wringing the hair like she wants to strangle it. She notices me watching and stops, then looks away.

I watch over both her and Kyle for some time, though. None of us seem inclined to talk, even though we have so much to talk about. We're all traumatized in one way or another. Kyle is likely reliving his near death at the hands of Mitch. Lara is perhaps conjuring revenge fantasies in her head. I can't blame her. I had threatened to make Mitch scream after all. I even told him I'd enjoy it. If it came down to it, I would balk. I wouldn't be able to do something like that, even to someone who deserved it. Lara, though... she's had to live with the injustice of her father driving both her sisters out of their family home, then had to assume the role of her father's punching bag. I can see how the feeling of helplessness might overwhelm her, how she might take any opportunity, however ill-advised, to exact revenge on Kyle's behalf.

When I can't stand the silence anymore, I say, "Guys, I know it seems hopeless, but we're about as safe as we can be for the moment. Maybe we should—" I close my eyes, shake my head. I can't think of anything that will alleviate this feeling. The only thing, the one thing that might tip the scales in our favor, is getting that bottle of Oxy, and I just want to wait until the constant feeling that one of us is going to die to stop for a minute so I can catch my breath before I venture out, maybe volunteering to be that person.

Lara shoots a look my way. When she speaks, it's with a raised, desperate voice I haven't heard before and don't want to hear again. "Safe? You said it yourself. Mitch has keys. He's incredibly strong. He can control the train. He could just make this carriage not exist, then we'd all be floating around in the grayspace."

I don't open my eyes. I don't want to argue. I nod, then speak as gently as I can. "I know safe is a relative term. But Mitch doesn't know we know that he might be able to control things. I'm betting he won't tip his hand unless he has to. He'll want to keep up the pretense for as long as possible."

Kyle sits up straight and lets his head fall back, exhaling noisily. "Eden's right. I think we have some time."

Lara looks at me, then at Kyle, then back at me. She sighs. "Fine. So, we have time until he tries to kill Kyle again." I wince. "What are we going to do with it?"

We spend the next few sleeps in relative boredom, but the good kind, at least as far as I'm concerned. The kind where nobody comes to kill your friends for no reason, and where our situation doesn't get appreciably worse. I keep an eye on Lara, but she seems okay. My main worry now is Kyle, who seems sluggish and subdued. It's like being dangled out of the train as if he were a toy held by a careless child has stolen some of what made him who he is.

We talked about plans, but everything we could come up with has problems. I have resisted going to get the Oxy because it seems like it risks our safety for a less than guaranteed gain. Lara offered to get the Oxy by herself, which I objected to strenuously.

Lara and I have taken to spending time in the passenger car behind her sleeper car. We've rearranged the chairs to make it more homey, and we've brought some of the stuff from Lara's room as well. She and I are there one morning while Kyle is taking one of the frequent naps he now needs since his run-in with Mitch.

"I don't know how much longer I can do this, Eden," Lara tells me. Her voice is quiet, but I still hear every word against the backdrop of total silence. My heart sinks a little.

"What do you mean?"

"Languish back here and pretend everything is okay."

"We're regrouping," I say, trying for humor. It sounds wrong, even to me. We stopped regrouping a few days ago, now we're just waiting for something to happen. We're waiting for me to do what I said I would. "Okay. What do you want to do instead? Do you want to confront Mitch?"

Lara shakes her head, then screws up her face and rubs at her forehead as if I've missed the point entirely. "No. I mean... there's so much to think about. There's Mitch, obviously, but we're also on a train speeding through some shit we don't understand. Where are we going? Why are we here? We had plans. We were going to wait until the train stopped so we could go outside and figure out when we're all from. The train hasn't stopped since we had that idea. It's like it knows or something."

I had the same thought when it appeared to wait just long enough for us to get to carriage eleven before taking off again. I'm grateful Lara is thinking about this rather than about more immediate problems.

When I don't say anything, she goes on. "I just want to do something. Doing nothing all day is stressing me the fuck out. Don't get me wrong, I think you and Kyle are great, but is this enough for you? Is this what we're planning to do for the rest of eternity? That's what Emma said, right? We don't age while we're on board. Time doesn't exist. I don't think I can just sit around until the end of the universe, waiting for Mitch to kill us."

"We won't," I say, though our only workable plan is still the Oxycodone. As much as it pains me to admit it, Lara is right. We're drifting. We don't have any good plans and I'm scared of the fragment of plan we do have. She is looking at me expectantly. I sigh, "I think when I stopped believing I could see my family again is when I... well, I didn't exactly stop caring, but I checked out a little. You're right, we're just coasting. But I don't know what to do. Kyle seems...wrong somehow? You seem angry. I haven't stopped being scared since Mitch... you know."

She gets up and comes over, sits down next to me and puts her arm around me. I let my head fall to the side, resting on her shoulder. "It seems we're in the same boat, you and I. I can't stop being angry at the universe, you can't stop being scared by it. Neither one accomplishes anything."

"You're remarkably insightful for however old you are."

She laughs at that. "We need a real plan; one we can actually put into action. I don't want to spend the rest of eternity on this fucking train. I want to go home. I want to have a boyfriend. I want to have sex, Eden. Maybe I want kids. I still have a life..." she slaps her hand over her mouth. "Oh my God, I'm so sorry!"

I lift my head from her shoulder. Her eyes are bulging. "It's okay. You're not telling me anything I don't already know. You *do* have a life back home. You'd be better off without your asshole dad, but aside from that I can see how you'd want to go back."

"I just... you don't have anything. Anyone. I can't imagine..."

"You don't have to. That's for me to figure out."

Lara frowns. "No, Eden, that's not how it's going to work. I'm starting to think I—" she hesitates, "— we're becoming close, right? If you have nothing to go back to, then you come back with me. Maybe we can all get an apartment together or something. We already know Kyle can't go back to his life. He'll be arrested and executed."

"What if we find somewhere new?"

Lara's face registers surprise. "Somewhere new?"

"Yeah. I've been thinking about what Emma said. What if the train stops somewhere and it's beautiful, and there are people and we think we could be happy there? Maybe we can even figure out a way to control the train and make it go somewhere specific."

She thinks about it. Her head nods almost imperceptibly a few times like she's making a list of pros and cons. "Yeah. I'd be happy with that. It's not my specific life I have to go back to. There are things there I'd happily never see again. I'd miss a few people – Paige and Sam mainly, - but when we do see each other, it's often too painful to bear anyway. And none of that is anything compared to your loss. Starting over appeals. It's the experiences I'd miss out on by being on board that are what I want."

I nod and feel a warmth blooming in my stomach. I feel the beginnings of something that's maybe stronger than my terror. Is this hope? "Okay. So, let's see what we can do about getting ourselves off this damn contraption."

TWENTY

THE ARGUMENT

I'M AMAZED AT how quickly I've taken our relative safety for granted. It's been a few sleeps, and while I was nervous about Kyle being somewhere on his own at first, I'm okay with it now. Mitch hasn't broken through the locked door into carriage twelve and Kyle hasn't been abducted or murdered. We find him in Lara's room. He's awake, laid on his stack of blankets the opposite way to usual, facing the window. The blind is rolled all the way up, revealing the shapeshifting horror outside.

"What are you doing?" I ask as we enter.

He starts, then cranes his neck around, looking a little pissed. "Nothing," he says, then turns back.

I stride over to the blinds and pull them down, then turn to look at him. "Good nap?" I ask, trying to sound neutral. I'm unnerved though, and I can see Lara is too. Neither of us can stand looking out into that horrible gray infinity for long. Kyle was lying here staring at it for, well, hours, probably. He said it himself; he hasn't felt right since he was exposed to the outside. If that stuff is capable of infecting, or possessing, or whatever... well, I'm trying not to think about it.

Even more reason to get ourselves off this damn train once and for all, and I'm starting to think that it doesn't really matter where we go. Perhaps the next time the train stops, we should simply get off and not get back on. The important thing is that we're together.

"Fine," Kyle says, but he doesn't meet my gaze. He's staring at the blinds covering the window.

"Good. Lara and I have been thinking about a plan again," I say, and he finally looks at me. "We need to get off the train, right?"

"Mmm," Kyle intones. "I don't see how. Unless we can make it stop."

"Well, that's a start. We need to figure out how to access the controls," I say.

Kyle hauls himself to his feet with an effort. The sluggishness I've noticed in him since his exposure to the outside worries me. The experience he had at Mitch's hands was probably traumatic and exhausting, but shouldn't he have recovered by now? Unless he hasn't been taking naps when he says he is. Maybe he's not sleeping at all. Maybe he's still traumatized. Or maybe he spends all his time staring at the shapes outside. Do they dance for him the way they danced for me? Maybe they no longer need to.

"The controls are going to be in the locomotive," Kyle says. "And you can't even face a trip back to your room. How do you expect to get to the controls?"

I glance at Lara whose expression mirrors how I feel: hurt. I try not to let it show.

"They may not be," Lara says, and Kyle turns to face her. She recoils a little when their eyes meet. She's standing over by her bed and it seems like she's trying to keep some distance between herself and Kyle. "There's at least one car behind seventeen. Maybe there are more."

"Whoever heard of a train you drive from the back?" Kyle asks with a derisive laugh, and Lara frowns. This time, she doesn't look hurt, she looks pissed.

"Wherever the controls are," I blurt, jumping in before Lara can say something she'll regret, "it makes sense to check out the back of the train first. There's nobody back here to stop us, and it's closer."

Lara nods, but only I can see it. Kyle has turned back to me. Mockingly, he says, "And poor Eden doesn't have to do anything scary."

I watch Lara bite her lip. I'm confused. I don't understand what's going on, but seeing Lara's anger ignites my own. "What the fuck is your problem, Kyle?"

"I'm not the one with the problem."

I take a step closer to him, getting in his face. I don't want to feel this way, but he's seriously pushing my buttons. "What's that supposed to mean?"

He steps forward so I have to look nearly straight up to meet his gaze. His arms stay rigidly by his side as he speaks, as if he's having to fight to keep them still. "You've got us trapped at the back of the train when everyone who knows anything about it, about how we might get off, about how to control it, and even where the controls are, is at the front. We shouldn't be cowering here like trapped rats, we should have grabbed anything we could use as a weapon and we should have beaten all the information we need out of that fucker and his friend, and then we should have killed them and thrown them outside!" I flinch when he steps back and punches the wall to punctuate his point, leaving a crater behind. "We'd be home already if not for you."

I blink rapidly at the violence in this suggestion, my eyes flitting between him and the hole in the wall. "I didn't hear you complaining when we all agreed to lock the door."

"Like you'd listen if I had."

Lara is watching, wide-eyed. Occasionally her gaze darts to the door. She's checking her escape route. I realize we're scaring the shit out of her and my anger deflates. We must have looked like we were about to start getting violent with each other, and I take two quick steps back from Kyle and hurry around him to Lara. Her eyes are filled with tears as she steps backwards and sits down hard on the bed. I reach her and sit down, putting my arm around her.

"I'm so sorry," I whisper. "It's okay. Everything's going to be okay."

Kyle watches us without an ounce of empathy in his eyes.

"I think you should take a walk and cool down," I say to him, then turn my attention back to Lara.

"Whatever," Kyle says as he leaves the room.

Lara cries for a short time, each one of her hitching sobs breaking my heart a little. I stroke her hair and mutter words of comfort. When she's finished, she looks at me with those earnest eyes of hers. "It isn't him anymore."

I weigh up her words, but whatever way I choose to look at it, I know she isn't wrong. Slowly, I shake my head. "No, it isn't."

I feel as if Mitch won. He took Kyle from us without ever having to throw him off the train.

"What are we going to do?" she asks. She sounds like she's on the edge of giving up, but if she can survive her father, she can survive anything. I'm not going to let her give up, but I still can't think of anything to say in answer to her question.

"I don't know, honey." I wish I did. We don't know Kyle is done changing or if he's going to get worse, but it already seems like he's no longer exactly on our side. I could still go and get the Oxy, but I can see several possibilities. First is that I'll encounter Mitch on the way, and that doesn't end well for me. Mitch once said that it was remarkable what you can see if you know where to look, and I think it's quite likely that the Oxy simply wouldn't be in my room anymore. If he or Rona saw me board, they would have seen what I was carrying. Maybe they can read minds too.

"I don't want to be here anymore," she says. She sounds on the verge of tears, but she looks determined.

"Same." But, as she observed the last time we had this conversation, we have nowhere to go. Selfishly, I worry that Lara's view will change from us all being in this together to one where she simply aims for the easiest exit available and to hell with me and Kyle. I wouldn't necessarily blame her, but it would hurt. I'm rapidly coming to understand that the thing stronger than terror, the thing that got me moving again, isn't hope. It's something else.

I wonder where Kyle is, and what he's doing. I'm assuming he'll be in the dining car or in one of the two passenger cars we have access to now that the door to eleven is locked. Those are the places he spends most of his time, and it wouldn't surprise me if he started sleeping in one of the passenger cars if he hasn't already.

I spend some time trying to organize my thoughts, considering everything I know. I mentally link them to other things. It's therapeutic. As I'm doing this, my mind makes a leap it hasn't made before. "Do you think the gray stuff is what made Kyle start acting differently?"

Lara nods immediately. "Pretty certain."

"What if..." I pause, not sure how to put it into words. My brain is running faster than my mouth and finally I just blurt, "What if that was the point?"

"What do you mean?" Lara asks, shuffling back so she can look at me properly.

"I don't know exactly," I say, trying to figure out what I'm getting at. "What if the plan were never to kill Kyle? What if Mitch's plan were to just expose him to the gray stuff all along?"

Lara considers this, sucking one cheek in as she does. "And we came along, and he had to make it seem like something else?"

"Maybe, yeah. Throw us off the trail." I'm starting to get animated now. We have no evidence, but this is feeling more and more like it might be right.

"What would be the point, though?" she asks.

"I guess it depends on what the gray stuff is supposed to do."

Lara sighs. "Well, it made Kyle mean."

"It did. But that also explains why Mitch apologized so quickly, doesn't it? And why he didn't simply kill me when I was alone with him? If the guy could overpower Kyle, I don't stand much of a chance if he wanted to hurt me."

"Maybe. I don't know anymore. I don't have any idea what's happening." She sounds dejected rather than excited that we might have a new angle to consider.

I can understand how she feels though. I feel the same way. It's not like anything on this stupid train has ever made any sense. Resignedly, I say, "Yeah. Whether it's true or not, it doesn't bring us any closer to understanding anything."

"Do you think the crew might know anything about the outside?"

Maybe they do and maybe they don't. The real question is whether a fifty-fifty chance on something that might not lead in the right direction is worth wasting the last of our water. But what else do we have?

TWENTY-ONE

Explanations

LARA AND I each take a mouthful of water. It's a risk, doing it this way. There are probably only two mouthfuls each left in the bottle, and we might need to use all of it here. We sit in silence as we wait, both facing the corner where Emma appeared last time. When she doesn't, we each drink another mouthful. And sometime later, the final one. We don't say anything about it, but this is now our last chance. It's not long before a woman blinks into existence in the corner.

Lara's expression registers surprise. "This is so cool!"

I smile, but it doesn't belong on my face. "Hi, Emma."

"Eden," she nods. "Lara, is it? Nice to meet you properly."

"You, too."

"What can I do for you this time?" Her expression is one that says she wishes we'd figured out a way to solve our own problems, and I start to feel disheartened.

Lara takes the lead. "We were wondering if you know anything about the grayspace outside."

Emma spends a second scrutinizing her, then says, "I know it is what exists between the places the train goes. Maybe it didn't always, I don't remember. I don't know what it is, exactly, only that it is not inert and may be dangerous."

That's exactly what we were afraid of. I say, "Mitch exposed Kyle to it."

Emma nods. "Mitch has ejected some of the crew into it in the past if they questioned him or did not perform to his liking."

I don't know why, but that shocks me. It's what I assumed Mitch was going to do to Kyle, but to hear that he has actually gone through with it with other people chills me to my core. "Jeez, you should have kicked that guy's ass a long time ago."

Emma looks at me coldly. "Perhaps that is how you solve your problems, but our problems play out on a timescale you can't even comprehend, and our lives do not matter. The train comes first. Please do not presume to judge our action or lack thereof."

Suitably abashed, I say, "I'm sorry. I'm just frustrated."

She appears to take pity on me, offering a kind smile. Then she's all business again. "You have noticed changes in Kyle?"

I nod.

"I am sorry to hear that, but I cannot say what fate will ultimately befall him, or any of you. If, as you sense, Mitch's intention was not to kill Kyle, but to expose him to the creatures outside, then I suspect Mitch understands far more about it than we do."

"It's quite unnerving when you read our minds," I tell her.

Lara chimes in, "So, let's talk about retaliation. You say kicking Mitch's ass isn't how you do things. How *do* you do things? Does Mitch just get away with throwing you outside?"

"We were created to serve the train. Our lives are of no importance, and that being the case, we cannot risk going up against Mitch directly unless it is guaranteed he will be removed from play. If he survives our action, he may kill all of us, and the train would be left without a crew. That is unacceptable."

"Why? What is the train? Why is it so important that it has a crew?" Lara asks.

"You have to remember, child, that we're in the dark as much as you are about a great many things. We may work on the train, but we do not know how it works, how it's controlled, or even the full extent of the powers it has. Only one person knows that: The Creator. The Creator told Rona some of what he knew, enough to keep certain things running, but he did not tell us. We were created to serve the train and those aboard, not to run it."

Lara looks annoyed at this answer, so I jump in. "What can you tell us about The Creator?"

Emma looks at me for a long moment, her mouth forming the faintest smile. She finally appears engaged rather than looking at us like we're pests who she wishes would go away. "Now that is an interesting question."

"How so?"

"Would it surprise you to learn that there is not, in the cosmic sense, a creator?"

"Not really," I say at the same time Lara asks, "No God?"

"Quite. There were once pockets of life scattered throughout existence, which spans farther and wider than you have ever imagined. Many of those sentient beings have conjured up similar origin stories to the ones your people have, but none that we've heard are close to being accurate. No, The Creator of whom we speak is better thought of as a caretaker of creation, not its composer.

"We refer to him as The Creator in the context of the train. He made it. Nobody ever told us how everything else came to be, if indeed anyone truly knows. The train's creator, our creator, may simply be playing the hand the universe dealt him, much as we are. Perhaps your big bang theory is correct, perhaps not. While The Creator has the power to create and destroy, he did not create the universe. He exercises his powers in certain limited ways. He created this train, and gave it *its* powers, as a means to an end. A way to travel creation, tending to what needs tending to. Where the spark of life faltered, he helped it along. Where it developed poorly, he guided it. Where it refused to be guided, it was snuffed out. Despite what you may think, life is important. Death is important, too. But there are older and more frightening things in the universe than planetary life that is anchored to the rock that hosts it. Someday, you may see that."

"Wait, so we're traveling through space?" I ask, glancing automatically at the walls of the carriage where the windows should be if this car had any.

"In a manner of speaking. The train takes shortcuts. If it did not, getting anywhere would take millions of what you call years."

"So that's what grayspace is," Lara muses. "The shortcuts go through it?"

"I suppose so," Emma says, then takes a breath. I take a quick look at Lara. She's clearly captivated by the old woman's words.

"You said you were created?" Lara asks. "Not born?"

"The Creator made us to serve the train. We were not born in the traditional sense that you mean. Some of us have been here since the beginning, most of us have not."

"What happened to him?" Lara asks.

"The Creator? We don't know. He wasn't always on board. He had many duties to attend to, and not all of them could be dealt with on board the train. One day he left, and hasn't yet come back. It was an extremely long time before we saw anyone else. We worked, we tidied the train, we cooked meals for ourselves and we kept up the train's schedule of supply pickups. This continued for lifetimes. Occasionally, we would see people in the distance when we stopped for supplies. Eventually, they dared come close enough to board the train. We served them as we served The Creator, because that is what we were put here to do."

"How can you track time when we can't?" Lara asks.

"We can't either. We just have reference points. As you yourselves know, getting off the train allows you to think in temporal terms again. We simply got off every time we stopped and made a record. It was hard to begin with. We had to judge time by the shape of rock formations in the distance and how they changed between visits, or by how deep a river was. When sentient life started visiting the train, we simply asked them how they measured time and hybridized their approaches."

"Jesus," I mutter. Measuring time by the erosion of rocks puts the timescales involved here in the millions or billions of years.

Lara asks, "There are aliens?"

"There were life forms on planets other than your own, yes. We do not see them often, do not know if they still exist. Mostly, The Creator limits his interest to humans. There may be a reason for that, but I don't know it."

Lara looks flustered and takes a second to continue. "So, how do the rooms work? I mean, they don't exist before someone gets on, right?"

Emma nods. "That is correct. The train constructs the rooms based on the person's psyche."

Lara glances at me. "I wonder what rooms an alien's psyche conjures up."

I smile and shrug, then ask, "So, it's not Mitch making the rooms?"

"No."

My eyes meet Lara's and her sad expression makes me sure we're thinking the same thought. That Kyle may be the one responsible for his prison cell compartment. Maybe he thinks he doesn't deserve his freedom, such as it is. He may not have killed his wife and daughter, but he didn't prevent their deaths either. Maybe he believes he deserves punishment. It's not something I'd considered before, and I feel terrible for the guy.

Emma goes on, "Before Rona arrived, The Creator simply left the train as it was whenever he had to tend to matters elsewhere. After she boarded, he started leaving her in charge. I don't know why he chose her for this duty. For many lifetimes, things ran smoothly in this fashion. It was only when Mitch boarded the train that everything changed. We suspect he has somehow corrupted Rona. He got a taste of the power he could have. I do not know where he came from nor what his story is, though I know what he tells people is a lie. He took our home from us and made us prisoners and slaves. We still get visitors such as yourselves, but many of them seem... downtrodden."

My spine is tingling with dread. "So, Mitch has been here a long time," I say.

"Not as long as Rona, but still a long time. We have not been allowed off the train since he boarded, so we have no way of knowing how long. He confines us to our rooms when the train stops for supplies and he loads them himself, or more often, gets another of the passengers to do it for him while he acts out his frail old man routine."

Lara suddenly blurts, "Shit! I lost her!"

This isn't lasting as long as I'd hoped. Last ditch effort, then. "Do you know where the controls for the train are?"

"There are controls everywhere, though I do not know what all of them do. Kyle even found some, though I don't believe he knew what he had found. I watched him do it when he took a notice board off the wall. There are controls in the engine. There are controls at the rear of the train, though there is security back there. There are controls in carriage seven, too."

"Carriage seven?" I ask, counting in my head. "That's... the room with the cross?"

"That's right."

"But... it's just out in the open?"

And that's when I lose sight of her.

TWENTY-TWO

The Plan

"I SHOULD HAVE known that asshole couldn't tell the truth about anything," I say.

"What? What did she say?" Lara asks.

Lara hasn't seen the oddly empty carriage seven with its metal grille covered walls and floor, and the strip of light that mirrors the one on the outside of the train. Mitch took me through it as part of his tour of the train, but he downplayed its significance. He even claimed he didn't know what the stuff in there actually did. Mitch has lied about everything, right from the moment I met him. He lied about his wife's death, he lied about how long he's been on the train, he lied about his belief that the train is taking him to Heaven. He lied about trying to kill Kyle. Why wouldn't he have lied about what's in carriage seven?

"Emma said some of the train's controls are in carriage seven. You remember I told you about the cross on the floor in there?"

She nods. "Any idea what it's for?"

"Nope, and Emma didn't know. She said there are controls there, though. Controls everywhere. In the locomotive, and in the carriages at the back we can't access."

"I think I might know," a deep voice says from the corner of the room behind me.

Kyle.

I stand and put myself between him and Lara. "Kyle," I say. "Cooled down?"

"I have. I'm sorry, Eden. Both of you. My head... something's wrong. It's like there's a fog over my thoughts and I can't think about anything clearly or rationally. It's scary, Eden. I'm scared. I'll keep my distance because it might not be done getting worse."

I stare at him, willing his words to have the feel of lies, but they don't. I can't help but wonder if this is what happened to Mitch. Was he exposed to the outside? Is that what made him the man he is? Is that why he couldn't answer me when I grilled him on why he'd threatened Kyle's life? The determined set of Kyle's jaw makes me think that part of him wants whatever's happening to him, as his punishment for not being able to save his daughter. I blink once and my eyes begin to fill with tears. I want to go to him, to offer comfort, and it kills me that I can't. If the gray stuff makes him mean, maybe it makes him violent or murderous, like Mitch. I can't risk leaving Lara alone.

"You said you might know what carriage seven controls?" Lara asks.

"I think it controls the route," Kyle says. Turning to me, "You remember what I said just after we climbed up into carriage eleven after going outside?"

"I do; you said the color of the line on the outside of the train might denote a location, or maybe the next stop."

Kyle nods. "If that's right, it makes sense that the room with the same color line might control the route, right?"

I nod slowly. "Yeah. Yeah, that does make sense."

Lara, wide eyed, declares, "We need to learn how to use that room."

"I agree," Kyle says. "And you have to let me go check it out."

"What?" I gasp. "No! We all go."

"No, Eden. You need to stay with Lara, and you both need to stay safe. At least for now. I don't know what's happening in my head, but there's every chance that whatever it is might get worse or might be irreversible. You stay here in safety, end of discussion."

I can't even pretend to disagree with him. As much as I want us to stick together, he is absolutely right: we can't. I nod, then sigh, closing my eyes. "I'm not disagreeing, but I just want to point out, for the record, that "safe" is still a relative term. What's your plan?"

"Recon first. I'm going to get a good look at that room. If Mitch shows up, I'll be ready for him this time. I'll come back and let you know what I find, and we can come up with a more complete plan then. If I can figure out how to make the train go somewhere, I'll pick somewhere good."

Lara and I both nod and now it's her turn to tear up as Kyle stands and walks to the padlocked door. I follow and we stand three feet apart, facing each other. He waits for me to unlock the door, and I gaze up at him. Fuck it. Whatever's going on in his head, he's about to head off into enemy territory. I step forward and wrap my arms around him.

"Be careful, big guy," I whisper, then I hear Lara's chair clatter to the floor as she sees what's happening and runs over to make this a group hug.

I pretend not to notice the way his voice breaks when he says, "I will. Stay safe."

I slide the door shut and lock it when Kyle has passed beyond the next car. Lara walks slowly back to the table and plops herself down. I ask, "You okay?"

She shakes her head, and it's the action of a young child who hasn't learned how to deal with her emotions yet.

"Kyle will be fine," I reassure her, though I don't know if I believe it. I wanted to question his assertion that he'd be ready for Mitch this time. The old man already overpowered him once. Why couldn't he do it again? I try to push those thoughts away.

"You don't know that."

I walk over to her and sit down in the seat next to her, then scoot it over to her, putting my arm around her shoulders.

"You're right, honey, I don't. But he's going to be careful, and that's all any of us can do."

It makes my stomach hurt to see Lara this upset, and I wish there were more I could do for her. We sit that way for a time, Lara occasionally sniffling, but mostly we're silent. I am thinking back over everything that's happened. Boarding the train, discovering my room, meeting Mitch and Rona. I wonder if there were things I missed in those early days; something that would have alerted me to the fact that Mitch isn't a good guy. And who knows where Rona sits in all of this. Mitch seemed alarmed that I might tell Rona of his attempt to kill Kyle, but we're also working on the assumption that everything about that was staged, and that everything he says is a lie, so who knows?

Did Rona tell Mitch how to use the train willingly, or did he do something to her to get the information? Torture her? Threaten to expose her to the gray stuff? If he did, could Rona be of help to us? If she's not on his side, maybe she'd be on ours, and her knowledge of the train, of being left in charge by The Creator, might come in extremely handy.

There are too many unknowns. What we need to do is wait for Kyle, hope he finds something, then get ourselves off this train once and for all. Lara deserves to have a normal life. I do, too, for that matter. And Kyle.

I pull Lara closer and rub her upper arm. "I love you, kiddo," I say. I didn't mean to say it, but it's not wrong. It is, I realized earlier, the thing that pulled me out of my terror about Mitch. She deserves to know that somebody does, and she should get to know it unambiguously. Our lives seem to be getting more and more dangerous, and it feels like only a matter of time until something irrevocable happens.

She's silent for a moment. I'm not offended. She doesn't have to say it back. It's a very parental feeling, the closest I've come to feeling anything truly maternal. I'm just happy she knows.

"I love you," she whispers.

"And nothing can ever change that."

She nods against me. Silently, I wonder if that's true.

TWENTY-THREE

Reprise

KYLE'S VOICE COMES suddenly and clearly through the door and I hurry over to open it. Mitch might be on the other side, maybe holding Kyle at gunpoint or something, but I force the thought away and open the door anyway. Maybe that's reckless, but we need progress. We have to stop standing still. Thankfully, only Kyle stands on the other side of the door. He looks exhausted.

"What happened?" I ask, stepping aside to let him into the carriage, then locking the door behind him again.

"I got to carriage seven and didn't see anyone," he says. Lara is behind me in an instant and she steps forward to hug Kyle. He hugs her back, but his expression is one of bewilderment.

"Did you figure out how it works?"

"No. I found controls, but it's not clear what they do. Or maybe it's my head. The more I studied them, the less sense they seemed to make. But everything's quiet. No sign of Mitch or Rona. Maybe we should take the opportunity and all head down to seven now and take a look, maybe grab your Oxy?"

I'm nodding before he's finished speaking. "Yes. Yes, let's go."

Lara offers no resistance and we file out of the door after I unlock it again. I debate relocking it behind us, but decide against it when I imagine Mitch giving chase and all of us dying while I fumble with the key. Instead, I bring the lock and key with us. Maybe I'll get to hit someone with it.

The journey to car seven is uneventful. Lara comments on the lavish decorations in the front half of the train, but those are the only words spoken by any of us.

When we get to our destination, the first thing I notice is that the cross on the floor and the colored line behind the metal grilles that cover the walls are yellow today. Kyle moves off to the side and opens a panel I must have missed the last time I was here, and I walk over to examine it, Lara by my side. Behind the panel is a screen like the noticeboards, images rendered half an inch above the surface. There are buttons with icons on them, but I can't tell what any of them mean.

"Does it make any sense to you?" Kyle asks.

I shake my head. "Lara?"

"No... but, wait. Maybe we're making a mistake. We're expecting this to control the route, right? Maybe it's for something else."

I think about it. She could be right. "Like what?"

She makes a sound of deep concentration. Kyle and I stand silently behind her and watch. Eventually, she says, "I'm going to try something, okay? Stand back against the wall."

"What do you expect to happen?" I ask as I position myself as suggested.

"Emma said the train could create matter, right?"

My eyebrows shoot up. "Lara, are you about to kill us all?"

She tears her gaze away from the panel for long enough to shoot me a *please, what do you take me for?* look. "Give me some credit, Eden. I think this is actually pretty intuitive. Watch."

Lara presses a sequence of buttons while I hold my breath.

With no fanfare at all, a chair appears on the cross in the center of the room. One second it's not there, the next it is. I feel like there should have been a popping sound or something, but it happened silently.

I blink, then look at Kyle to make sure I'm not hallucinating. He looks just as shocked as I feel. Lara, meanwhile, walks to the chair and drops herself down in it. It's one of the red and gold upholstered armchairs from the passenger carriages.

"Pretty comfortable," she says with a massive smile.

I can't help but grin. "How did you know it'd do that?"

"The system is pretty self-explanatory. At least if you want to create something it already knows how to create. I don't know how to make something from scratch, if that's even possible."

We walk over to scrutinize the panel, and I have to admit, it is pretty logical, and I would never have guessed that something so unassuming would have the power this thing seems to have.

It's just a screen set into the wall, about 9 inches across. It's positioned perfectly for Lara's eyeline, so I guess it's about five feet up the wall. Typically, the display is rendered half an inch above the surface. The entire interface is just four buttons across the bottom of the screen, two of them to scroll through the things the machine knows how to make, which appear in the top two-thirds of the display. Another button actually creates the object, and a final one that presumably destroys whatever happens to be on the cross. Immediately, I wonder if we could lure Mitch in here and use that. It's another option, I guess. If only I'd found this earlier, I might have been able to create something to keep us all safe.

As if picking up on this thought, Kyle crosses to the brand-new chair, picks it up and smashes it against the wall until he has two splintered chair legs and a whole lot of mess. Lara retreats behind me while this is happening, but I think I know what he has in mind, and it's not his brain going all screwy again. I hope.

When he's done, he hands me a chair leg and holds out another to Lara who takes it hesitantly.

She blinks. "Thanks? What—"

"Weapons," he says.

"What about you?"

"I could probably kill both of you with my bare hands, and my mind is not completely under my control. I don't think you want me to be armed."

Suddenly the yellow line and the cross on the floor fade to black and we all stop what we're doing and look around nervously. "What's going on?" Lara asks as the line and cross switch back on. They are no longer yellow.

A weight on my chest. I can't breathe. All I can manage to say is, "White."

"Isn't that..." Kyle begins.

"Yes." That's what color it was when it came to pick me up. The color it was in my dream. If Kyle is right about the meaning of the colored line, that means the train might have brought me home. The one place I have no interest in going. Sure enough, as soon as I've had the thought, the train starts to slow down for the first time in what seems like it could be weeks.

My gaze flits between Kyle and Lara searching for help, for any way to stop this.

We head back to carriage nine to see what's happening outside. We're still high above the world. I look down, trying to spot landmarks that might tell me where I am. If I press my face to the window and look left, there's ocean in the distance, but that's the best I can do. Looking the other way, all I can see is forest covered hills.

"Do you recognize anything?" Kyle asks, looking worriedly at me.

"Too high."

Lara is staring out of the window. She turns to look at me, and her expression is all wide-eyed excitement. "Are we going to get off?" To her credit, she manages not to sound excited, at least.

The immediate answer that springs to mind is absolutely not. We agreed to leave the train, but there's no point getting off here. This is a dead place filled with ghosts, the kind that don't dance for you. Still, maybe we should get off so we can think about time again. Who knows, maybe Kyle's issues will disappear once he's off the train. "I don't know."

We're silent for some time, watching as the world flies by. We gradually dip lower and I start to think I can make out landmarks.

"I think this is Oregon." I pace up and down the car wondering if it's possible to tell from up here. "Is this Mitch? Is this the kind of sick fuck he is, bringing me back to this hell?"

Kyle puts his hand on my shoulder. "I don't know, Eden. As usual, we don't know anything. Maybe the train is just following a giant loop. Mitch controlling the route is only a theory."

"A pretty convincing one," Lara adds.

Kyle nods sadly. "Agreed. But let's wait and see what we see, okay?"

My shoulders are tense and I want to scream, but I try to force myself to feel nothing. "Okay."

We wait and we watch out of the windows until we're low enough to make out buildings. The train moves gradually lower and slows down further. I shuffle unnoticed away from the others when it becomes apparent where the train is taking me. It couldn't have picked a worse place. No, wait. *He* couldn't have picked a worse place. *Mitch* couldn't.

The view is different from above, but the tennis court and swimming pool render it unmistakable.

"Eden?" Lara asks. "Are you okay? Do you know what this place is?"

I can't bring myself to speak, so I turn to her and shake my head in answer to the first question, not the second. I don't think she gets it, because she turns back to the window as if she might be able to identify the building given more time.

"Oh," Kyle says finally, then quietly to Lara, he adds, "The swimming pool, the tennis court. Look at the front door. It's wide open."

I didn't remember if I'd told them all the details about what happened here, but I guess I must have. Greg's still here, somewhere in that building. Worse, Alice is still where I left her on that bed. The bed she and I should have shared. Where I could have told her that everything was going to be okay, even though we both knew it wasn't. I think I can almost feel her presence.

"Oh, God," Lara says, but as soon as her wide-eyed empathy turns my way and she starts taking hesitant steps in my direction, my sadness is overwhelmed by anger. She stops in her tracks.

"I'm going to kill him," I say, my tone completely calm because I absolutely mean it. I head for the door before either of them has time to reach me, and each step increases the rage I feel. I hurry out of the vestibule and into carriage eight on my way to Mitch's room. I'm serious, I'm going to fucking kill him.

I've had enough of this. Either he'll tell me what he knows, or he won't. But one way or another, he's dead.

"Eden, wait!" Lara calls.

"Eden!" Kyle shouts.

I ignore them.

TWENTY-FOUR

The Realization

"MITCH!" I SHOUT, hammering on his door with the splintered chair leg Kyle gave me in carriage seven. I pause long enough to listen, but I don't hear anything from within, so I start pounding again. "Mitch! Get out here right the fuck now!"

My uncontrollable rage has propelled me around the train like a mad woman with Lara and Kyle in tow. They tried to talk me down. At one point Kyle looked like he was going to physically restrain me. Maybe he'd have been able to or maybe he wouldn't, but I'm pretty sure in that moment that he was regretting having armed me. So here we are. I push the handle down and give the door a shove, but it's locked. Frustration overwhelms me for a second and I drop the chair leg and throw myself at the door shoulder first, grunting as I make contact. It doesn't open.

"Fuck," I spit, and slam my open palm against it.

My heart is racing and I'm struggling to get enough air into my lungs, but that doesn't stop me from turning to head to Rona's carriage, hoping I might find Mitch there. Lara steps in front of me. She's a couple of inches shorter than I am and a lot thinner, but she stands there with her arms crossed, daring me to try to get past her. It's enough to begin to calm me down.

I close my eyes and turn my back to Mitch's door, lean back against it then slump to the ground with a colossal sigh. "I *hate* this fucking train."

"You're in good company, then," Lara says.

I look up at her and sigh again.

She grins down at me and uncrosses her arms. I can't help but smile back. I look around and find I have no recollection of getting to this carriage. I was on rage-fueled autopilot. Then I notice Kyle sitting against the wall further down the corridor, head in his hands. "You okay, big guy?"

He starts to rock back and forth as if my words are pummeling him. "Get..." he says, his voice strained. "You have to... get... away from me."

"Kyle? What's wrong?" Lara asks as she starts to approach him. Kyle's hands are balled up in fists which he's using to rub at his temples. Lara has to know the answer to her question, but her desire to help overrides her caution.

I get to my feet. "Lara, stop," I say, my voice taking on the loud and clear tone of command. She stops and glances over her shoulder at me. "Come to me, honey."

She looks conflicted. She wants to go to Kyle and help him. She looks like she might be about to turn and do just that when Kyle roars, "Go!"

She whips her head back around to look at him in shock, stands frozen for a second, then finally runs to my side. "What's happening?"

"It's whatever happened earlier coming back, I think. We have to leave him alone for a little bit. He'll be okay."

My chair leg is closer to Kyle than I'd like, and he's now between us and our ability to make other weapons. Regretfully, I leave the weapon behind. Lara's will have to be enough. I lead her in the only direction we can go, toward the front of the train.

I take Lara to my room because it's the only place that exists which offers anything approaching safety. Once we're both inside, I lock the door and cross the room to sit on the bed next to Lara who has already made herself comfortable.

"This is a nice room," she says, but her voice is flat.

"It's not bad," I admit. "Shame it's on this fucking train."

She grimaces and closes her eyes.

"Can you—" I start, then falter. "Would you mind looking outside? Have we moved at all?"

"Sure." She hops nimbly off the bed then pokes her head behind the blinds. "We've moved. It looks like we're over water now."

I breathe a sigh of relief. "Thank fuck for that. I can't believe that of all the places we could have revisited, it took me back there."

"It does seem a bit on the nose," Lara agrees. "Do you really think Mitch did it?"

"Maybe. If the train is just on one big loop, it wouldn't make sense for it to stop somewhere other than where it picked me up."

"Why would he, though?"

"To fuck with me? I threatened him with violence, I don't imagine he likes me very much." I exhale, shaking my head. "I don't know if someone like Mitch needs a reason. He could have been fucking with us in all sorts of tiny ways ever since we got on. I just wish I could figure out how and why he's doing it. If we can't control the route from carriage seven, we need to figure out where..."

"Eden, shut up," Lara says, one hand in the air.

My earlier fear about her being infected by the gray stuff outside the train comes back to haunt me for a second before I see she's deep in thought. I snap my mouth shut.

Eventually, she says, "You said Mitch could have been fucking with us ever since we got on, right?"

"I did."

"What would he do if that didn't work?"

"If what didn't work?" I'm not sure what she's getting at.

"If fucking with you wasn't having the desired effect?"

I think about it, but after a moment I say, "I don't think I understand what you're asking."

"Think about it. There are three passengers on this train except for Mitch and Rona. You and me and Kyle. What do you and I have in common?"

"Well, quite a lot, I think."

She gives me a tiny smile that's gone as soon as it appears. "Yeah, but there's one big thing we have in common."

"Still not getting it. We're both female?"

Lara smiles. "Well, maybe that's part of it. No. I'm talking about our shitty fathers."

"Oh," I say.

"And how does Kyle fit in?" she asks, and my spine begins to tingle.

"He was convicted of killing his wife and... oh... his daughter." I'm catching on now, and the implications of what Lara is saying are almost too horrible to contemplate. I take over her train of thought. "If Mitch can control the route, perhaps he can control who he picks up somehow. So, he chooses two girls with daddy issues and a father who is supposed to have killed his daughter. He *has* been fucking with us all along!"

The more I think about this, the more the idea runs away with itself. Lara shakes her head as if she can't believe any of this and continues, "And either Mitch didn't realize Kyle innocent, or he didn't expect us to believe he was innocent. He didn't expect us all to become friends."

"Oh, shit," I gasp. Lara is still a step ahead of me, but I reach the punchline just as she says it.

"And so, he does something he knows will turn Kyle into the monster Mitch already assumed he was: he exposes him to the grayspace."

"Fuck," I mutter. "I mean... fuck!"

"I know."

"But... if Kyle keeps getting worse, he's going to kill one or both of us. Is that the point? Are we just sport? Jesus." I rub my temples and Lara just shakes her head. I'm out of words now. Is this just one big game for that fucking psycho?

The train suddenly accelerates, and Lara pokes her head behind the blind again. "We're back in grayspace."

I nod slowly.

Time passes. Obviously, I don't know how much. We stay in my room. I venture out to the dining car twice and return with stacks of junk food. I make a point of thanking whoever in the crew prepared and delivered it, but of course, I don't know if they heard me. We survive in this way for several sleeps.

"I thought Kyle would be better by now," Lara says. I have spent a lot of time convincing Lara that leaving him alone is our best course of action. If her theory about Mitch is right, the damage is already done, and Mitch is unlikely to try anything else. The best thing to do is to let events run their course and hope for the best at this point. I don't have the heart to tell Lara that Kyle might not get better. Maybe whatever his affliction is comes in waves at the beginning, but after a while, perhaps it's permanent. "Me, too."

"Or I thought Mitch might have come to visit. You know, to kill us."

"Those are some dark thoughts, little lady." Mine are no better, though.

"I can't help it. It's this fucking train."

I can do nothing but nod my agreement. I know how she feels because I feel the same way. As much as I'm all for letting events progress naturally, something needs to happen soon or we'll both go insane. We're waiting for Kyle to come back before we enact our plan to try to alter the course of the train, but maybe we shouldn't be. We don't know if he's coming back.

I'm almost afraid to ask the question that comes to mind, but it needs asking. "How long do we wait for him?"

Lara glares at me, but she obviously doesn't have an answer, and seems annoyed to have to confront that fact. "I don't know." She holds my gaze for a while, her expression slowly degenerating from horrified to devastated, but eventually goes back to staring at the ceiling above my bed.

More time passes. We talk about Kyle, about the things we like about him, and the things that make us laugh. We talk about ways we might be able to help him. We come up with some options. Taking him off the train is number one, but if we can't do that, we can restrain him. His room is the perfect place to do that, being a prison cell. We'd both feel bad doing that to him, but if we can keep him from harming us, and from harming himself, and figure out how to take Mitch and Rona out of play, maybe we can eventually come up with a way to undo what Mitch did to him.

Yet more time passes. Lara asks if I can teach her some violin, but she gets frustrated too quickly and we give up. I play for her sometimes. We eat. We sleep. We don't talk often, but when we do, we try to make sure it's about things from our lives before the train.

The bottle of Oxycodone – still present in my room after all – becomes a sort of talisman during this time. I cling to the idea of it like its mere existence can protect us when the most damage I can do with it in close quarters with Mitch is maybe to throw it at him and hope it hits him in the eye. I can't very well force feed him the ten or twenty pills that might constitute a fatal overdose and then restrain him for an hour while he slowly dies.

And then, one pseudo-morning, Lara wakes me by shaking my shoulder. "Eden, wake up. We're slowing down."

TWENTY-FIVE

The Outside (2)

LARA AND I stand facing the door I used to board this awful contraption. Boarding is easily the worst decision I've ever made; I feel pretty sure of that now. If I'd downed the Oxy and checked out, I'd never have met Kyle or Lara, but maybe we'd all be better off.

Kyle should be here. Instead, he's off somewhere doing God knows what, feeling his mind unravel. I can't even imagine. I don't have any idea how we could even begin to reverse what Mitch did to him. Maybe it's not possible. Maybe Mitch has finished the job by now. We'd never know.

"Are you sure you want to do this?" I ask. "We might leave Kyle behind."

She doesn't look at all sure, but she says, "Time doesn't work on board, who knows what else might be blocked from our minds? We need to have this conversation; I just wish Kyle were here to have it with us. Let's not venture far from the train, okay?"

I nod and the train finally pulls to a stop. Lara looks out of the window and something in her expression shifts.

"You okay?" I ask.

"I... there's something familiar about this place."

"You think this is where you came from?"

She hesitates. "I don't know. I guess it doesn't matter."

"Right," I agree, then slap the illuminated Open button. The doors slide apart and Lara descends to the ground while I follow behind.

When I jump down beside her, I find she's tipped her head back and is grinning widely. "That's some weird shit! I was standing in the train trying to think of my birthday, and I couldn't. As soon as I get out here, it's like a switch has flipped. I was born in 1977." She pulls out some paper and a pencil from her back pocket and starts writing.

I can't help but return her grin. "1989 for me. I really feel like I shouldn't be older than you. Emma said the train can't time travel—"

"She also said she didn't know the full extent of the train's abilities."

I nod. "That's true." I cast my gaze around, taking in these new surroundings. It's clearly somewhere in America. The cars are familiar from old movies. We're in a city somewhere, or the

237

outskirts of one. There's some angular brutalist architecture rendered in rough concrete in the near distance and some dilapidated apartment buildings off to one side. I glance at the colored line on the train and find that it's a bright orange.

"So, wait," Lara says, interrupting my thoughts. "You're how old?"

"Thirty."

"That means you boarded the train in 2019?"

"That's right. How old are you?"

"I'm seventeen."

I'm surprised; she's older than I would have thought. "So, you boarded... when I was five years old."

"Agh! This hurts my head." She rubs her forehead to illustrate her point, but it just makes me think of the way Kyle rubbed at his temples when trying to control whatever has invaded his mind.

"If it's not time travel, it has to be some kind of parallel universe situation. Doesn't it? Unless time is so malleable on board that you were waiting twenty-five years before I arrived. Does it feel like that could be true?"

"Eden, that isn't helping!" Lara says with mock exasperation. I laugh, and she goes on, "Can you think of anything else the train might have concealed?"

The door of a squat gray concrete building opens about a hundred yards away and a man wearing a brown suit steps out. I turn to Lara. "Nope. Nothing. I think it's just—"

"Lara Mae!" a voice calls. It's the man. He's standing maybe forty yards away now, having covered the rest of the distance quicker than seems possible.

"Oh, fuck!" Lara gasps, her voice suddenly breathy and panicked. She starts to hyperventilate almost immediately, but I don't need her to tell me who this man is. If we'd been thinking, and if we hadn't been so desperate for something to happen, we could have predicted this. The train took me back to relive my grief about Alice. Why *wouldn't* it bring us to see Lara's father? I turn to face him.

"Stop right there!" I shout, then I whisper to Lara, who is cowering behind me, "Get back on the train." She doesn't move. Maybe she can't move. She might be paralyzed with fear, or rage, or both.

"Who do you think you are?" the man shouts. "Get away from my daughter!"

"You're funny, I was going to say the same thing." Antagonizing him probably isn't my best move, but I'm unable to resist. I take a step forward and Lara's father does the same. He's not what I expected. He looks respectable with his neat hair and cleanly shaven face, though I guess I shouldn't be surprised by that. We're all just people, that's what makes it so hard to spot the bastards.

"Give me my fucking daughter," he growls.

"Or what? From what I hear, you like beating up girls. How about it? You think you can take me?" He doesn't look physically fit, but he's also not obviously unfit either. He's got a couple inches on me and I'm not sure who would win that fight. I took martial arts classes for a while when I was younger. I know how to defend myself if I need to, at least in theory, but it's a big risk.

"Lara," he says, apparently trying to bypass any influence I might have, "come on, sweetie, we're going home."

"She's not going anywhere with you," I say. He's turning a dark shade of red and starting to shake. These are not good signs. I turn my head slightly to the right without taking my eyes from the man. "Lara, honey, get on the train now. We have to go."

"You think I'm going to let you take my daughter with you?"

"You think I'm going to let you take her home so you can beat her up some more?" I hear Lara start to move behind me, shoes scrambling on concrete. She's breathing hard, gasping almost, but she's moving. Good.

"I don't know what she's been telling you, but—"

"Save it," I take a careful step back.

The man's eyes bulge, and I hope that means Lara is back on the train. "Bitches like you need to know your place!" he snarls. "Lara, get down from there!"

"Eden," Lara's voice comes from behind me, barely above a whisper. "Let's go."

I take another quick step back. "I know my place, and more importantly, so does Lara. It's far away from you." I spin around and start to run the few yards to the short ladder up into the train. Lara is standing just inside the door, ready to pull me up. I hear the scuff of shoes on gravel behind me as Lara's father begins to give chase. I already know I'm not going to make it.

A few steps later, Lara screams my name, putting so much force behind it it's as if she's experiencing the violence that I expect to be upon me in moments. In the split second I allow myself to glance up at her, I see she is bent at the knees and holding both palms out toward me, her entire face a portrait of desperate, frantic hope that I understand her meaning. Thankfully, it's hard to mistake, and I stop abruptly, taking a quick sidestep to my left as I do.

Lara's father lands face first in a heap just to my right having evidently tried to leap on top of me. I almost laugh, but instead I make a surprised squawk when the man's left arm reaches out and grabs my ankle. Pure instinct takes over and I stamp on his wrist with my free foot with enough force to break it. He roars with pain and profanity, but he lets go. Then he's getting up almost at once. I run the rest of the way, then throw myself up into the train, barely touching the ladder, and Lara hits the close button just as her father starts to climb awkwardly, one hand held against his body. The doors slide shut.

"Shit," I breathe. "These doors open from the outside. Where's your chair leg?"

She doesn't answer, but I spot it on the floor on the other side of the vestibule and bend to pick it up.

Lara's father is hammering on the door with his forehead, smashing it against the glass in an utterly blind rage, snarling and shouting profanity. He's using his good arm to hold on to one of the handles that are affixed on either side of the outer doors while standing on the top rung of the ladder. Seems it hasn't occurred to him to press the open button, but it's only a matter of time.

He shouts something, but the carriage is soundproof and I can't make it out. His face is now beet red and blood trickles down his face. I can see spittle on the window.

"Jesus," I say as I watch him go to work again with his forehead. This might be the worst thing I've ever seen. Someone driven so utterly mad that they are practically beating themselves to death to get what they want. Lara is just staring, her expression making a clear statement: *I do not know this person. I may never have truly known this person.*

I hold the chair leg ready to bludgeon, all the while hoping I won't have to. He might not be fit to be her father, but watching him die would still fuck her up big time. I look around for a way to stop him doing what he's doing, because watching this is almost as bad as watching him die.

It's then that I notice the lights by the door are no longer illuminated, and the train is starting to move.

"Oh, no."

Lara's father continues to pound his head against the glass, though more slowly and with less force now, but even if I wanted to, I couldn't let him in. The doors are locked. The train begins to move faster. Lara's father stops, looks around, then clings on for dear life as best he can, now using the hand of his bad arm to try to maintain his balance. His wide-eyed face swivels this way and that, trying to understand what's happening to him.

Lara whimpers and my eyes fill with tears. "Lara, don't watch," I say, but I'm not about to make her stop. It might be better for her not to see this, but I don't get to dictate the last image she has of her father.

When the train starts to rise into the sky, I'm disappointed that he manages to retain his grip on the handles. At least if he fell it would be over quickly from Lara's perspective. When we enter back into what Lara calls the grayspace, I don't know what's going to happen.

Luckily, or not, it's not long before we find out. Lara has sunk to the ground, her back against the opposite door. She doesn't cry, but her face morphs from expression to expression almost too fast to follow. Occasionally she whines or makes an involuntary squeaking sound, or something that could be a sob if not for the utter terror that's all I can hear. I assume she must be imagining every possible way this can end and that's what she's reacting to. There is no good way for this to end. I go over and sit next to her, wrap my arm around her, and we watch. It's awful, but we can't do anything else. I can't leave her here, and she's not going to leave her dad.

When we break out into the grayspace, the tendrils start to work their way over his body almost immediately, touching him, tasting him, deciding if he's worth taking. The train is, thankfully, soundproof enough that we can't hear what are obviously screams as he succumbs to his fate. Lara buries her head in my shoulder, and I bring my other arm around to shield her from the sight of her father being plucked from the ladder by the gray shapes outside. Finally, blessedly, he passes out of sight.

PART FOUR

TWENTY-SIX

THE DISCOVERY

LARA DOESN'T CRY at all, she just rests against me with her head on my shoulder. We sit that way for a long time while I think. We're no closer to getting off the train. Indeed, we just tried and were confronted with Lara's father. What happens next time? Are we going to encounter mine? If Mitch is controlling the train's route, he could ensure that we never get off simply by taking us to places too horrible for us to want to. Or he could just never stop the train. Maybe the food would run out if he did that? Emma said the train can produce matter, but also that it takes on supplies.

Lara's father is now dead, consumed by the ghosts outside the train. I try to imagine what she's going through, but I'm not sure that I can. I once remember wishing my dad dead because my life would just be so much easier that way. I felt horrible about it for days afterwards. Words are cheap, but watching your father *die*? I wouldn't want that. I watched Lara's die and that was bad enough.

I'm glad he's dead because now he can never hurt her again, but I can only imagine the conflict going on in her head right now. When she thought he was dead before, back when I told her that the world had ended, she made her peace with it quickly, but that was abstract, not something she actually saw.

I don't want to break the silence. I want her to take all the time she needs. I assume she'll tell me when she's ready to stop sitting here. Until then, I am simply planning to be here for her. And so, my mind moves on to other things.

We're unsafe out here, sitting in the vestibule of carriage one. All I have is a chair leg to defend myself. Mitch could find us here and we'd be more trapped than we usually are. Kyle could find us here. Maybe he'd have recovered from this latest bout of mania and maybe he wouldn't. I'd rather have a way of escaping before I find out, and all I have is hope that they leave us alone.

I think back to when we caught Mitch about to kill Kyle, or so we assumed. I was the one who stayed behind to talk to Mitch afterward. I was the one who threatened him. Assuming we're right about Mitch controlling the route, why did he take Lara back to her father? Why is Mitch taking out his frustrations on her rather than on me? Maybe he deduced, correctly, that hurting her will cut me much deeper than simply targeting me directly. Still, I would expect him to be planning something more for me. I need to keep my wits about me, and

I need to keep Lara close. I'm not going to lose her to that sick bastard. I don't want to lose Kyle either, but I don't know what I could do for him. I don't know if his episodes will get better or worse. It's the same problem I've had ever since I boarded: I don't know enough. Even the things I've learned aren't helpful in any real way.

Lara's breathing slows and I think she falls asleep. I wonder if I could lift her, and if I could, would she stay that way? Maybe I could get us back to the relative safety of my room. I decide against it. I'd be incredibly vulnerable with Lara in my arms, and Mitch would probably choose that moment to make his move.

Think, dammit! I *must* know something I can use. There must be something I've discovered on this fucked up train ride that can help. What is it?

My mind is blank and I want to cry out in frustration.

I wonder where Mitch is. He could be in his room. He'd have heard me hammering at his door, trying to break it down, but he might have simply ignored me. Maybe he's in the carriages at the back of the train, where Emma said some of the controls are. I have to assume that no areas of the train are off limits to him.

I shift my weight slightly, slowly so as not to wake Lara, and I feel something under me. I poke at it through the carpet with my free hand. It feels like a shallow hole with something circular inside it, right at the edge of the carriage floor. It's probably nothing, but... I remember when I boarded, noticing that the carpet in here had much more wear than the carpet in the main passenger area. Kyle justified taking the train apart with a screwdriver as "being thorough." We didn't think to look down, though.

"Lara, honey?" I whisper.

She stirs. "What is it?"

"I'm sorry to disturb you, but there's something under the carpet here."

She shifts away from me slowly and watches disinterestedly as I get my fingertips under the carpet and start pulling. It's fastened down well, and it takes a lot of energy to get even an inch of it to come away. Lara sees my struggles and comes to help. Between us, we pull enough carpet back to reveal a black metal ring set into shallow square recess in the floor. A handle, and it seems attached to some sort of movable panel.

We continue working on the carpet, and once we have a mostly bare floor, I pull on the handle and a large section of the floor, almost the entire front half of the vestibule, comes out. I prop it up against the left door.

"What's down there?" Lara asks.

There's not a lot. It seems like it's basically just a step down, and I can't figure out why it would exist until I see there are three small buttons against the front wall of the car. I step down into the new space and crouch to get a closer look. "There are some buttons over here."

Emma said, *who's to say doors cannot cease to exist? Or walls?* Was that a hint?

Lara trots over to examine them with me. Two have obvious meanings, though it's not clear what they affect. They are miniature versions of the Open and Close buttons on all the doors. The third has no discernible meaning, having only a single solid white circle rendered above it.

"What do you think?" I ask.

"I think you should press the Open button. I'm sick of this fucking place and if there's a door we haven't found yet, one that will open for us, I want to see what's on the other side of it."

I press the button, and the whole front wall of the carriage ceases to exist. I gasp.

We can see into the locomotive.

Together, we step forward.

Finally, somewhere that makes sense on this damn train. At long last!

Everywhere else is completely, disconcertingly silent. In the locomotive, it sounds like the inside of an airplane cabin in flight, like we're actually doing the thing we're doing: flying through a swirling gray hell. The more I think about this, the more alarming it becomes. Am I hearing those twisting, churning shapes outside as the train carves a path through them?

"This is..." Lara begins, then trails off.

"Yeah," I say. There's a tone of wonder to my voice that I'd rather wasn't there. I still want to get off, but I have to admit, this is fascinating. The interior is poorly lit. Most of the light here comes from some kind of display panel on the left, but there are pinpricks of light of differing colors from a bunch of other instruments. None of it looks modern, though it doesn't exactly look dated, either. If the train is as old as Emma said, that's potentially interesting. Maybe there have been upgrades along the way, or maybe this thing was just way ahead of its time. Moving closer to the instruments, I can see that many of the buttons and dials are roughly hewn from what looks like metal. A few even appear to be made of stone. There's nothing obviously made of plastic in here.

I glance over my shoulder. "I wonder if we can put the vestibule back the way we found it without the door closing."

Lara turns to face the same direction. "I don't know." She walks to what used to be the back wall of the locomotive and bends down. "There are the same buttons on this side," she says, indicating a small recess at ground level containing an open and close button, plus whatever the third one is. "I'll go and do it."

"Wait. No. I don't want you trapped on that side if Mitch comes for us. I'll tidy up. You keep the way open, okay? But lock it up if Mitch shows up."

She nods reluctantly and I step over the threshold and start putting things back as they were. The carpet is the hardest part, and upon closer inspection it looks like this ritual has been done over and over again. There are layers upon layers of glue, and some of it looks much older and yellower than the most recent layers.

"Is there any glue in there?" I ask Lara, and she heads off to look, returning a moment later with an enormous squeezy metal tube which is half empty. I return to my task while Lara gazes around the interior of the locomotive. When I'm done, the vestibule doesn't look half bad and the way through to the locomotive didn't close. I step back through and press the close button. Immediately, we lose sight of the carriage as the wall rematerializes. There's a screen on it which displays an image of the vestibule. I guess we get some advance warning if someone's trying to get to us. I imagine Mitch in here, doing whatever it is he does. Maybe he watched me board the train from right where I now stand. He'd have the perfect vantage point, and I'd have been none the wiser. Or maybe it was Rona.

I shudder at that.

"You okay?" Lara asks.

"I'm good. How are you doing?" Given the magnitude of this discovery, it would be easy to forget she just watched her dad die.

She nods slowly. "I'll be fine. It's just... I keep thinking of the happy memories I have before... you know."

"He wasn't that person anymore," I say, remembering Lara once saying something similar about Kyle. I suppress another shudder.

"I know."

"I'm sorry. I really am."

She shakes her head, then starts inspecting the locomotive's controls. I turn to do the same. I should try to prioritize, but I have a lot of priorities, and no clue where to start. I want to fix Kyle, if that's even possible. I want to make the crew visible again, and hopefully disable the ability to make them invisible. I want to find somewhere to go with Kyle and Lara where we can start new lives. I want to learn more about the train and its purpose and its abilities.

"Look at this," Lara says, and I walk over to find her tracing a finger over a huge dim screen showing a diagram containing thousands of different blobs of color, all of them slightly bleeding into each other. Hovering half an inch above the display is a white dot. It's in the middle of a sea of dark blue and is slowly heading up and to the left. Down and to the right is a blob of bright orange.

I put my finger on it. "Bright orange. That was the color of the line on the train when we stopped. That's where you came from originally." My eyes dart around the diagram looking for a white blob, and I find it near the bottom left of the display. "That was me. This is the route map."

"Weird route map."

"Yeah. What do you think each of these blobs is? A different timeline? A different universe?"

"Maybe something like that. Do you know what color Kyle's home was?"

I wrack my brains. "Brown, I think." We locate the blob near the top in the center. I study the display further and note that there's only one white, only one orange and only one brown. There are hundreds of shades of blue, green, yellow and red.

"Doesn't matter, I guess. None of us wants to go back to where we're from, do we? We need to find somewhere new."

The display seems to be full of possibilities, if only we can figure out a way to make the train go to one of the colored blobs.

"Yeah. Any indication of how you set a route?" I ask. Lara's closer to the console under the diagram, and she seems to have a knack for this stuff.

"I guess it's one of these buttons or dials, but there's no way of knowing what each one does. It's not like the matter generator, these icons make no sense."

I nod. "Let's see what else we can find. Who knows how long we have in here."

TWENTY-SEVEN

The Controls

THE MOST OBVIOUS thing here is that we can never hope to learn even a tiny bit of how this works, let alone all of it. Not with the ever-present threat of Mitch looming over us. The controls are so archaic, defying even basic understanding. There are some cubes of rock stacked under a metal bench on one side of the... what? Cockpit? Is that the right word? Anyway, these rocks could just be rocks, but they appear to serve some actual purpose. How can I tell? It's because they subtly change color in sync with other more traditional instruments. Rocks. Where I come from, rocks just sit there.

The whole cockpit is like that. Everywhere I look is another thing that defies explanation. The whole ceiling looks like some great electronic spider has made its home up there. Seeing the tangle of cables of varying colors makes me feel far less secure than I did before coming in here. Then again, if the train has lasted millions or billions of years, maybe the state of the locomotive doesn't matter. Maybe the whole thing is a construct designed to be familiar, wrapped around some even more inexplicable entity.

"What's this?" Lara asks from the very front of the cockpit. She's holding up a pale green object, about the size of a paperback book.

"Looks like oxidized copper."

"Hmm." Lara turns back to whatever lies in front of her. "There are others in different colors about the same size."

I walk over and we discover dozens of materials under a bench, stacked haphazardly on top of one another, or shoved in the gaps between other things. Some are easy to identify. I can tell which is iron because I decide licking it is a good idea. The block of charcoal – carbon – is obvious. There are some other smaller blocks of material sealed in cubes of clear resin. One of these has the letter K etched roughly into it, and I suppose that's probably potassium. When we're done looking through, we've counted about forty different materials.

"Chemical elements?" Lara asks.

"Looks like. I'm not sure why, though. I thought Emma said this train could create matter."

"Maybe whoever created the train used these to tell it how."

I find that concept a hard one to wrap my head around, so I don't even try. "Maybe," I say, then I leave Lara to her explorations. There's a dark gray sphere almost the size of my head in front of the large display on the left side and I've been thinking it looks like something I could try to use. I approach and tentatively put my right hand on the sphere. It's cold to the touch and rough like stone. It glows faintly when my hand makes contact and I fight the urge to pull back.

Sure enough, the screen in front of me brightens, then an interface of sorts appears. Like the other screens we've seen, the display is rendered half an inch or so above the actual surface. What's there is mostly pictographs, and I struggle to decipher any of them. One looks like a planet with a ring around it, but the ring has a small arrow pointing to the left. One is simply a white rectangle. There are two more that I do recognize: open and close. In a different color at the bottom of the display there are five smaller icons which, after some staring, I decide represent the numbers one through five. The first has a single vertical line, the second has two, then three, then four. The fifth has one line and a dot and seems to be dimmer than the rest. There are maybe ten others I can't make any sense of.

"What do you think these might mean?" I ask Lara, and she comes over to look. "I think the ones along the bottom might be numbers. There's open and close."

"Looks like it might be the main control panel. If such a thing exists."

I nod my agreement. I'm taken by the rectangle icon. It could be just about anything, but I'm wondering if it simply represents matter. Maybe that's the key to creating new objects from scratch rather than whatever's already in the system in carriage seven. Or maybe not. I'm reluctant to try anything without understanding it first, but I don't think we're ever going to be in that position. If we want to get off, we have to use trial and error. If one of these buttons inexplicably vaporizes whoever is operating the control panel, then so be it.

Lara points at an icon which depicts a bunch of haphazard white dots. "Stars?"

"You might be right. What about the planet?" I ask, indicating the circle with the ring around it, and the arrow.

"Hmm. Could it be... time? Emma said they had to measure the passage of time by rock erosion. Maybe the spin, or position, of a planet might serve a similar purpose, at least in terms of describing concepts with icons."

"Huh. Has anyone ever told you that you're pretty smart?"

"Everyone usually clamors to tell me the opposite," she says with a wry grin.

"Assholes."

She laughs. It's a nice sound. I've missed her laugh. I've missed being in a situation where laughing feels more appropriate than screaming. I gaze at the icon that may or may not relate to time in some way. Emma said the train can't time travel, but she might be wrong. If it can, it might make more sense for there to be two of these icons, one with the arrow pointing left and one pointing right. But there's only one, so I think it must be something else.

"Press it," Lara says.

"I... what if something bad happens?"

"Plenty of bad stuff has already happened. What's one more thing?"

"What if we die, Lara?"

"Then we die."

I hesitate for several seconds, then I move my hand on the sphere. It works like a giant trackball except I realize it's not tethered to anything. It's just hovering in midair. A red outline gradually jumps from icon to icon until it's on the planet-like one. I don't know how to select it, so I try pressing on the sphere. It moves forward a little, then rebounds as the screen changes. This time, all the icons are the same: stars, and next to them are sequences of the numerals.

"What are these?" I ask, but I'm mainly just filling the silence. Neither of us knows.

"One... three... three... uh, zero, I guess... one... one," Lara says, reading the numerals that accompany the first icon. Under that is one, three, two, three, two, one. There are more, hundreds more. They extend off the bottom of the screen and I figure out the sphere also doubles as a method of scrolling through the information.

"Select one," Lara says. "We won't figure anything out if we don't try things."

"Okay, okay." I scroll back to the top and select the first entry.

The icons on the screen fade away and we're left with a black display. This persists for a few seconds until several numerals appear at the top left. They change rapidly and we're not fast enough to decipher them, so we don't try.

Gradually, a sphere appears in the center of the display. It's gray, featureless and static.

Slowly, it starts to spin.

"What is this?" Lara asks.

I'm silent as I watch cracks appear in the surface of the sphere on the screen. An icon appears in the top left with some other pictographs under it, but I have no idea what they mean. The icons fade away once all the cracks have been rendered in detail on the sphere.

"It looks like a planet," I say.

We watch transfixed as other things happen. Each time the planet changes, an icon at the top of the screen appears with some characters we don't understand under it. The planet is hit by another object and gains a moon. A short time later, volcanoes sprout from the surface. It becomes obvious where this is going after a while, but Lara and I both watch in mute astonishment as the Earth is formed before us. Water appears and continents move gradually into the configuration Lara and I are both familiar with. It looks like a satellite photo.

"I have a really terrible feeling about this," Lara groans.

"I don't know what to think," I confess. My mind is swirling with ideas. If Emma is right, The Creator made the train to travel around the universe tending to things as if all of creation were nothing more than an enormous garden. Was Earth one of his creations? Is the list of things a record of creation for each planet, or star, or galaxy? Why would Earth be at the top? It's pretty old.

"Go back," Lara says. "I want to see the next item down."

We figure out how to go back to the list and select the next item in it. The same thing happens again, Earth is formed before our eyes.

"Do you have a theory?" I ask her.

"I have a wild notion."

"Do I want to hear it?"

"I'd be very interested to!" We both spin around at the sound of Mitch's voice. We must have been too engrossed to notice him entering. Kyle is behind him, standing in the now open vestibule. Shit. We're no match for both of them. If Kyle has joined Mitch, willingly or otherwise, we're screwed. We might as well just give up now.

I glance at Lara who is glaring at Mitch. She takes a deep breath, then says, "You made us, right? All three of us."

Mitch inclines his head, and his eyes widen with surprise. He nods approvingly. "I'm impressed."

"Wait, what?" I say, astonished.

"Your little friend here is correct. Mostly. I can't take credit for figuring out how this all works, that was Rona's doing. Once she showed me, once she explained... well, it was easy after that."

"You made us?" I ask. "What does that even mean?"

Mitch grins as if he's humoring a foolish child. "Not just you, your entire worlds. Granted, it's not a true creation. They're modeled on the real Earth, but I changed certain parameters once I figured out how. Then I looked for people to bring aboard. You three seemed perfect, though you're still not quite what I'd hoped for. Maybe my criteria were too subtle."

"Wait, wait... this is insane!"

Mitch looks at me as if he's expecting me to say more. When I don't, he asks, "What's so insane about it?"

"What isn't?"

He sighs. "When it became clear that I was staying on this train forever, I started to crave company. Rona... she suffered an unfortunate incident, though she was once brilliant. A more stimulating conversation you would never find. Sadly, she's not what she once was. I talked to the staff — a tiresome bunch, I hear you've met them — and they told me about The Creator. It gave me an idea. Maybe I could create some company. People came and went from time to time, of course, but it was often decades between seeing anyone new."

"So, you manufactured friends?"

"No, no, not at all. I manufactured worlds. I chose people from those worlds to board the train. It started off simply enough. I would pick people at random, follow their lives, watch as they grew and developed, then pick the most interesting ones."

I rub my forehead. "That's why our ages don't make any sense. We're all from Earth, but... different ones."

"Yes, indeed."

Lara interrupts. "And when did you decide that wasn't enough?"

Mitch's sneer makes my skin crawl. "Right around the time of the first murder on board. It was wonderful theater; I have to say. So much emotion, so much drama. I was conflicted at first, but these were people I created, they weren't real. None of this is real, why should I care if these unreal people kill each other? I began to get a taste for it, to look for ways to make it happen again. Don't look at me like that, I won't apologize for it. You wouldn't exist if not for me!"

"Why create new planets, though? Why not just pick people from the real Earth?" The moment I voice the question, I realize that *my* Earth isn't the real one. Not the original. Mitch created it. That leaves me feeling a little like my tether to reality has finally snapped.

"Why not? I created my first planet quite by accident, but I've refined my understanding since then. You should see it, Eden. Watching a planet coming to life... It's incredible."

I can only shake my head.

Lara asks, "I was right, wasn't I? When I said you picked Eden and me because of our fathers? And you picked Kyle because of his daughter?"

"All of that may be factually accurate, but none of it matters! You're not real! I made you. You exist because of me."

"We still exist!" Lara shouts. "We're still human!"

Mitch's smile remains in place and he simply shakes his head. It makes me want to go over there and punch his teeth in. The only thing that stops me is that I don't know how Kyle fits into this situation. Would he stop me? Would he help me? His glazed-over eyes make me hope he would just stand there and do nothing, but hope is a dangerous thing.

I take a deep breath. "So, what was your plan? You wanted us to kill Kyle, right? So that you'd have some entertainment? Like people killing each other in front of you is no different from watching the fucking television. You didn't expect we'd befriend him."

"No, I admit my predilections have caused me to underestimate certain emotions."

He says it like it's normal. Not for the first time, I wonder how I ever saw any good in him at all. "Your predilections have... how many Earths have you made?"

"Oh, dozens. It took a long time to get the parameters right. It's not just Earth, either—"

I cut him off. "And those people are still out there?"

"For the most part, yes. Where you came from is a slightly different matter." He smirks.

"Jesus," I say, because I can't understand any of this. I can't understand why he thinks this is okay. He's created dozens of Earths, is responsible for the creation of tens of billions of lives, and yet all I can think is that maybe, somehow, something on this train will let me create a replica of my world and live on it. As much as I want to kill Mitch where he stands, I also recognize that he is my best hope of seeing my family again. They may not be my actual family, but it sounds like it might be possible to come close. Maybe even close enough that I can't tell the difference.

"Wait. You said you based these worlds on the real Earth?" Lara asks, and she sounds completely calm. "Does that mean each one of them has a version of us?"

Mitch tilts his head slightly. "No, no, no. It's not like that. I only created the worlds and set some basic parameters. They developed organically, though usually along the same lines.

There's a version of Earth that has such a weak magnetic field that most consumer electronics are impossible. Solar flares, you see. Another is further away from its sun and much colder. It's interesting the kinds of people those places produce. You had it easy. I will admit that I followed your lives, though. Maybe I saw opportunities to... alter your trajectories."

"Like when you killed billions of people and left only me alive?"

"Quite. That wasn't something I'd tried before. There were glitches. Alice and Greg, for example. They weren't supposed to survive. But I admit, I wanted to see how you'd handle it. Adversity of that magnitude tends to change people, which makes for more interesting... guests."

I make a frustrated sound that he doesn't seem to hear. Lara asks, "Did you create whole solar systems for these new planets?" It makes me realize I've only scratched the surface of the horror.

"It started that way, but I realized it won't make any difference to the little people. They just need a sun in the right approximate place, so I started placing the planets around existing stars. It will certainly be interesting when technology advances sufficiently for one Earth to find one of others. That'll be a head scratcher!" He laughs that same laugh I heard on my first day here. The one that I thought pegged him as a pleasant, jolly man, but he's discussing this as if it's purely theoretical, not something he's done. Like he hasn't created billions of lives just so he can toy with them.

"So, you altered our trajectories," Lara says. "Does that mean you made my father the way he was?" Her words steal the air from the lungs as I wonder what else he might have done to us. We're just toys to Mitch. Everything I achieved, everything Lara achieved is just background noise to the purpose Mitch had planned for us. I shake my head to clear it. No, I've been down that path before. I used to believe that because my father only valued me for the money that I could provide to him, willingly or otherwise, or the situations I could bail him out of, I had no intrinsic worth of my own. It wasn't true then, and it isn't true now. He was just an asshole. Mitch may have technically created us, but we're still better than him.

"Actually, no," Mitch says. "Have you ever studied humans? They're terrible. They get off on hurting one another. Your fathers may be why I was interested in you, but I didn't make them the way they were. Listen, as much as I enjoy discussing my train's abilities, I think I can count this experiment as having failed."

My eyes flick to Kyle. He doesn't seem to have registered anything that has been said.

"What about Kyle?" I ask. "You exposed him to the outside to make him violent?"

"Something like that. It seems to have different effects on different people, so I wasn't sure it would work. It hasn't done exactly what I hoped. With Rona, it was very different. She withdrew into herself and gradually lost her mind. You should see what she spends most of her time doing now. She sits in her room painting the outside. It's awful to look at, truly."

I feel like I've been punched in the stomach again. Even people he claims as friends aren't safe from his depravity. "You exposed Rona to it?"

"I did. She had different ideas about how the train should be used."

"She showed you how to use the train and that's how you thanked her?" Lara asks.

Mitch shifts his gaze to her, apparently disinterested in her tone of anguish. "I thanked her by saying thank you. This was a separate matter."

"Right, of course. Silly me," she says. I want to warn her not to provoke him too much. I don't know what he's going to do with us now that he's found us in the locomotive, but I can't imagine it'll be good. It's likely that our lives are over, and with Kyle on his side, there's nothing we can do about it.

"So how does it all work?" I ask, obviously stalling for time, but hoping he won't be able to resist talking about his great and terrible toy.

"It's quite simple, really. The locomotive contains most of the basic controls. On, off, forward, backward, that kind of thing. It also keeps records of every place the train has been, every action that it has carried out. There's a kind of universe explorer in that system," he says, pointing at the screen we were using, "It lets you see everything that's out there. You can set the route in there too. At the rear of the train is where creation, destruction and alteration of the physical world is controlled. In the middle of the train is where small matter is created. Chairs, tables, that kind of thing."

"You redecorated the front half of the train, right?" I ask.

"Yes. That black color scheme is unflattering. I much prefer the red and gold."

A flash of desperation causes me to try to be friendly. "Me, too."

He nods, as if he hasn't been trying to systematically destroy my life. I glance around, searching for the chair leg. I see it leaning up against the wall just inside the locomotive, just to Lara's right.

"What does the colored line on the outside of the train mean?" Lara asks.

"Kyle guessed correctly. It's the current location. I assigned colors to places so I can keep track. White is the version of Earth Eden comes from, orange is where Lara is from, and so on."

I feel like when we run out of things to say, he will take us and throw us after Lara's father, so I quickly ask, "What about my dream? You sent me that dream of the train?"

Mitch hesitates, then stares at me. "I... no. I haven't been able to figure that one out. I thought you were lying when I first met you, but then you told the others the same thing and apparently haven't strayed from that story. You really dreamed of the train?"

"I did. And the line on the outside was white. That's a color you picked."

He scratches his chin. "That is a concern, I have to admit. One I should probably resolve. Kyle, grab Eden, I will bring Lara. It's time to go, ladies."

"No!" Lara shouts immediately. She grabs the chair leg, raises it above her head and runs at Mitch. I almost think she's going to make it, but Kyle bends and lifts her off the ground before she's in range of Mitch. She struggles and cries out, then Kyle grabs her wrist and twists, and the chair leg clatters to the floor. I swear I hear bones snap. Lara's scream of pain is like nothing I've ever heard, so violent and so full of betrayal that I'm surprised she doesn't damage her vocal cords. I fight to stay silent and I don't try to move. What would be the point? We're on a train, there's nowhere we can go that we can be safe. I choke back the tears that threaten to come. I don't want to give Mitch the satisfaction of seeing me cry. When I hear Lara whimpering, though, I can't help it.

"Kyle!" Lara pleads, her voice shrill and uncontrolled. "You don't have to do this. Please!" Nobody replies. I try to catch her eye, but she doesn't look my way. Kyle hands her over to Mitch then comes for me. I hold out my hand for him to take, and, gently, he does. We're marched out of the locomotive.

TWENTY-EIGHT

The Truth

WHEN MITCH MARCHES us right through the first carriage, I start to hope that our fate isn't what I assumed. I am fully expecting to be thrown from the train into the amorphous horror outside. He walks us past my room and through the dining car. We trudge past Mitch's room, through the storage car, then through the small matter creator. Lara's sobbing is getting louder the farther we go. I want to reach out to her, but Mitch has her by both shoulders, making her walk ahead of him. It hurts me physically that I can't offer any kind of comfort, and even if I could, I doubt I could make it convincing. She's a smart kid, she knows this is the end of the line just as much as I do.

Finally, Mitch comes to a halt in the rear vestibule of carriage nine. This is where we got off the train to head to carriage eleven for the first time, and I briefly wonder if there's anything to that rather than mere coincidence. Is Mitch trying to communicate something? If he throws us out, will we be able to get back on in carriage eleven?

Mitch turns to address me. "I'm sorry, Eden. I truly did believe your name was perfect. It's a shame you weren't."

I can't help the bitter laugh that escapes me, nor the sudden and unstoppable tears that follow. I bite down hard on my tongue to stop them. I shake my head, trying to communicate my disgust for everything that Mitch is. "So, now what?"

"I'm afraid this is where you get off."

Lara tries to back up, but Mitch yanks on her broken arm, causing her to scream again. I feel it as a primal urge to move, to charge forward, to seize her from the grip of her captor.

"Let me go!" she howls. I try to catch her eye, but she's too terrified. Where is my fire? Where is my determination to do something, anything? I can't bring myself to fight this, despite the anger that's on a slow burn deep in the pit of my stomach. My eyes dart around, looking for absolutely anything that might help. They land on Kyle, who has said nothing since Mitch found us in the locomotive. He's just staring straight ahead. What did Mitch do to him? Is it something that can be undone?

I turn and, trying to keep the pleading note out of my voice, I say, "Kyle, Mitch is going to turn you into the man you were in prison for being, a man you never were! Are you going to let him do that to you? Is that what you want?" There's no reaction.

"Kyle, you have to be in there!" I try. "You don't want it to end like this. You don't want our blood on your hands."

His gaze flicks down to me for an instant, but then flicks away again. It feels dismissive. I'm suddenly sure that's all the time we have. It's game over. There's nothing more I can do.

The fact that Lara's father didn't suffocate as he clung to the train while we flew through the grayspace suggests that, by itself, the outside isn't lethal. It isn't like space. We might live among the ghosts until we starve. Or we might live forever out there, lost. At least Lara and I would have each other, but honestly, that's not much of a consolation considering our minds might unravel out there.

Mitch has finished struggling with Lara and now holds her in front of him, his forearm around her neck. "Kyle! Open the door!"

Kyle pulls me forward to the door controls. I could maybe push him out as soon as they open, but he's holding on tightly to me and I'd only go with him. Lara would be next. There's no point. Kyle presses the open button and the door slides silently open. Those tendrils of gray waste no time in gripping the door frame and soon they begin to flail around just inside.

Kyle gasps, but he looks just as vacant as before when I turn and glance at him.

"Please," I beg. "You don't have to do this!"

"Eden!" Lara cries. Mitch is advancing toward the door, pushing her as he goes. I'm torn between not wanting to watch and...

"Wait!" I shout. "Me first. Put me out first." I don't want Lara to see me disappear into the gray, but if I have any control over myself once I'm out there, I'm going to do everything in my power to pretend it's not as bad as it undoubtedly is. Anything I can do to ease her fear, just a little bit.

"As you wish," Mitch says and steps aside, taking Lara with him. She's sobbing and gasping and makes the briefest eye contact as Mitch readjusts his grip on her. I very nearly lash out at him as Kyle maneuvers me closer to the threshold between this life and whatever comes after.

Then I'm standing on the edge. The gray tendrils snake around my feet and ankles then pull back, tasting me, not knowing what to make of me. I think about everything I'll never get to do, but then I notice Kyle is no longer holding me. He must be getting ready to push. I close my eyes and try to picture Lara's face, then I hear something solid hitting metal.

"No!" Mitch roars. "No, this isn't..." Then that noise again.

I turn, grabbing hold of the door frame to steady myself and see Kyle, his face contorted into what I imagine pure rage must look like. He has Mitch's head in both of his hands. I can see the force he's using to keep a hold of it. His muscles stand out from his arms, his fingers shake. Blood runs down Mitch's face. His nose is bent, his lips smashed, his eyes darting around in terrified, angry confusion. Kyle roars as he uses the power of his entire body, pivoting from the hips, propelling Mitch's head into the vestibule noticeboard, now smashed and sparking, for the third time. I feel a savage thrill when it makes contact.

Lara watches this happen, still terrified, but no longer sobbing. I make my way over to her and touch her good shoulder. She flinches and turns to face me, then wraps her good arm around me and won't let go. I briefly consider sidling over to the door and closing it.

"It's okay," I whisper. "Everything's okay."

"No," she whispers back, but that's all she says.

Whatever Mitch is, whoever he is, and whatever he's done, he can't possibly be the balding old man he pretends to be. Maybe he was caught off-guard. Maybe he assumed whatever he'd done to Kyle would last longer. He must now understand his mistake. Moments before his head hits the noticeboard a fourth time, Kyle's wild roar falters and falls silent. I watch, terrified all over again as Mitch pries Kyle's fingers from his head as if they are nothing more troublesome than flies, dispersing as soon as they perceive movement. He then stands with such force, he sends Kyle sprawling to the floor just inside the open door.

"Kyle!" I shout. Lara buries her head in my shoulder.

"Get out of here, Eden!" he shouts as Mitch moves almost supernaturally quickly, like stop-motion animation with frames missing, to where Kyle lays. Mitch puts his foot on Kyle's face and presses down.

"Sweetie, I'm going to need you to let go for a minute, okay?" I whisper.

Reluctantly, Lara releases me from her grip, but surprises me by whirling around. In a second, she's taken in the scene before her. She darts forward and lands a hard kick on the side of Mitch's knee, the one supporting him as he crushes Kyle's skull. He roars in pain and stumbles.

"Lara!" That was what I was going to do.

Kyle rises to his feet quickly and heads for Mitch, grabbing him by the shoulders. Mitch lands a punch on Kyle's nose and Kyle responds in kind, devastating Mitch's face further. The two men grapple with each other, punching where they can, kicking when their arms are otherwise engaged.

"Kyle! Be careful!" Lara shouts. They are so close to the door now.

Kyle turns around forcefully, bringing Mitch with him so that the older man's back is to us. Kyle looks at each of us in turn, then smiles, his bloody teeth visible. He nods once. "Thank you both," he says. "For believing me."

My eyes almost pop clean out of my head. "Kyle! No!" It's only six or seven feet. I start running.

I'm too late. Kyle sidesteps neatly out of the train, taking Mitch with him. I stop a foot inside the door and Lara arrives by my side a split second later. Mitch's flailing hand, now no longer gripping Kyle, reappears from the gray and grabs Lara's hair. She screams, and I immediately sink to a sitting position, bracing my foot against the door frame, pulling her down with me. She attempts to relieve the pulling at her scalp with her good arm and I loop one arm around her to stop her from being dragged away.

"No, no, no, no, no!" I hear myself babbling as I go to work on Mitch's hand with my free one, trying to lever his fingers up one by one. "No, you can't have her, too." I want to scream when his fingers refuse to move even a little bit. I have to be able to do this. I have to be strong enough. There is no alternative. There has to be some way...

I do the only thing I can think of.

I lean forward and clamp my teeth down over the joint where Mitch's index finger attaches to the rest of his hand. I do it as hard as I can, ignoring the pain exploding in my jaw, ignoring the flood of hot, metallic tasting liquid in my mouth. It must work, though, because I hear an echoing noise from outside and the hand finally lets go of Lara's hair. I push off with my foot against the door frame, pulling her further inside the carriage and start to get up to go for the door controls. At the last second, I look up and see Rona standing there.

She hits the close button.

I can't breathe. I feel like I've just run a marathon up a mountain. I'm sure I'm going to pass out, or just drop dead from sheer exhaustion. I try to focus on the old woman standing before us, wondering what we're going to have to deal with next, already knowing I don't have the energy to face anything else. Lara crawls to me, her bad arm held awkwardly in the air, and grabs hold. I don't think she'll ever let go again, and I'm not sure I want her to. It hits me: Kyle is dead, or as good as. He sacrificed himself to save us. My vision swims.

"I'm sorry about your friend," Rona says, quietly and to the floor. She's also breathing a little heavily. "But I'm glad that black hearted son of a bitch is gone."

I start to feel something unwelcome: hope. Maybe Rona isn't here to finish the job. I try to say something, but all I can do is make a croaking noise.

"I'm sorry I wasn't clear enough, too. I was the one who sent you the dream. I thought... I hoped it might stop you from getting on. I don't know how much you know, but I don't have a lot of time. I have clear, lucid moments, but they don't last long. I have Mitch to thank for that."

"The grayspace?" Lara rasps.

Rona nods and looks down at the girl with such kind sympathetic eyes that I think we really might be okay. "I don't think we've met," she says.

"I'm Lara."

"Ah, yes. I'm Rona. I wasn't sure whether he'd bring you aboard. He seemed awfully fixated on Eden."

I wince. I wonder how long Mitch was watching me. My whole life? I imagine him in the locomotive, laughing as I cry over whatever latest scam my dad pulled on me. "You tried to warn me, that day at breakfast, right?"

She turns her kind gaze my way. "That's right. I didn't do a very good job, I'm sorry. Maybe I could have saved us all some pain if... well, you know."

I nod.

"I can feel the disturbance coming back. Don't hesitate to come and visit me, okay? I used to know a lot about the train, maybe I can still remember some. And if you could restore the crew, I'm sure they'd appreciate that." She turns to go while she's still speaking.

"Wait! What are we supposed to do now?"

Rona turns back, her eyes playful. "The train is yours. I daresay you'll do a better job of running it than Mitch ever did."

Lara and I both watch as she hobbles through the door in the direction of her room. When she's gone, we turn to look at each other. What I see in Lara's face reflects what I feel. Deep pain, but also, somewhere, something like joy. We're safe. Mitch is gone, but Kyle is gone, too. I have to imagine that whatever Mitch did to him wasn't something he wanted to live with.

I think he got his redemption.

He couldn't save his daughter, but he saved us.

TWENTY-NINE

EDEN

"LET ME GET it. That's what I'm here for," Emma says.

"You need to go and get ready," I tell her. She does. She still isn't dressed. She watches me for several seconds, weighing up the pros and cons of arguing with me further, but eventually turns to leave the room.

It took us a while to figure out how the train works, but we mastered the small matter generator quickly. It takes a lot of effort to create something from scratch, though, so we usually just pick something from one of the planets we're now *de facto* stewards of. There are plenty of designers down there and they make some stunning dresses. They make some pretty nice tuxes, too.

Lara steps out into the carriage in a shimmering dark green floor length dress. Her eyes dart around the carriage and she fusses at her elaborately piled hair, which I've never seen not in a functional ponytail before.

"Wow, look at you!" I say, mostly to ease her obvious discomfort. She told me when she chose the dress that she wasn't used to getting gussied up, had only done it once before in her life, in fact. I assured her that what she'd chosen would look incredible, and it does.

"It's not... too much?"

"That's really kind of the point of all this." She grins, but keeps glancing down at herself. "You look great, seriously."

"Where is everybody?" she asks, making her way farther into the carriage.

"Getting ready, I hope."

"Speaking of which..."

"Yeah, yeah, I know. I'll go change in a minute. I just want to get a last look at this. Parties are stressful, you know? Especially when you're the host. I want to appreciate these last few minutes of calm."

Lara nods and gazes around the room. It's nothing like it used to be. None of the first ten carriages are. One of the first things we did was redecorate. We picked a color scheme that was as far from Mitch's choices as possible. Earth tones, mainly. It seemed appropriate. We replaced all the chairs and tables, carpets and light fixtures. One of the nice things about the small matter generator is that it can also destroy things. Just, you know, don't stand on that big cross on the floor while you're doing it. It was cathartic, destroying every last remnant of Mitch's reign.

We've been busy. Rona showed us what she could remember, but she's happy to be considered retired. She just wants to paint. That she paints the ghosts outside the train is a little worrying, but she says it's therapeutic. Maybe it stops her from suffering the same mania Kyle did after he was exposed to the grayspace, and if it truly helps, I'm not about to stop her.

Mitch's room had reverted to vacuum by the time either Lara or I thought to check it out. It may have done that as soon as he stepped off the train. Whether that's a failsafe he put in place or whether it happens to everyone's room remains to be seen. I desperately hope that he's not still alive out there someplace, because if he is, that means Kyle is too. The idea of the two of them grappling with each other until the end of time, floating out there among the shapes is unnerving. We decided almost immediately that we weren't going to mount a rescue mission for Kyle. Maybe that seems cold, but as far as we know, the grayspace is not something one can be exposed to and remain oneself. We have no idea what we'd be letting back into the train. He made his decision clear: this is how he wanted it. We just hope he found some peace.

It took us a while to figure out how to make the crew visible again. Rona couldn't remember how, and we obviously didn't have any notes to work from. It ended up being a ridiculous amount of trial and error, and mostly Lara's doing. She spent days of her time in the locomotive, puzzling out the pictographs. She can read a lot of it now, and she's getting better every day.

We had a memorial for Kyle once the crew was visible again, and most of them attended, which surprised me. Emma told me that Kyle came to the dining car often after Mitch had exposed him to the outside, and he would often sit and talk. I wish he'd talked to us, but she told us much of what he said was incoherent. Not all of it, though. Emma told us how he preferred to be in the dining car because it had no windows, but how he couldn't seem to resist the pull from the outside. She also told us how he already seemed to know what his fate would be even back then, and how his strongest desire was to avoid hurting either myself or Lara. We got some seeds and created some pots and planters, lamps and an irrigation system, and I maintain a small garden in the rear vestibule of carriage nine, where Kyle saved our lives. It makes me feel like some part of Nana lives on in me.

Lara and I figured out how to move our rooms next to each other, and better than that, we've figured out how to alter the physical structure of the train. We have an adjoining door now. I don't honestly know if we're just friends or if there really is more of a mother-daughter relationship going on, I just know we're happy as we are. She's at the age where she has less and less need of a mother-figure anyway. That said, her life isn't going to be what she wanted it to be. We talked about it over the course of several days after Kyle saved our lives: what were we going to do now? Lara once expressed her desire for a normal life and living as gods on a train that can create whole solar systems is not in the least bit normal. Maybe one day she'll decide she wants to leave. Actually, I think that's pretty likely, but that's okay. One of the functions of the train is that it can keep track of people, so even though she won't be able to talk to me directly, I can still keep tabs on her and she can always come to visit. Maybe her life will be better now her father's gone from it. I think she'll stick around for a while, though. Firstly, because it feels like the right thing to do to honor Kyle's memory. Secondly, because there's a lot to learn, and she's very good at it.

As for me, well, I don't have anything to go back to. Mitch took it all away. Lara asked me if I thought I'd make a new planet for myself once we figured out how. I was non-committal then, but the answer is simply that I don't know. Is it worth creating all those lives with all the attendant unhappiness of the human condition just so I can have a normal life? I don't think it is. Besides, if I left the train, who would run it? Neither the crew nor Rona want the job.

We still have no time. Being timeless is apparently just a function of the train. I thought Mitch may have done something, but no. I wonder sometimes if The Creator will come back, and what he'll make of everything that's happened in his absence. If he's still out there, and the crew is adamant that he is, then I'd very much like to meet him. Would I give the job of caretaker back? If he asked me to, sure, but I think I'd be sad about it. I don't have a home, and maybe I can do some good with this train if I can learn how.

Unfortunately, I'll have to do it without the internet, though I can access it if we're in the vicinity of an Earth that has it — some of them don't, how weird is that? — and I've been reading about the timeline of the universe as humans understand it. Assuming they're – we're – right, there's a pretty high chance humans aren't going to be around for more than another eight million years or so. Sounds like a long time when you don't live forever, right? Even without humans, who knows what else might be out there? Both Emma and Mitch mentioned other life forms, maybe I'll find them someday.

Things get a little hazy when I start to read about the heat death of the universe. Is the train affected by that? Will it gradually be torn apart over trillions of years? Or does the train exist outside of our universe? Am I supposed to use it to create a new universe when this one tears itself apart at the seams? Is that what generation upon generation of caretakers have done? I don't know the answers to any of these questions. I guess I get to decide, if I'm still here when that time comes.

"I think I hear them," Lara says, and I realize I'm out of time to change. Never mind. It's not like anyone will care.

The door slides open and Emma walks in followed by Rona, then everyone else on the crew. They take their seats and I stand there with Lara, watching, listening to the chatter. After a minute, the noise dies down and Lara whispers to me, "Knock 'em dead," hugs me quickly, then goes to take her seat.

I turn to face everyone. I'm still not sure I want to do this. It feels self-indulgent, but Lara keeps assuring me that it's fine to indulge yourself once in a while. I reach down and pick up my violin, position it under my chin, then start to play. It's a short piece, just an excerpt from a Brahms violin sonata, but it's one of my favorites.

When I'm done, the room is silent. I put my instrument down and face everyone, noticing several of them are now smiling. Lara is beaming at me.

"Hi," I've been practicing this in my head for a while now. That's not how it was supposed to begin, but I guess it doesn't matter as long as I say what needs saying. "For those of you I haven't met, my name's Eden Lucas. The girl over there is Lara Parker. We're what I guess you would call the current caretakers."

I leave a pause, but nobody objects. That's a good sign. Emma said they wouldn't. She also said this gesture was unnecessary because they are servants of the train. The position of caretaker is not their concern, but she said they would appreciate not being treated like garbage.

"I know you had problems with the previous holder of this position," I say, and I hear faint chuckling around the room. That is putting it mildly, I suppose. "I just wanted to tell you that this is the beginning of a new era. Mitch is gone. He's taken something from each of us, but he can't take anything more. This is a new chapter."

That's all I have. I'm about to tell people to enjoy the party when Emma starts to clap. It's slow at first, but her applause is joined by other people's. Soon, everyone in the room is clapping. I can see Lara's eyes glistening with tears.

I smile, shake my head and stifle my own sob with a laugh. "Enjoy the party!" I shout over the tail end of the applause, then I walk over to take my seat next to Lara as everyone else stands and begins to mingle. There's a buffet table along one side of the room, filled with all sorts of exotic foods. We had to stop the train a few times to get it all, but I'm not about to make these people cater their own party, so it was worth it. I also created them another carriage of crew quarters, so everyone has a room and a space they can go to unwind. It seems only fair. They're still on the train to do a job, but I'm not going to treat them like Mitch did.

Lara and I remain seated, two islands in a sea of activity. "Good speech," she tells me.

"Thanks, kiddo."

She fixes me with a gaze, a knowing little half smile on her face. "You're going to stay, aren't you?"

We've talked about this, but I've been avoiding giving anyone a direct answer. I wanted to see how this went first. Despite Emma telling me that the caretaker is of no consequence to the crew, I still clung to some vague anxiety they'd reject me. I owe Lara an answer, though she obviously already knows what it will be. I gaze around the room. I can barely believe it, given what we've been through, but there are much worse places to be than here, and I've been to some of them. I still miss Alice and Mom and Nana and even Greg, in a way. I will never stop missing Kyle, nor forget what he did for us. But all those people are gone. Everyone I ever knew in my old life is gone. Lara, and Emma and James and Rona and all the other people I haven't yet had a chance to befriend are here. And who knows the kinds of people I might meet on our travels?

I smile. "Yeah, I think I am."

The End.

If you enjoyed this story and you're interested in finding out what happens next, I'd be thrilled if you'd consider joining my newsletter or following me on Facebook.

If you join my newsletter, you'll receive a short e-book with deleted and alternative scenes from this book, plus some commentary. There are also a number of short stories in this world on my website which are accessible only to newsletter subscribers.

www.neilwritesthings.com
www.primordials.net

facebook.com/neilwritesthings

ACKNOWLEDGEMENTS

I'LL KEEP THIS short, but there are people on this particular Earth without whom there would be no book, or perhaps there would be, but it wouldn't be this book, and it wouldn't be anywhere near as good as it ended up being. I'll start with my wife, Charlotte, who read the early versions of the book and provided a lot of help in shaping the final story.

My beta readers, Neil, Valour and Chris, helped so much in terms of figuring out where I was spending too much time on things or not spending enough. The shower scene and the fact Alice gets to live as long as Greg (she didn't originally) are directly attributable to those fine people, among a number of other things.

I'd like to offer special thanks to Sarah Lyons Fleming, who not only beta read this book, but also spent hours of her life answering my incessant questions and providing encouragement. If you're unfamiliar with her books, you should really rectify that. Check out her website at www.sarahlyonsfleming.com.

Thanks to Red Line Editing for their editing services.

Finally, thanks to you for reading this. I hope you enjoyed it. Let me know: neil@neilwritesthings.com.

An excerpt from the next book in the series...

ONE

Lara

I WONDER SOMETIMES whether I'm the most traveled human alive. It's likely Rona has me beat, but she can't remember, so I don't think it counts.

Of the hundred-and-eight Earth clones, this is the eleventh I've set foot on: my own home planet and ten others — clones three through twelve. I can smell the difference immediately. We usually touch down a stone's throw from a populated area where the stench of traffic, pollution, factories, dumpsters and whatever else is pervasive. Here, everything smells clean, almost fresh, a counterpoint to the stifling heat. I'm standing in the middle of a small, wooded area — that helps with the smell — on the outskirts of what may or may not be Salina, Kansas. The trees and flowers are lit by angled sunbeams making their way through the canopy, giving the space a magical, dreamlike feel. All I need now are cartoon animals to emerge from behind the trees, seat me on a giant toadstool throne and declare me their queen. I smile to myself, then glance around to make sure I'm alone. Around the base of several trees are unusually striking dark red flowers whose petals darken to black around the edges. Somewhere distant, I hear a small yappy dog barking excitedly about something, but I'm not unduly concerned. We've got this down to an art now. The train can check for life signs and heat signatures while it's still in grayspace. We've rigged up a perimeter alarm, too. Eden would have checked everything before we emerged.

I walk away from the drop-off point, the wooded area gradually becoming a small meadow filled with tiny flowers and humming insects. A trail of compressed grass hints that I'm not the only person to ever come this way. At the far side of the meadow is a fenced off and boarded up gas station. There's a gap in the fence and something that looks suspiciously like a sleeping bag visible through a fist-sized hole in one grimy window at the back. I skirt around the edge, managing to avoid tangling with a thorny bush. Once I reach the roadside, one reason for the clean smell becomes clear: the cars are all electric. They rush past me with none of the engine noise I'm used to hearing, just the smooth noise of tires on asphalt. Gleaming tram lines run down the center of each lane of traffic.

I traverse the road at the nearest crosswalk and head deeper into the city, gawking up at the buildings, amazed at how spotless everything is. No litter, no dirt coating the buildings, nothing like that. Everything is immaculate. In the distance, I see a group of cylindrical robots working tirelessly to keep everything shining and pristine, so I guess that explains that.

The avenue I follow is lined with mid-sized white stone buildings, around five or six stories. The first two side streets feature townhouses rendered in the same unblemished white. I pause at the intersection of the third, draw back the sleeve of my hoodie and check my watch. I tap the screen and navigate to the timer which informs me I have an hour and thirty-five minutes until I'm supposed to check in with Eden. I get two hours in theory, but she freaks out if I'm late, so I've been giving myself about an hour forty-five.

Eden is my mom-friend. She's kind of my adoptive mom and kind of my best friend. The plan was that we would explore the Earths together, visiting each in turn, learning what we can. Fate seems to have had other plans; Eden hasn't left the train since we inherited it almost six months ago. I get it, she went through a lot. For a time, she truly believed — not unreasonably, I might add — that she was the last of her species. Mitch, the sick bastard who ran the train before his death, sterilized Eden's planet, leaving her the only survivor. I can't even imagine. She has every right to be upset, angry, pretty much any emotion, but she insists nothing's wrong. I try to talk to her about it, but I don't know how. It feels too big.

Mitch is also the reason there are so many Earths. He cloned them using the train's frankly mind-boggling power. Why? Well, that's what we're trying to find out by visiting them. So far, we have no idea. Maybe it was experimentation, or maybe there was a point to it. What we do know is that this Earth is the twelfth. I came from the forty-fourth, Eden from the twenty-ninth.

The last time Eden left the confines of the train was also the last time I saw my father alive. He came to take me home, but, well, I didn't want to go. I ran away for a reason. I was done letting him hit me, and Eden wasn't about to let him take me against my will. He grabbed hold of the train as it entered grayspace, and the grayshapes that live there engulfed him. I guess you could say I've been through a lot too.

But Eden has suffered more than anyone should ever have to suffer. More than anyone should be able to cope with. We're supposed to be there for each other, and I get it if she needs time. I get it if she doesn't know how to process everything that happened to her. I understand if she prefers to spend her time moving boxes around and writing instruction manuals because she's terrified to set foot off the train and just wants to stay busy. I get it, I do. But I wish it wasn't so. I wish she were here with me.

Instead, here I am, exploring a galaxy of Earths all by myself. It's lonely, not to mention dangerous. The fact that nothing has happened to me yet doesn't mean nothing ever will. I'd prefer some backup, but more than that, I want my favorite person in the universe with me.

The city we touched down near isn't called Salina. It seems to be called Sterling, Kansas, judging by the various signs I see above the stores that line the third side street. There's the Sterling Grill, which is dark inside, but the kind of darkness that speaks of upmarket dining rather than closure. A few other restaurants, too. There's a kiosk set into the wall beneath a jaunty sign that reads Sterling Wok along one portion of street where a robot arm is serving noodle dishes to a group of young men and women who seem like they could be college students. They're the only people I've seen who could be described as casually dressed. Behind me, a sudden whirring makes me turn just in time to see a green and white tram sweeping into view, all curves and slopes and reminders of home. It stops a little way down the street, and a handful of besuited people get off while a couple more get on, then it starts to move again. I don't see a driver as it passes me, and I stand there and watch it speed off into the distance.

Already, this is my favorite Earth so far, and it's not even a close call. Most of the Earths haven't differed that much from mine. When we decided to visit each of the clones Mitch made, we did it because that seemed like the logical first step. Learn the extent of Mitch's meddling with the universe to learn if there were any problems we could fix. The first two, created over a century ago according to the train's records, were dead places, and it seemed like that had always been the case. The continents had formed in roughly the same configuration they do on all the Earths, but life had never taken hold. It was all just bare rock and water. We briefly wondered if all the early ones might be like that, but so far, it's only those two. Failed experiments, perhaps.

The next nine Earths didn't have much to tell them apart. They were like home. People living their lives, falling in love, singing, dancing, driving, working. And of course, the politics, the wars, the greed, the ecological collapse. Humans are humans everywhere they exist. We know it took Mitch a while to figure out how to vary aspects of each clone successfully, so our thinking is that the early ones will all be similar to the elusive original.

That's right; if the original Earth is out there, we don't know where. There's no record of it on the train like there is for each of the clones, or at least not one that appears in search results. It may be that Mitch erased the records, or perhaps he erased the planet. Anything seems possible with that psycho.

I check my watch again and realize I've spent fifteen minutes just staring at things and thinking. I need to figure out if there's any reason to stay here, aside from the obvious fact that it's so very different from all the others we've visited. Why would that be? The main thing that's linked the Earths so far has been their similarities. Mostly similar levels of technology. Same continent shapes, same countries for the most part, though we have noticed a few variations. Most of the same states in the United States, though again, we've seen some differences. City names are occasionally different, like this one. On my Earth, the city in this approximate location was called Salina. It's where I was born, which is why I picked it. There was a Sterling some miles southwest, so perhaps that place and this place swapped names on this clone. We have theories about how all of this works, but nothing concrete.

I cross the street and peer through some of the restaurant windows. Most are about half full, and almost all appear to be staffed by machines of varying types, from static robot arms to roving screens with animated human faces. The Sterling Grill, though, has only one occupied table and an honest-to-God human standing behind the bar.

I push the door open.

The stale dryness of the air conditioning hits me immediately, reminding me of being on the train. It's quiet inside, most tables empty, but it's twenty to four in the afternoon. Lunch is over, dinner hasn't begun. The human worker I spotted through the window, a floppy haired blonde guy in a loose-fitting white shirt, has moved from his position behind the bar and now stands at the only occupied table talking with a quartet of well-kempt businessmen.

I wait. Eventually, Floppy Hair glances over and sees me standing just inside the door. He bounds over, his hair trying to leave his head with each bounce.

"Welcome to the Sterling Grill," he says with a smile. "Table for one?"

I shake my head. "Can I sit at the bar?"

He appraises me suspiciously. "Are you old enough?"

"Nope. Can I sit there anyway?"

He casts a glance over his shoulder at the table of businessmen. "I... guess? Go take a seat, I'll be over in a sec."

"Thanks." He retreats down the central aisle of the restaurant, past the occupied table to the photo-strewn wood-paneled rear wall, then through a door. I head left to the bar and slide onto a stool that blocks the businessmen from view behind a pillar.

There's a television mounted high on the wall in a corner of the room, tuned to some kind of documentary. It looks like an exploration through an abandoned city, though it's hard to tell where it is. The architecture is distinctive, but that's all I can say about it.

After a moment, Floppy Hair appears through a doorway behind the bar, grinning. "What can I get you?"

I scan the brand names of the various bottles and cans, ignoring the alcohol that he won't serve me – and I don't want anyway – focusing on the soft drinks. Thankfully, there's plenty I recognize. "Coke, please."

He nods. "Fountain or bottle?"

"Oh, fountain, definitely." So far, Eden has been reluctant to grant my request to have a canister of carbon dioxide and a soda fountain installed on the train. She doesn't think it tastes any different to the bottled or canned varieties we already get. It suddenly hits me as I fantasize about sugary liquid that I'm aging right now. That's not something I do much anymore. I spend most of my time on the train, which blocks time's effects. It's hard to keep track, but I once worked out that by the time we get around to visiting our erstwhile companion Kyle's Earth, number fifty-six, I will have finally made it to a biological eighteen years old. I'd like to get to twenty-one at least. That gets me all the good stuff.

Floppy Hair smiles and goes to work pouring my drink. A few seconds later, he sets it down in front of me and I guzzle a quarter of it greedily. When I pause for breath, he says, "That'll be five bucks."

Muffling my surprise at the exorbitant cost in a fake cough, I hand over a ten-dollar bill, the smallest thing I have. He looks at me strangely as he takes it. "I—ah, I don't have change."

"I guess consider it a tip then."

He smiles and struts a little. "A hundred percent tip? Must be doing something right!"

I grin and twirl my straw, watching the bubbles surge to the surface of the dark liquid. I glance back up at the television as the view changes, then zooms abruptly, everything blurring before resolving back into focus a second later. In the distance are what appear to be two adults and two young children running away from whoever is filming. I nod to the television. "What's that about?"

He looks. "Las Cruces, I think. I saw this advertised."

I cock my head in an invitation to explain further.

Floppy Hair continues, "They're poking around for the first time since the city was officially abandoned. Seeing what was left behind."

"Why was it abandoned?"

"Same as most places out that way, I guess. It's too hot and the weather is too unpredictable. The Rio Grande is dry most of the summer now."

"Where did everybody go?"

"North," Floppy hair says. "Same as always."

"Except for those people, I guess." The camera still tracks the people who are fleeing. Where there's one family, there are probably more.

"I guess so. Anyway," he says, "What brings you to town? I

don't think I've seen you around before."

I'm still thinking about the situation in Las Cruces. If it's that bad in the United States, how bad will it be in Mexico and farther south? I blink, realizing Floppy Hair asked a question, and I blurt, "I was born here, actually." I immediately wish I hadn't. The sudden noise of chairs scraping on wood, the shuffling of feet and hushed whispering announces the table of businessmen are leaving.

He says, "Really? Me too! You don't meet many natives anymore. Almost everyone is from out of state. Should I remember you from school or anything?"

My mind immediately jumps down a rabbit hole. He looks like he might be a similar age to me, so it's certainly conceivable we could have been at school together. One of the curiosities of the Earth-clones is why their dates don't match with each other. Eden and I have talked about it and theorized that it could just be down to the fact that the local humans measure differently or consider different events important. I don't think it's that, though. From what Mitch told us, and from the bits and pieces I've learned on my own, it seems that when the train clones a planet, it somehow accelerates it through its development at a massively increased rate. I don't know how long, having never tried it. It could be minutes; it could be months. It seems unlikely to be longer given how many clones Mitch was able to make in barely a century. However long it actually is, the train created our planets in a fraction of the time we were taught in school. My theory is that Mitch simply stopped this accelerated development at arbitrary points as part of his experimentation.

This Earth is two years behind Eden's. Back home, I was born in 1977. It was 1994 when I boarded the train. On Eden's Earth, it was April 2019 when she boarded, and I would have needed to be born in 2002 to be the age I am. Here, it's July 2017. It's all so complicated. "Probably not, I moved around a lot as a kid," I lie.

He nods and produces a rag from somewhere and starts wiping down the bar. I watch his fluid motions for a moment, then babble, "What's it like, the city? It's been a long time."

He puts his rag down and considers. "It's a busy place, not a lot of room for people who didn't go to college, like me. Mostly food service jobs or street sweeping, but a lot of that's being done by robots now. It's only because this place caters to a certain type of clientele that appreciates the human touch that I have this job. That, and my dad owns the place."

I nod as I consider my journey here from the train. "Impressive. It's mostly electric cars?"

He nods, and his eyebrows move fractionally closer together. "Has been for years. Most of my life probably."

Dammit. If I'm pretending that I was born here, I should know about technological developments in the wider world. I sip my Coke and consider how to figure out if this world needs our attention or if we can move on to the next one. Eventually, because I can't keep calling him Floppy Hair in my head, I ask, "What's your name?"

He looks up. "People call me Ty."

I smile at the impending rhyme. "Hi, Ty. I'm Lara."

He grins. "Nice to meet you. So... let's try this again. What brings you back to Sterling?"

I think fast. "My... mom just moved back." Technically not a lie. Eden is family, and she's around here someplace. Nobody would be able to see her, but she's definitely there.

"Cool. Does she work at The IP?"

I sigh internally. This is the worst part of the job. If this is something I should know, I will lose even more of Ty's trust. "IP..." I say slowly.

He screws up his face and squints at me, his head cocked. "It's actually called the IAIPR, but that's a mouthful. Mostly we just call it The IP."

"Okay. What's that?"

He puts the rag he's been fiddling with down and stares at me. "You must know. Everyone knows."

I shake my head.

"The International Alliance for Interplanetary Research. Ringing any bells? Biggest employer in the state. One of the biggest in the world."

I consider blurting *Oh, of course!* But that would convince nobody. I wish I'd never mentioned that I was born here. "Look, when I said I'd been away a long time, let's just assume it was someplace I didn't see a lot of the outside world."

He shrugs while at the same time frowning.

"Anyway, no, my mom doesn't work there. I'm not sure we'll be here long."

"Ah. Military family? My brother's in the Air Force."

I nod. Yes, that works as an excuse. I wrestle with my sleeve and check my watch. Just under an hour to go before I'm due back at the train.

"Is that real leather?" Ty asks, an apparent non-sequitur until I realize he's staring at the device on my wrist with barely concealed awe.

I frown down at the round silver case and the white leather strap. "It... is."

"Wow. That must have been expensive."

It was about a hundred bucks in a random electronics store on Earth #4, the cheapest smartwatch I could find, because no matter how often I see people fiddling with their phones, I can't seem to ingrain the same habits in myself. Most of the time I forget I have mine with me. But as that isn't something I can say, I search for something else. I guess leather isn't common, which I guess means the animals it comes from aren't common either. Suddenly, I find myself wanting to know what a place calling itself the Sterling Grill actually serves. "Uh... it's an heirloom, kinda."

"It's nice."

"Thanks. I should probably get going." I down the rest of my Coke and stand while Ty watches me, unmoving. "Thanks for the drink," I say, then hop down from my stool and turn for the door.

"Wait."

I almost don't. I almost make a run for it. I've made too many errors here, and I don't want this guy looking at me strangely anymore. I hesitate for several seconds, then turn back to find Ty smiling awkwardly with half of his face. His eyebrows look like they're trying to get to orbit. "Do you... I mean, would you like to—"

I cock my head and raise my own eyebrows.

Ty takes a deep breath. "Would you like to grab a coffee later?"

I blink. I keep blinking for seconds, a little bit dazed. Then I gaze around the room like an idiot. I don't know what to say. Nobody has ever asked me out before. Not because nobody wanted to, but because everyone knew the reputation my dad had. At least, that's my theory. "I... uh..."

"It's fine if you don't," he says, a little too quickly.

I once told Eden that I wanted to have a normal life. Things have changed so much since then. We inherited control of a train with the powers of a God. I finally have a family I can love unconditionally. The desire for something more normal hasn't disappeared, though. I don't want to leave Eden, but I start to wonder if leaving Eden and having a more mainstream life are mutually exclusive. If I find the right guy — and I feel sure it would be a very long search involving a lot of vetting for psychopathic tendencies — why couldn't he join us on the train?

"It's not that," I say, surprising myself. "It's just... I hate coffee. Is there a place we can get sushi?"

He hesitates, seeming to consider. When he smiles, it's like the sunrise.

AVAILABLE NOW

Earth Twelve is available now on Amazon.

Printed in Great Britain
by Amazon